Griffins of the Knighthood

The Beginning of the End

dedicated to Angela Ranalli

2

ISBN-10: 0578141388

ISBN-13: 978-0578141381

Daniel Ranalli

Index

Prologue

Civilization, it is a gift as much as it is a curse.

In the land of Arktorion, this has proven truer than anywhere else. Ever since the dawn of civilization, chieftains and emperors, kings and tyrants alike have battled over this realm. Far to its south though, the realm of Raishany had long since unified into a single fatherland populated almost entirely by the red griffin race. Raishany wished to build an empire and spread their race around the world, and four millennia after the dawn of civilization they would begin with the wealthy and war-torn Arktorion.

In the years to come, each successive Raishan king expanded on the dominion of his predecessor, conquering lands beyond Arktorion, yet each successive king proved more tyrannical, growing greedier with each new colony. In time, Raishan kings would find it increasingly difficult to rule over their vast new empire, only their home fatherland felt the full sting of their iron fists. Many Raishans then fled, only to settle in Arktorion, and land not only free, but rich. Those who settled there knew that they would die before returning to their fatherland.

Two and a half centuries after the Raishan Invasion, their king so named Saish died without an heir. His widowed queen, Hayleed, needed a suitor, and she knew where to find him. For in Arktorion, there existed an ancient lineage of griffins – known as the Fyzar. Marrying into such a lineage would aid in unifying her vast empire, however, Queen Hayleed possessed an ulterior motive. For those within this lineage possessed great powers given to them by heavenly beings in the times before written word, just after the great retreat of the ice.

In due time, Queen Hayleed found her new king and gave birth to a son, a son who would be raised in Raishany. There, he grew to love the Raishan feudalistic state of the lord over the serf. Just prior to his being crowned king though, the prince then visited his father's homeland of Arktorion, a land far different from his own. There, he witnessed the freedom that his father's countrymen enjoyed, and their brazen resistance against Raishan oppression.

Soon after, this prince was crowned king, and once on the throne, he immediately imposed his will unto Arktorion, only to see it resisted against, the king then forced his will yet further, but this only ignited a Revolution. Outraged, the young king then attempted to annihilate the rebels, yet this only enhanced their resolve. Arktorion would eventually earn its independence by gradually decimating its oppressor over the course of many bloody years. These victories inspired other colonies to revolt, and so the king, with a withered army, lost them all.

In time, Arktorion would fill the power vacuum left by Raishany. Yet the still young nation had no experience in wielding such influence, and by the time it neared the tricentennial of its independence, Arktorion had squandered its wealth, made enemies, and inevitably began to wane. Meanwhile, her oldest nemesis, Raishany, had resurrected herself, and a Cold War commenced.

For centuries, Raishany had longed for vengeance – something that it would soon have. Yet from this rancor, came a prophecy, one which proclaimed that a Fyzar would soon be born, and choose his side of the war – and that whichever side he chose – would be victorious. Yet, this prophecy warned that in winning this war, he might just have to make the ultimate sacrifice. And so, as Raishany prepared to launch a World War, for both soldier and civilian alike, it would soon be the beginning of the end.

Chapter 2

Morning on the isle of Hyleeda as a white fog rested over a thick green forest with the ocean to the west. Five Arktorian scouts, one of many scouting parties in the area, flew from the island's interior toward their home base on the coast, Fortress Hammer, which had the tree line up against one side, and the tide washing up against the other. It sat a mere couple hundred meters from a river that marked the colonial border between the Arktorian and Raishan colony.

The octagonal Fortress Hammer remained unfinished because its roof, a defense against aerial attack, had not been completed except for the roof's skeleton and three platforms, one above the other, where the archers would stand during battle. The scouts landed in the middle of the fort at the foot of the command post. A wooden building with a slanted, shingled roof, it housed the officers, including the fort's commander. On either side of the command post's entrance stood two guards, one of them opened the entrance door, "sirs, the night scouts have returned."

Gray light peeked in through the one small opening in the post's roof, the fort's skeleton roof above that. The few windows in the post's common room also let in a bit but most came from the lit fireplace. Huddled next to this fireplace and wrapped in fur were the commander, a major and his second in command, a shivering lieutenant. Their breath becoming white mist despite the fire's heat, "damn this cold," shuddered the lieutenant, a red griffin.

The commander, a white-browed griffin, breathed into his cupped hands and rubbed them together. Gray feathers and white spots covered his body except for his white brow, giving them the name. "Time to debrief the scouts, lieutenant," the major groaned as he stood.

"If you don't mind, sir, I would like to sit this one out," shuttered the lieutenant.

"Why?"

"I cannot feel my toes, sir," this complaint made the major frown, "it is too cold."

"Oh get up!" he wrenched his lieutenant to his feet, walking him to the door and outside. The two guards and the scouts clicked their heels as they snapped to attention. The major saluted, and then the scouts saluted back. "What have you to report, sergeant?" he asked the lead scout.

"Nothing to report, no detectable enemy activity, sir," replied the sergeant before rubbing his index finger on his beak.

The major's eyes gave a flash of fear. He cleared his throat. "Thank you, sergeant," he saluted, and the scouts did back.

The major motioned for the sergeant, the lead scout, to come inside as the other four went off. As the lead scout passed the major in the doorway he said, "I didn't want to cause a scare, sir. I didn't want any rumors flying about."

The major turned to the guards at the door, "we are not to be disturbed, understand?"

"Yes, sir," replied the guards as the major closed and locked the door.

"Now, what's really going on out there?" the major asked the sergeant.

"Do you have a map, sir?" As the rest of the fort's officers, about a half dozen, came in a junior officer fetched a map of the island of Hyleeda and laid it out on a table as the sergeant spoke. "Now just so we're clear, this is the Raishan colony," the scout pointed to the red half, "and this is our colony," he pointed to the blue half.

"And where are we again?" another officer asked.

"Right here," the scout pointed to a black square on the western coast, "the border is right here where that river just south of us is. And just south of there, around the coast's bend, is where the Raishans are approaching from."

"How strong?" asked the major.

"It is a small fleet, sir, eight ships strong, four destroyers and four large transports."

"How long till they arrive?"

"Within a quarter the hour, sir."

The major thought for a moment, "four large transports?"

"Yes, sir."

The major nodded, "a single large transport can carry four or five hundred soldiers, times four may be as many as two thousand, more than twice our forces here." He paused, "and it is Raishan military doctrine that to seize a fortress they must have at least twice as many soldiers as their fortified enemy, meaning us." The other officers watched him intently. "Sound the alert," he finally ordered a junior officer.

"Yes, sir," the junior officer grabbed a bow and arrow sitting next to the fireplace, the arrow's end being wrapped in a piece of cloth which he lit with the fire. A red flame shown and the junior officer pointed the bow and arrow straight up at the roof's opening, letting it fly.

The soldiers outside sprang into action, some darting to their barracks to put on their armor while the rest fetched weapons from the armory as the officers and lead scout came outside. The archers took their positions atop the three platforms circling the roof's skeleton and the major flew up to the highest one with his officers following. From there he looked on, the fog only allowing him to see as far as the nearby river. "That fleet should be coming right around the bend in the coast, sir," said the scout, "any time soon."

A half-mile south the coast took a sharp turn toward the interior of Hyleeda. It remained hidden from the fort behind the thick forest. Along this stretch, nothing moved. There was nothing to move. No creatures sounded out from the trees, and the only sound that could be heard was that of the rippling tide. Out over the water sat the fog, which broke as eight war ships skulked out of its whiteness. The four destroyers, with their cannons sticking out, flanked the four larger transports with two on each side. The transports dropped anchor mere feet of running aground. There they rested for a minute. Then a metallic ringing emanated out and their flat bows opened up into doors and smashed down onto the sand.

Five hundred Raishan soldiers marched out from each transport. Four types came out, grenadiers first who were specifically selected for their large stature and specially trained to siege fortresses. Behind them came lancers who held spears in one hand and shields in the other. Next were the hoplites with their sabers and shields, followed by the crossbowmen all of them creeping along the beach. A general landed just at the edge of the tide with his immediate subordinates following. This general began to walk alongside his soldiers who seemed miniscule compared to his towering stature. His red armor covered him from his shoulders down. Behind him flew his yellow trimmed red cape, his hands clenched together beneath it. He watched his soldiers with a disciplined scowl, one tattooed onto his face from decades of military service, below this gleamed two yellow eyes that tracked his small army's every move. Below them bulged wrinkles and bags from a life of being on the front lines.

Close behind him, trailed his two spear-brandishing guards, and behind them his immediate subordinates, a rear admiral, and a few colonels. One colonel whispered to another, "I don't understand, why are we not taking this fort by air?"

The other colonel shrugged and the general cut in, "I have explained this already, colonel, we are to walk along the tree line until we reach the beach's bend. There we will be hidden no more. It is at that point that the soldiers be ordered into the fog to take the fortress."

"With all due respect, sir, why not send our forces into the fog to begin with?"

"Because that is what the enemy expects, we must take off only from where they do not expect, and that is from the coast, right up against their own territory."

In a tree at the coast's corner slept an Arktorian sentry in a small, camouflaged nest. His ear to the floor, a thumping sound woke him. Groaningly he forced himself up, rubbing his eyes as he did. Upon taking his hands away from his eyes he saw the enemy army just to his left, "Raishans!" he whispered to himself.

Back on the beach, the general's ear twitched.

The Arktorian sentry grabbed a bow and arrow, lit the cloth at the tip with the small pit of embers next to him. WHAM! A spear ripped through his neck and he tumbled through the tree branches all the way to the ground.

Back on the beach, the general was still in his throwing stance, "General Trajetton, sir, how did you know of the sentry?"

General Trajetton, still peering at the forest, hesitated before answering, "It is difficult to explain," when he noticed his soldiers were about to reach the coast's bend and reveal themselves, "HALT!" and his troops then did as ordered. The general started forward, his two guards and subordinates followed, "stay here," he ordered, and they stopped as he continued all the way past the tree line.

One officer whispered to another, "what is he doing?! He is revealing himself!"

Back at the fortress, "hmmm, the fog seems to be clearing," said the major.

"Sir, look!" alerted the scout.

The major spied at a solitary figure, a mere speck in the distance. The major took out his telescope and put it to his eye. His brow raised as he peered through the glass, "sir?" asked the scout, "sir, what is it?"

The major did not utter a word, he remained still as if frozen by the brisk air before he finally spoke, "it's Trajetton."

General Trajetton then slowly raised his right hand, his middle and index fingers pointed to the sky.

Back at the fort, "soldiers," began the major, "brace yourselves!"

Trajetton extended his talons, paused, his troops clenched. He ripped his hand down, and his troops then launched themselves into the air in V formation.

The Arktorian archers pointed their bows up, their enemy still out of range.

As two thousand Raishan soldiers rocketed up, the noise of their clinking armor and rushing wings filled the air before they disappeared into the fog above.

The Arktorian soldiers and major searched the skies yet could see nothing but the white and gray fog. The major then noticed that General Trajetton had vanished as well. Nothing happened for an eternity. The archers scanned above them, their bows fully tensed.

Suddenly a rain of arrows streamed down. The Arktorians all ducked and dodged, the screeching of the wounded echoing through the fortress walls. The major, his hands over his head and his body against the floor, jumped to his feet once the steel rain had ended, "get back into formation!" he ordered as he ran, "get back into formation before the next volley!" He stopped, his soldiers dashing about, some trying to get into formation, others trying to help the medics. Some tending to their wounded friends, others crying over their dead ones. The major's heart sunk, not out of sorrow but out of hopelessness, if and when the enemy returned his forces would not be prepared. To what was left of his archers he ordered, "keep your bows pointed up!"

"We have nothing to aim for, sir!" another volley rained down. The major jumped to the floor and hid underneath the lowest platform. From there he watched his soldiers get chewed up even worse than before.

The major darted into the chaos, pulling those who were still battle worthy onto their feet, "TO WINGS! TO WINGS!"

The lieutenant ran up to him, "but sir, they are not in formation! They will be ripped to pieces!"

"Then they will form up in midair!" His soldiers clambered upward and out over the beach with barely any order. The Raishans screamed down out of the mist, the lancers spearing their enemies with an organized precision. The major watched helplessly as his army was shattered like glass.

"Sir! Sir!" screamed his lieutenant, "SIR!" he slapped the major's face, "what do we do now, sir?" Meanwhile his still living soldiers came tumbling back into the fort, their pursuers on their heels.

"There is nothing now, lieutenant." The major ripped out his sword and charged at the lancers, screaming as he ran, his lieutenant following. Soon, with no other choice, the rest of the Arktorians turned and fought as well, both sides tripping over the wounded and dead as they fought, many of the wounded being crushed by those falling on them.

The major finished off a hoplite when he felt a rumbling fly over him, a second later, the ground trembled as if startled. He turned around and there stood General Trajetton, his wings extended, his eyes fixed forward. The general unsheathed his saber, the major vengefully groaned, then charged, thrusting his sword forward. Trajetton blocked and swung, the major ducked. Trajetton lunged forward, the major struggling to block his blows, getting cut up along the way. Trajetton ripped his saber down, the major blocked and the two blades struck and let out a sharp clang. The major tipped his blade sideways, deflecting Trajetton's, then the general punched the major's face, sending him twirling to the ground.

The major jumped back to his feet, yet as he did, he saw what laid around him, all of his soldiers were either dead or surrendering. General Trajetton put his saber up to the major's neck. With one final expression of hopelessness, the major dropped his sword. "Colonel," ordered Trajetton, "collect the bodies and burn them. Put the prisoners in the stockades, see if they know anything."

"Yes sir," and the colonel went off.

The major fumed, "those dead deserve a proper burial." He slapped away the saber, leapt up and punched the general in the face. The general lifted the major by the throat, holding him in midair, then impaled him. The major opened his beak, yet could not scream. Trajetton dropped him to the ground and wiped the blood off of his blade. He picked up the major's sword and after examining it for a moment he placed it in his belt. "Colonel, you are in charge now."

"Yes sir," replied the colonel. The general flew up to the fort's perimeter wall where he surveyed the battle's aftermath. He took off down the coast, his fleet passing him by as he headed towards the island's interior, off into the fog.

Chapter 3

Somewhere off in the distance was General Trajetton's home, a tree with a nest on top and rooms carved into the trunk. It was somewhere in the middle of an ocean of evergreens, leagues away from even the smallest droplet of civilization. Soon he began to pass steep, blade-shaped spires of rock hundreds or even thousands of feet high. He was constantly dodging left and right as they popped out of the fog before he reached the valley his tree-home was in.

The general's two sons were lying in their bedroom inside of the tree's trunk. Both of them were wearing the same tattered linen uniforms as they stared up at the wooden ceiling. With the exception of their young faces and their lighter feathers they resembled their father. As with all red griffins the backs of their ears were yellow so that when angered their ears would flatten against their heads and the yellow side would be exposed.

Their father landed on the nest, "father's home!" announced the younger as he ran out of the room and up to the nest. The eldest who was a couple years older kept his eyes on the ceiling. Just lying there, staring. After a minute he let out a sigh, rolled off his bed and slumped up the stairs.

Up on the nest, the younger greeted the general, "hello, father."

"Dyricio," responded the general.

"You're home early today. You don't normally return until nightfall," inquired Dyricio.

The general didn't respond as the elder came up and greeted him too, "hello father."

"Tysorious," said the general, "how be you?"

"I'm fine."

"Good...good." responded the general who seemed rather distant. Tysorious, the elder, then noticed the second sword in his father's belt.

Dyricio was curious as to why he was so distant, "father, is everything alright?"

The general hesitated before speaking, "Tysorious, why don't you take your brother hunting?"

Dyricio cut in, "but father, I already know how to h-"

"Dyricio, just go," the general commanded and Dyricio bowed his head. He went to the ground floor with his older brother following. When they got down there they each grabbed two spears.

"Do you want to talk about it?" asked the elder, Dyricio shook his head. "It's alright, he yells at me too, you just have to learn to ignore it."

"Well I'm not you, Sory!"

There was a silence before the elder spoke, "why do you call me 'Tysorious' around father, but 'Sory' everywhere else?"

Dyricio shrugged, "you said you wanted to be called 'Sory.'"

Sory started back upstairs, "alright, let's go," he walked a few feet into the staircase before stopping.

"What's the matter?" asked Dyricio.

"I forgot the packs. Go up to the nest, I'll be right back." Sory was rummaging for the packs when he heard a stick snap outside. He paused with his eyes on the door leading outside. He opened the door, peering into the darkness between the countless trunks.

"Sory!" yelled Dyricio from behind as Sory flinched, "come on! We must leave before it gets too dark!" Sory was about to follow when he gave one last look into the forest.

When Sory had returned to the nest four officers who he'd never seen before were speaking with his father. Sory watched them as he approached the edge of the nest, his father returning his suspicious gaze. "Tysorious, come on," urged Dyricio before taking flight, Sory following, the general watching his eldest.

Soon they had arrived at a river flanked by the thick forest. Dyricio stood at its muddy bank and threw spears at the small gray fish under the water, growing more and more frustrated with each unsuccessful throw. Sory sat on a tree branch and peered up at the gray clouds, "why do you think those officers were there?" Sory asked Dyricio.

"What?" asked Dyricio as he only half listened, eyeing another fish, then tossing a spear. He leaned on the weapon to see if he had caught anything, but hadn't. "Ugh! I thought fish were supposed to be dumb."

"They are," Sory said, then to himself, "you're just dumber."

Dyricio shot him a look, "well alright then, if you think you're so good then you come down here and get one."

"Alright," he glided over to Dyricio who handed him a spear. Sory scanned the river, pulled back his arm and threw. He pulled the spear out with a squirming fish around the blade.

Sour grew on Dyricio's face, "how did you do that?"

"When you throw the spear into the water, it scares the fish and they swim forward. So you have to aim just in front of them." Sory gave the weapon back and returned to his branch. "You didn't answer my question."

"To what?" asked Dyricio.

"The fish really are smarter." Sory said to himself.

"What?"

"Those officers, what did you make of those officers?"

"I don't know."

"Well what were they doing there? Ramous has never had anyone from the army at home before."

"It is odd I suppose. And you shouldn't call father by his first name." the air whipped as Dyricio threw again, "Hah!" he pulled the spear out with a fish on the end, "Sory look, I got one!"

"Congratulations." Sory waited for an answer to his inquiry, "you still haven't answered me."

Dyricio slumped, "you are making a great deal out of nothing."

"It's unusual for Ramous to have anyone over."

"Maybe they're just friends that just decided to stop by."

"First of all, father does not have friends," Dyricio nodded in agreement as Sory continued, "second," Sory jumped off the branch and started walking toward his brother, "why now? No matter who they are, why now? Why in all the years that we have been living in that tree have there never ever been any visitors and today we get some, hm?" Dyricio shrugged, "and what about that sword?" asked Sory.

"What sword?" Dyricio asked.

"That sword, the one father had in his belt."

"He's always had that."

"No not his saber, there was a second one."

Dyricio shook his head, "again, I don't know."

"Yeah, it's probably nothing. Come on, I caught a few fish already let's just go home." By now the fog had cleared nearly to the horizon as the brothers weaved through the spires for sport. They'd come in as close as they could as fast as they could without hitting the mountains. Soon though they had arrived in the small valley their tree-home was in. Some fog having been trapped within the valley.

The two brothers landed just as the four officers left. Ramous examined the few morsels of fish that Dyricio had in his pack, "is this all? You were supposed to be teaching your brother how to hunt and all you brought back was some fish?" Sory said nothing, "go downstairs, Dyricio." He sulkily did as told as Ramous turned back to Sory, "I know that you wish to leave this tree and see the world, and you will, soon. Soon you will be seeing a great deal of it."

"How much?"

"Whatever the King wishes to claim as his own," they stared at each other for a couple more seconds before Ramous headed downstairs, leaving Sory to contemplate what he meant. Sory stood alone, silently and still, absorbing the brisk air when he felt the sun's warmth on his back. He turned to see it showing through the clouds for the first time in days. A reddish light blushed the nest and warmed Sory as the clouds above and fog below now glowed red in two parallel blankets of fire. Blankets that were split by the pitch black shadows of the spires which appeared as though they were the fingers of carbon titans, cascading in between these two fiery plains. Sory's breath too turned red as he longed for what he saw because he knew it would be a long time before he could reach it, if he ever even did. He knew that his father and Raishany would be the reasons for this intolerable procrastination. After a bit, he turned and dragged his feet back inside the tree, the warmth of the sun once more on his back.

Dyricio was reading one of his royally issued propaganda books on his bed as Sory laid on his and tossed his little leather ball up and down, "what are you reading?" asked Sory.

"A book about Raishan weaponry, how to build cannons and stuff like that."

Sory winced, "I don't understand why you like that stuff."

"What's with you and father lately?"

"What do you mean?"

"For a while now you and he haven't been getting along." Sory shrugged, Dyricio squinted as he tried to remember something, "remember that time, a while back, when you were lost out in the forest?"

"Yeah?"

"Well, it was around then, after you came back, you seemed different." Sory caught the ball and didn't toss it back up, "you seemed, I don't know, changed."

There was a silence, "how was I changed?" Sory finally asked.

"I don't know, you were just more," Dyricio looked for the word, "defiant...of father."

Sory tightened his beak, "I'm not defiant," he declared as he rolled over and blew out the lantern next to his bed.

Dyricio rolled over and to himself said, "then what do you call that?" and blew out his lantern.

*

It was dark, gradually a yellowish light began to illuminate a figure in front of Sory with his back to him as more light came in. Soon Sory could see a giant facing them who was speaking, but Sory couldn't understand what he was saying. The giant's words were just whispers getting louder and louder and soon they were rattling Sory's brain and he couldn't even hear himself think as his head was flooded and he wanted to scream but couldn't.

Sory's eyes opened, the nightmare was gone, and as reality came back he could hear hushed voices up on the nest. He sat up, his heart still pounding as he looked up in the direction of the whispers. Dyricio was still asleep and snoring. Sory snuck upstairs to the slightly opened door that led to the nest, and poked his head through. The sky as gray and chilly as the day before, and so far as he could tell the same four officers from the day before were talking to his father. After a few seconds they shook hands and flew off. Sory brought his head back inside and wondered why they were there again and why it was in secret. Ramous opened the door, Sory jumped, "father–"

"It is rood to eavesdrop, boy."

Sory bowed his head and took a step back, "my apologies, sir."

"I am returning to the coast for the day. You can take care of your brother until then, right?"

"Yes sir." Ramous managed a step away before Sory asked, "why are you returning to the coast?"

Ramous hesitated, "for military matters," and with that, he flew off.

Sory then noticed his father's saber resting against the nest's edge, but the other sword had gone. He decided not to give it much thought and returned downstairs.

Sory quietly walked down and into the hall, to his immediate right was his and Dyricio's bedroom, a little further down on the left was their father's. At the very end of the hall was the spiral staircase that led to the floor below and all the way down to the ground floor. Sory went into his room and grabbed his ball from the end table next to his bed, knocking the lantern onto the floor and causing a clatter. He froze, making sure Dyricio hadn't been awoken. Convinced he hadn't been, Sory left the room and went downstairs. Dyricio, who had pretended to be asleep, followed.

Dyricio continued after Sory as he went all the way to the ground floor and then outside, into the abyss of the trees. Dyricio hesitated for a second, he had heard countless odd and eerie noises come for those trees over the years. Going to the river was one thing because they flew there, but Sory was walking and in those thick branches if something were to lunge out at him he wouldn't have the room to spread his wings and fly to safety. But curiosity soon got the best of Dyricio as he waited until Sory was far enough away for him to follow without notice.

Never had Dyricio seen the forest from within, from above it seemed mysterious, from inside, the trees themselves seemed to be closing in. They creaked and as Dyricio continued, he thought he heard them moan. Creatures scampering about disturbed the ferns and shrubs around them. Tufts of mist and leaves blocked out the light and made it difficult to see, only adding to the fear. Everything looked like something. Like a hatchling without a candle at midnight Dyricio whipped his head about in an anticipation for something to just jump from the darkness and pounce on him.

Then he did see something, it was bigger than him and covered in dark gray fur with black stripes. It was hanging from a tree about twenty feet away, facing away its wings were wrapped around itself. It stretched those wings as it yawned. Wide-eyed, Dyricio watched this bat-like beast, but it seemed fast asleep and so he kept on. He realized that he had lost sight of Sory and frenetically looked about. Moving his eyes up and down and around the infinite vegetation until he finally saw Sory well into the distance. Dyricio leaped after him.

Dyricio followed Sory for some time before he finally started to climb another tree-home. Dyricio waited until his brother had climbed up over the nest before he too went up. He could hear Sory calling for someone from within the tree as he went to the doorway that led downstairs, then turned to find a knife at his face.

Sory went back to the nest to find Dyricio being held hostage, "what-?"

"Sory!" yelled Dyricio with a knife to his throat, wriggling as his captor held him from behind, "tell this Lesser to let me go!"

"Dyricio, what the hell are you doing here?!" exclaimed Sory.

"I saw this cretin following you, Sory," said the armed griffin.

"Let him go, Ayro. He's my brother."

"Really?" Sory nodded and Ayro released his grip, "gods, well, that was my excitement for the week." He was a blue-backed griffin, his body covered in white feathers except for his back. He was also young, only a few years older than Sory.

"Who is this Lesser, Sory?" asked Dyricio.

Ayro jumped up, "what did you call me?!"

"Relax Ayro, he doesn't know any better." Sory turned to his brother, "Dyricio, this is my friend, Ayro."

"That's an odd name."

"Oh right, because Dyricio's not the name of a whiny little bigot." Dyricio took a step forward, "ah-ah-ah," said Ayro as he held up the knife.

"Dyricio, why did you follow me?" inquired Sory.

"I was just - just wondering why you were sneaking out."

"Well I hadn't seen Ayro in a while."

"How did you two become friends anyway?"

Sory took in a deep breath, "remember last night when you said that I had become defiant of father ever since that time I had gotten lost. Well when I was lost I saw this tree-home and figured that whoever was here could help me. But when I saw Ayro I realized I'd crossed the colonial border-"

"WE'RE OVER THE BORDER?! We're not in Raishan territory?!" screamed Dyricio.

"Ayro helped me find my way back. He had been living alone for a while and he knew his way around. But by showing me the way home, he showed me the truth."

Ayro smiled, "That's beautiful."

"Thank you, I just made that up off the top of my head. Anyway, it was then that I realized that all the propaganda that father had taught us all our lives was wrong."

"It is not, your friend was going to stab me!" Dyricio pointed at Ayro.

"Yeah and that's because you deserve it!" called back Ayro.

"Ayro," said Sory, "have you seen any Raishan activity lately? Say in the past couple of days?"

Ayro thought, "I don't know if it's important, but I did see some smoke coming from the coast yesterday."

"Yesterday," Sory said to himself.

"It was over there, in that direction," Ayro pointed northwest.

"That's the same direction father came from yesterday."

"You should not be calling father by his first name, and stop telling your friend those things!" yelled Dyricio.

"Why?" asked Sory.

"Because-" Dyricio searched his mind for a reason, "because those are military secrets!"

Sory's eyes widened as he looked at something in the distance. The other two looked and saw someone flying by. "It's father. I've got to go, bye Ayro." Sory ran and jumped off the edge of the nest. Dyricio and Ayro gave each other one last glance before Dyricio followed his brother.

Sory was bounding over the forest floor as Dyricio caught up, "Sory, why aren't you flying?"

"I don't want to be seen."

"But do you have any idea how dangerous it is down here?"

"We can just fly if we need-" they jumped over a log, "to."

"No we can't, the branches are too dense for us to fly."

Sory stopped, "I never thought of that." From behind, something giant on the side of a tree that had been perfectly camouflaged scurried to the other side of the trunk. The brothers only caught a glimpse of what may have been a giant spider, "let's fly."

"Yeah," and they both scampered up another tree before darting into the air. They weaved in between the individual treetops to avoid being seen as Sory kept his eye on Ramous. Soon they were in their little valley and Ramous had beaten them to their home. He landed on the nest while the two brothers hid in a nearby tree. Sory watched as Dyricio came up behind and gasped for breath. Their father was walking to the nest's doorway and Sory had just enough time to make it to the ground floor door before his father discovered they weren't there. Not that it mattered, Ramous' hearing was uncanny from all those years of fighting all those wars. But at the last second, Ramous stopped, he was looking at something, he was looking in their direction. Sory squeezed Dyricio's wheezing beak shut, then froze. Ramous picked up his saber which was still sitting there.

Sory whispered a sigh of relief, "why did he come all the way back here for a saber?"

"All Raishan soldiers of the King must be armed at all times. Don't you ever listen to what father says? Oh I forgot, you've been 'shown the truth.'" Ramous flew right over them and they both ducked. After he was a distance away Dyricio got up, "come on, let's get inside before father comes back."

"You go, I'm going to follow him."

"Are you insane?"

Sory flew off without answering. His father was already a speck in the distance. Sory feared that he was heading for Ayro's tree-home. He knew it was crazy, but he couldn't help think it. Soon they had crossed the border into Arktorian territory, only amplifying Sory's fear. Yet after a little while he noticed that they'd passed Ayro's home, which made him wonder where his father was really heading. Sory then realized – he was going to wherever he'd been the day before.

Soon Sory could smell a stench, one he did not know. It was when he saw the horizon turn blue that he figured out the stench was the ocean. Ramous was still just a large dot in the sky as he descended into a fortress. Sory dropped and started weaving in between the tops of the trees like before.

Sory hid in a tree at the edge of the forest only a few dozen meters from an unfinished Arktorian fort manned by Raishans. His father was somewhere inside. A rush barreled through him, afraid and bewildered at the same time as to what was happening. Could they be at war? It must have been why those officers were at their home. "Put your hands up!" Sory's heart lurched as a Raishan voice commanded him from behind. He raised his trembling arms and the Raishan soldier grabbed the back of his collar, pulling him to the top of the tree. He then pushed a saber into Sory's back just enough to rip through the fabric of his shirt. "Fly."

The soldier forced Sory to the fort. They landed on the perimeter wall as other soldiers milled about. An older one came up to them, "I see you caught us lunch." The nearby soldiers laughed.

"I caught him spying," said Sory's captor.

"Spying? Do you speak Raishan, boy?"

Sory nodded, "y – yes, my name is Tysorious Trajetton."

"Hah! Trajetten? Did you hear that? You caught the general's son!" The nearby soldiers laughed again, "if you are his son than you won't mind if I go get him?" the older soldier smiled.

"Go ahead, it would be your head on a pike if anything happened to me."

The soldier grabbed Sory's neck and ripped out a dagger, pointing it at his face, "you've got a big beak on you."

"You're not going to kill me."

"Oh yeah, why not, because you're Trajetton's son? What if you're not?"

"What if I am?"

The older soldier considered this. He turned to the other, "get the general," the captor flew off. The elder pulled Sory in close, "if you're lying, I'll cut your tongue out so you can't tell anymore lies," he shoved Sory away.

Meanwhile on the fort's floor, half-naked Arktorian prisoners were being dragged in chains to the stockades, many of them limping. One prisoner collapsed, one of the Raishans pulling them kicked him to get up. The prisoner put his hands against the ground and started to push up, only making it a few inches before he froze. He couldn't go any farther. The Raishan then cracked him over the shoulder with an iron rod, the prisoner's wing fell limp as if it had been cut off. He curled his body in pain, too proud to acknowledge it with noise. The Raishan then started beating the prisoner wildly, then another joined in, and a dozen more gathered around. Almost all at once they let out their talons and dove in, roaring and snarling. The prisoner's one good wing stood in the air and rocked back and forth.

Sory's face morphed, "Tysorious," roared his father from behind, "why are you here?"

Sory just continued to watch the carnage below, "Tysorious! Why are you here?!" Sory flew off, "Tysorious!"

Sory's eyes dampened, his wings pumped but felt numb and he couldn't feel his body either. He just flew, not knowing for how long or where. He did not think about where he was until he saw Ayro's tree in the distance. Sory made sure no one had followed him before landing on Ayro's nest, who was sitting out there already. "Sory?" Sory heaved, "what's the matter?"

"Nothing, never-mind," he charged off for home. A minute later though he heard screaming, he turned to see two Raishan soldiers with Ayro in their talons. "Ayro," he shifted to turn when something grasped him from above.

"You – TRAITOR!" Ramous snarled as he held Sory. He raked his son's face with his talons and kneed him in the gut, knocking the Arktorian sword out of his belt. Sory cried out and Ramous tossed him to the ground, watching with a patronizing expression as his son fell, before heading toward Ayro's tree-home.

Sory tumbled through the air, thrashing his wings to right himself before the branches below could break them. He finally stopped tumbling a moment before smashing through the thick canopy. A second later, a thick branch stopped his fall. His stomach sore, Sory looked up to see his father's mysterious sword a few feet away. He snatched it, and then charged off after his father.

Chapter 4

Night had fallen by the time General Trajetton and Ayro had reached the fortress. The general brought Ayro to the stockade entrance where two guards stood. "I have a prisoner," the general told them. One opened the entrance with a key which the general snatched away. As Ayro was dragged alongside him he grasped at the general's strangling hand, his butt hitting each stair as they descended into the stockade. Ayro also noticed a hole in the entrance hall's roof from the recent attack.

At the bottom of the staircase they turned left into the actual stockade. A dreary hall lit by a few torches with three cells on each side, all filled to the brim with Arktorians. Ayro struggled even more upon seeing all these twisted and half dead bodies staring back at him. The general stopped at the end of the hall, unlocked a cell's door and tossed his prisoner in. He then slammed the door shut, the rusted metal bars of the cell ringing out. He relocked the door and marched off, the bars still ringing.

Sory sat crouched in a tree on the forest's edge. He had watched his father storm out of the stockades and into the command post. Then Sory dove to the bottom of one of the fort's walls. He squatted and thought what to do next, "Sory!" he flinched before realizing it was Dyricio.

"Go home, Dyricio."

His brother flew down beside him, "what are you doing?! What is wrong with you?!"

"What do you think I'm doing?" replied Sory as he slunk toward the wall's corner, scanning the stone above.

"We need to get out of here – right now!" Dyricio pleaded.

"No."

"Listen, Sory, you're already in enough trouble as it is, okay. Let's just go home," he persisted as they turned the corner.

Sory stopped as his eyes pointed straight up, "you go home."

Dyricio looked where Sory was, "what are you looking at?"

"There's a hole in the wall, right there."

Dyricio saw it. It was almost all the way to the top and looked like a bit that had not been completed. "Oh no, Sory-" Sory began climbing the ivy on the wall. Dyricio shook his head and started back to the forest, but then stopped and groaned, "wait! Sory!"

"Sh!"

"Sorry," he whispered, "wait for me." He started to grumble, "I can't believe – always something – never-" Sory poked his head through the unfinished bit and searched for the hall that his father had taken Ayro into. He soon found it, as well the hole in it which he figured was from the battle.

Dyricio reached him, "follow me," said Sory.

"W – wait, follow you where?" Sory jumped down, "Sory!" called Dyricio as his brother slipped down through the hole, Dyricio soon followed. A Raishan noticed them from near the command post and ran off to find some soldiers to send down there.

Sory was already at the bottom of the stairs when Dyricio came through the hole, "Dyricio, stay up there and make sure no one comes down." Sory then tip-toed down the stockade hall, whispering for Ayro as he went.

As soon as he heard Sory's voice, Ayro leapt to the bars of his cell, "Sory! I'm over here!" Sory rushed over to him, "get me out of here!"

"I will," Sory assured as he scanned the bars for any weaknesses.

"Come on!" urged Ayro.

"I'll get you out. Don't worry."

"Good luck, son," said one of the prisoners, "you'll never get these bars open." Terror overtook Ayro's face.

Sory's heart thumped in his chest, then Dyricio rushed down the stairs, "Sory! Sory! Soldiers are coming!" Sory could hear them approaching, their boots clanking with each step. He looked about for a place to hide, then looked up. Above them a series of rafters lined the ceiling. They might just have been dense enough to hide in. Sory jumped up, his brother grabbed on to a beam and Sory pulled him up just as the soldiers entered the room.

Frozen with their feathers glued to their skin as what happens when griffins are scared, the pair watched as the four soldiers searched the room but found nothing. They then each took a corner. Oddly though, Sory could feel and hear Dyricio's heartbeat as if his ear were against his chest. He tried to think of what to do, considering the window at the end of the hall. But he knew that the space was too small for even his head to fit through, besides there were two guards standing next to it.

Then Sory saw a hand from the outside put a cloth sack onto the windowsill. After a couple seconds a hissing flame climbed up the string that led into the sack. All four guards looked towards the window, then ran. Sory sprinted out of the rafters with Dyricio following. The prisoners who could stand struggled to flee to the far sides of their cells. They had only a second before the tiny flame reached the sack. BOOM. A shockwave flung everyone away as dust and bits of stone flew everywhere.

Their ears rung. Their bodies rocked to the core. Sory opened his eyes, searching for the Raishan soldiers. As the dust settled he spotted the silhouette of a figure standing in the hole in the wall. A couple seconds later and he could tell it was a female even though she had a helmet on, her camouflaged armor covering her entire body. She herself was slim and lean, but what stood out most was the intense fire in her eyes – clear as the sun, it perforated through the brown, dusty air.

She darted in between the brothers as they stumbled to their feet. With her sword she stabbed one soldier before he was even on his feet, then blocked the blow of another with her circular shield. She swung her sword over the soldier's shield and into his neck. A third lunged and as she fought him the fourth came up from behind.

Sory saw his sword laying on the floor, he snatched it up and approached the fourth soldier. They stared each other down, but Sory lost his nerve. The soldier realized this and started to laugh, his eyes closed and his beak wide open. Suddenly an instinct exploited the opening and Sory thrust his sword into the soldier's mouth.

The soldier collapsed and Sory stood traumatized. The female soldier finished off her opponent, then saw Sory standing there looking almost as dead as the dead soldier. She took off her helmet and took his hand in hers. They locked eyes for a moment. She was a magnus griffin, her body covered in light red feathers each outlined in black, a black that glistened in the moonlight. Ramous had once spoken highly of them because they were close relatives of the red griffin. "The trick is not to think of them as griffin," she finally said.

"Ruby!" called a voice from the hole in the wall, "what the hell did you think you were doing?"

She released Sory's hand and walked over to this soldier as more came in, "you know how I like to be the first one in, Bahren."

Bahren was a great-horned griffin with two tufts of black and white feathers sticking out of his ears, his body covered in brown, black, white, and red feathers. Bahren turned to the prisoners, "we are soldiers of the Arktorian Empire and we are here to liberate you!" The prisoners all cheered as the rest of the Arktorians flooded in and used axes to break the locks of the cells.

Dyricio whispered in Sory's ear, "come on, we need to get out of here!" Sory could hear Raishan soldiers at the top of the stairs whispering to each other what to do.

"What about Ayro?"

"He's fine, he's with his countrymen. Now let's get out of here before they figure out we're Raishans!" They dashed to the stairs which Bahren noticed. Sory started to think though. *What do I have in Raishany? What do I really have to lose if I go with the Arktorians?* He stopped at the foot of the stairs, Dyricio just ahead, "what are you waiting for?! Let's go!"

Sory, still staring into space, suddenly had an assuredness in his eyes. Nothing had ever made as much sense as what he had just decided. He glared at Dyricio with a steel face and asked, "why?" he then went off to help the Arktorians, his brother's face blank.

After a long pause Dyricio shook his head, "Sory!" but his brother kept going, "he'll come back." he looked up the stairs and saw a few Raishan soldiers at the top, "hello," he called to them in Raishan, but they didn't seem keen on listening. One threw a spear, Dyricio ducked. It stabbed into the stone wall just inches over his head. They assumed he was the enemy even though he had no armor or uniform on. Terrified, Dyricio sprinted for his brother, "Sory, I changed my mind! I'm coming with you!"

Raishan soldiers were scattering about in the rest of the fortress, readying for an attack. Archers flew to the platforms circling the roof's skeleton, some loading and cocking their crossbows while others manned the ballistae. Meanwhile the hoplites and lancers formed up into their rectangular phalanxes. General Trajetton was reading one of the books from the library when he heard and felt the explosion. When it happened he bolted to the stockades' entrance as hundreds of troops ran about and forced him to stop every couple of seconds as they got in his way. By now he could see smoke rising from the other side of the perimeter wall. He arrived at the stockades' entrance and was almost hit in the head by a soldier throwing a spear down into the stairwell, "what is going on?!" the general demanded.

"Sir, I – I didn't see you there, I – I didn't-" stuttered the soldier.

"What is happening?!" demanded the general.

"I – I think it's an attack, sir," replied the soldier. The general caught a glimpse of a griffin's leg as it disappeared at the bottom of the stairs. He unsheathed his saber and was about to chase after this griffin when the stuttering soldier stopped him.

"Sir, I suggest you don't go down there." The general could hear speaking from below, just as he was about to continue down an officer came up to him.

"General Trajetton, sir, you'll want to see this," he pointed out to sea. The general flew to the perimeter wall where he could see a ship floating in the distance.

The Arktorians stumbled out of the fort, the wounded being helped along by the commandos that had just liberated them. Sory, Ayro, and Dyricio aided as much as they could. Sory let one prisoner put his arm around him as they jogged down the sand dune to the beach.

The crowd raced to the longboats at the tide's edge. These were small boats powered by ores and were normally used as life rafts. Meanwhile a frigate, illuminated by the moonlight, sat waiting a few hundred feet out into the ocean. Sory helped the wounded soldier into one of these longboats before going over to the female soldier, Ruby, "hey, how did you know that we – that the Raishans had attacked this fort?"

"Distress signal, a red arrow fired into the air," she bluntly stated without making eye contact. "Now if you wouldn't mind hopping into a boat so that we could get out of here!" She swiftly jumped into one, "well, you coming or what?" Sory hopped in and started rowing with the others as hard as he could while Ruby crouched down and watched the fort.

The general could see the longboats with the prisoners in them escaping. "Fire!" he yelled. Hundreds of archers released a cloud of arrows into the night, creating a whizzing sound like a small storm. But the darkness prevented them from aiming accurately so they fired indiscriminately into the night.

Ruby's ears faced forward, Sory knew what he heard, "Incoming!" he yelled. He pulled Ruby under him. He covered them with a shield just as the arrows struck. The ordinance banged against the shield, making pointed dents. They clenched their eyes shut until it ended only a few seconds later. When it did, Sory was face to face with Ruby, "are you okay?" he asked.

"I would be if there wasn't something stabbing my hip."

Sory looked down at his weapon which was pressing into her, "that's just my sword."

"I don't care what you call it, get it off me!" She pressed her talons into Sory's ribs and he jumped off. She returned to her watch as Sory rubbed his hurting ribs. She turned back, "thank you," and she faced the fortress as it shrunk away.

Infuriated, General Trajetton raced into the stockades with soldiers and officers following. The first thing he noticed was the huge hole in the wall, then the four slain Raishan soldiers. "Bring me the soldier who threw the spear at one of them!" he ordered his entourage. An officer ran back up the stairs. Trajetton examined the four soldiers lying on the ground, disappointment on his face. "Where is that soldier?" the officer reentered with the soldier behind him.

"This is the private you requested, sir," the officer said.

"What did you see?" asked the general.

"I heard the explosion and when I looked down the stairs I saw one of them, sir. He looked me straight in the eye and told me 'hello.'"

"And what did you do?"

"I threw a spear at him, but I missed, sir."

Trajetton took a minute to think, "gentlemen, the element of surprise has been lost. They know we're at war." He pointed to Colonel Zarfis, "gather one hundred fifty of your best troopers and intercept the attackers!"

"Yes sir!" he clapped his heels and saluted.

"JUST GET ON WITH IT!" Trajetton yelled. The colonel darted up the stairs with Trajetton close behind. The colonel gathered his attack group then flew off, disappearing into the night.

Trajetton selected a junior officer, "you, go find Colonel Zarfis and tell him he's in charge." Ramous then headed home.

*

The Arktorians rowed frantically as the cries of the wounded sounded out into the night. When they reached the frigate a net was cast over the side and those on the longboats started hauling the wounded up with the ship's sailors helping. Once everyone was onboard, the longboats were brought up as well.

As the wounded were brought below deck Sory began looking for Dyricio. He found his brother hiding between two cannons. "Hey," Sory said, "are you alright?" Dyricio just stared forward, "I didn't mean for you to come with me. It's not too late, you can still go back." Dyricio still didn't reply. "What do you want me to say?! Why did you come along anyway?!" Dyricio mumbled something, "what?"

"I said why did you want to leave?!"

"Because – because I was miserable, that's why. I couldn't stand to live in that damned tree for another day!" Dyricio looked away and Sory crouched down beside him, "we can start a new life, a free one! We can go and do whatever we want. We don't have to do what father says anymore." Dyricio remained silent. Sory sat down next to him, leaning against the cannon Dyricio was, "you'll come around."

Meanwhile the sails were lowered as a half dozen wingless griffins started to hoist the anchors up by means of two giant gears. This enthralled Sory, who had never seen wingless griffins before. Ramous had talked about them plenty of times, how they were the sub-class of griffins. They were a race that had once been enslaved in most of the world and still was in some places, such as Raishany. Slavery had been abolished in other nations such as Arktorion. The wingless griffins on this ship were all wearing tattered and torn shorts and nothing else. Even though wingless griffins had been emancipated in Arktorion they were still considered second class citizens and so were forced to do the work considered beneath that of winged griffins. Most of their bodies were covered in white feathers except for the tops of their heads and backs which were red and their faces which were black. Yet what stood out most was their tremendous size, as much as one and half times the height of the average griffin.

Once the anchors had been raised one of the wingless went over and leaned against the gunwale, the railing at the edge of the ship. Ruby came up next to him, "hello, Gyric."

"Hello, Ruby."

"Smells like rain, maybe a storm's coming."

"Yeah, maybe."

Bahren walked up, "I am not sure about those two," he motioned to Sory and Dyricio who were well out of earshot.

"Oh Bahren, you're so paranoid," said Ruby.

"Am I? Then why don't they have uniforms on?"

"Maybe they were stripped of their uniforms when they were captured." Ruby replied before taking a second look at the brothers, "but when I got into the stockades they weren't in a cell."

"See, there is something wrong about them!" Bahren persisted.

"Maybe, I don't know," she shrugged as the frigate continued west and soon met up with more warships. All headed for Arktorion.

Chapter 5

Ramous landed on his nest and removed his armored boots. He noticed his second sword, the one he'd captured from the Arktorian officer, was missing. "Damn," he groaned before he headed downstairs. He peaked into his sons' room – and froze. They were gone. Instead of allowing his emotions to overpower him, he pondered where they could be. He remembered that Sory had seen Ayro get taken prisoner. He could have followed them to the fortress, he could have tried to break Ayro out, and he could have been in the stockades when the Arktorians came. Ramous blasted up to the nest and back for the fortress.

*

The waves rocked the frigate and kept Ayro, Dyricio, and Sory awake. They had never been on a ship before and so far their experience had not been so pleasant. They were in the crew's sleeping quarters within the bottom floor, a rather dank and dark place indeed. The bunks were small and stacked three high and the halls in between them were narrow. The bunks had white, stained sheets with stiff pillows, both of which stunk of sweat and brine.

Sory and Dyricio lied down as Ayro tried not to get sick by hugging and rocking himself back and forth. Dyricio was still pondering how much trouble they were going to be in, then a huge wave hit the frigate. Ayro darted to the end of the hall, with a hand around his beak, where he crouched over a bucket and hurled. Dyricio then stood up and laid his hands on the side of Sory's bunk, "well I guess now's as good a time as any to talk."

Sory opened his eyes and took a deep breath, "you still want to go back."

"What was wrong with the life we had back on Hyleeda? We were safe, well fed–"

"What's your point?" Sory asked in a low, slightly annoyed voice.

"Why didn't you come with me when you had the chance?"

"I wanted to escape. I've always wanted to escape." Dyricio hung his head as Sory continued, "why did you come? Why are you blaming me for your decision?"

Dyricio took a few seconds to answer, "one of the soldiers threw a spear at me."

"Hah! Now isn't that ironic?"

"Shut–up."

"Go back to sleep, Dyricio." Ayro sauntered back over wiping his beak, "feel better?" Sory asked him.

"Much better," there was a silence, "so Sory, have you said anything to that one soldier, what's her name, Ruby?"

"Ayro-" said Sory.

Ayro leaned against Sory's bunk, "you know, because I am well versed in the subtleties of the female species."

"'The female species?'"

"Oh yes."

"I am sure that they love to be called that."

Dyricio stood up and walked all the way up to the deck of the frigate. On the western horizon the first red rays of the sun were just starting to appear. With them he could see the rest of the fleet that they were at the end of. Half the sky had become a dark navy blue as the rest remained in blackness where the stars still shown. There was not a cloud in the sky, which was something that Dyricio had never seen before. The glassy air allowed for him to see countless stars in numbers that he didn't even know existed.

Dyricio went aft, the end of the ship, where he leaned over the gunwale and tried to see if Hyleeda was still visible, but it had disappeared long ago. Disappointed, he figured he might as well go back downstairs and sleep when he passed the ship's wheel without noticing that someone was manning it, "what are yah doin' yah night-crawler? Get back to bed." Dyricio flinched, now noticing this motionless silhouette against the blue and black sky. This griffin's raspy voice sounded ancient and had an accent. The mysterious figure who owned it faced on into the rising sun as he inhaled a drag from his pipe.

"What?" asked a bewildered Dyricio.

"You heard me, boy. What are yah doing up?"

"Oh, uh, I couldn't sleep."

The figure took another deep drag from his pipe. The ashes inside lit up and Dyricio could see part of his face and his beak which had a big chip in it. His face was covered in scruffy, gray and thinned feathers, some of which hung down around his beak like a mustache and beard. He removed the pipe from his mouth and blew out a cloud of smoke which was quickly whisked away by the wind. "What's your name, boy?"

"D – Dyricio."

"Dyricio, well that's not your fault," he took another breath of smoke, "you got a last name?"

"Uh, no, uh, I'm an orphan."

"Why do you say 'uh' so much? You get dropped on your noggin as a hatchling?"

"No!"

"Then what's the matter, boy?"

"Nothing, I – I'm just tired."

"Then how come you couldn't sleep?"

Dyricio was becoming frustrated with this character, "why are you so testy?"

"Just tryin' to make conversation, boy. No reason to get jumpy."

"I'm not getting jumpy."

"Whatever you say, boy." Dyricio had had enough, he trudged away while shaking his head. "Good, get gone, boy."

Just before Dyricio reached the trap door that led downstairs, another voice came from the darkness, "I see you've met Captain Zat," said Bahren who leaned against the center mast.

"Who?" asked Dyricio.

"Captain Zat. Don't mind him, he's a war hero you know? They say he went mad after some huge battle he was in years ago."

"Why did he go mad?"

"No one knows exactly. He won't talk about it, that battle I mean, but he's just lucky it made him a war hero or they'd have discharged him from the navy. I guess it makes him feel good just to be out at sea. They say he's spent more time on the waves than on land. Some say he was even conceived, born, and hatched out at sea."

"Why do they let him drive the ship if he's crazy?"

"He's only a little crazy."

Dyricio nodded, "alright, well, I'm going back to bed." he walked off, Bahren still watching, his eyes squinting.

*

General Trajetton pumped his wings, flying so rapidly the water in his eyes dried up. The sun began to rise over the horizon, a thin sliver of orange peaking up while the rest of the starless sky remained pitch black. Trajetton streaked into the fortress, nearly making the air crack and startling everyone within. He burst into the command post where the officers all jumped up and drew their weapons before realizing who it was, "general?" one asked.

"Did anyone see two red griffins sneaking into the fortress before the attack?"

"Sir?"

Trajetton leapt out of the room and flew to the roof of the command post, "did anyone see two red griffins sneaking into the fortress before the attack?!" The soldiers gathered and started whispering amongst each other before a voice rang out.

"I did, sir!" A trooper stepped forward.

Trajetton landed in front of him, "why did you not alert anyone?"

"I thought I'd caught a glimpse of something. I wasn't sure what and so I sent some soldiers down to the stockades because it looked like whatever I had seen had gone down there, sir. But I wasn't even sure that I'd seen anything and I knew sounding the alert for no reason would get me into trouble."

Trajetton said nothing. His ears folded back, showing the bright yellow on their back side. He grasped the soldier by the throat and lifted him off the ground, his talons fully extended, "you were the old one who was with my son the first time he snuck in," the old one gasped for air and pulled at Trajetton's hand who leaned into his face, "you may have just lost us the war you old fool!" He then whispered into the soldier's ear, "do you know how important they are to victory?"

The general constricted his hand to his greatest ability and the soldier's eyes rolled back into his head and a gargling sound came out of his mouth. Finally his hands went limp. Trajetton released his grip and his victim slumped to the ground, "let this be a lesson to all of you, take nothing for granted. Because those two griffins were my sons, and they have been captured by the enemy," a wave surged through the crowd, "and we are going to get them back." Trajetton took flight, his army of nearly two thousand following at full speed.

Chapter 6

It was a gray and cloudy mid-morning when Sory stepped onto the deck. Everyone was rushing around in a hurry when Ruby came up to him, "Sory!"

"What's going on?" he asked.

"Our sentries spotted a Raishan army coming in from the east only a few minutes behind us."

"Where did they come from? We're in the middle of the ocean."

"We think they're the same forces that took the fortress."

"Trajetton's forces?"

"Yes, I'm sorry but I must go."

Sory rushed down to Ayro and Dyricio in the sleeping quarters, "wake up! Wake up!" they groaned as he yelled, "father's coming!"

Ayro jumped out of bed, "what?!"

"He's brought his army with him. Dyricio, you and I must reach him before he kills everybody in this fleet." Sory started back to the deck with the other two following.

"Wait! Sory," said Ayro, "what are you talking about?"

"He's coming after me and Dyricio. If we can reach him in time he won't attack this fleet."

"But you can't go back to Hyleeda! You hated it!"

"I can't let all these griffins die because of that." They reached the deck and Sory turned to Dyricio, "are you ready?" Sory asked. Dyricio just stared blankly.

"Enemy at the helm!" yelled a sentry. They all turned to see two thousand Raishans only a few hundred meters behind them.

Ramous could sense his sons, "they are here."

"How can you tell, sir?" asked Colonel Zarfis.

"I just can. Ready for attack!" he ordered.

At the edge of the ship Sory spread his wings, "Dyricio, come on!"

Ayro stopped them, "Wait you can't just fly off! He's going to think you're Arktorians!" Sory froze, he knew Ayro was right. Hundreds of arrows then streamed down, hitting some of those on deck. The wounded cried out as everyone crouched or laid down. The trio darted behind the center mast.

"It is too late now," Sory whispered to himself. The archers flew up into the masts and perched themselves wherever possible before returning fire. Then the frigate starting turning, the rest of the fleet still moving forward.

"What's going on?!" exclaimed Ayro.

They ran up to the ship's wheel where Captain Zat was steering and belting out orders, "load the starboard cannons with all the flack we have and point them skyward!" Captain Zat was an old griffin with a gray mustache of feathers around his beak. On his head rested a black hat with a white feather sticking out of the right side, while the left flap was folded straight up.

"Are you crazy?! What are you doing?!" Ayro exclaimed again.

The captain stuck his saber at Ayro's throat, "don't call me crazy, boy! I know what I'm doing, and I'll be damned before some flightless hatchling tells me how to fight a battle!" Seconds later and the frigate's broadside was facing the Raishans when another hail of arrows rained down. Everyone had gotten a shield by then and the trio hid behind the soldiers protecting Captain Zat with their shields.

Bahren ran up, "Captain Zat, what are you doing?!"

"What does it look like?! I'm going to kill me some Raishans!" he threw his head back, "Hah-har!"

"There are reinforcements coming in. We'll put up a fight farther west." Bahren said.

"Nonsense, we're going to fight right here, right now. It's been a while since I've killed someone."

"We can't fight them with just one ship!" Bahren yelled when more arrows struck down.

The fleet's commodore on the nearby flag ship, Commodore Pdosvine, who was dressed in a dark blue naval uniform, watched Captain Zat's frigate through his telescope, "what in the name of all that is holy does that maniac think he's doing?"

"I don't know, sir," a lieutenant beside him replied, "but it looks like he's making a stand."

The commodore removed the telescope away from his eye, "damn that half-brained nincompoop." he whispered to himself, then yelled, "turn the fleet hard to starboard!"

"Sir?"

"We fight here!"

"A-aye…aye sir." The lieutenant ran to the signalman and gave him the command.

Dyricio noticed the fleet turning first, "Look! Look!" he pointed and everyone turned.

"Hah!" yelled Captain Zat, "hold onto your butts, lads, this will be the fight of our lives!" He waved his saber in the air and screeched at the top of his lungs. The sea was picking up, huge, squall sized waves began knocking the fleet about like corks.

Ramous couldn't believe his eyes, "they're moving to defend! Attack formation!" The lancers moved to the front of the formation and pointed their spears out, General Trajetton led the charge as his army dove and accelerated.

Sory fetched his sword from his bunk, then went to the armory and picked up a shield, it was round and silver, its edge sharpened. "That's a knight's shield," said Ruby.

Back on deck it had begun to rain as the archers fired as fast as they could. The cannons were being loaded with anti-air shells, which were cannonballs loaded with black powder and little bits of twisted metal that would explode midair. But the enemy was mere seconds away, the cannons couldn't be loaded in time.

"SHIELDS!" sounded a major. Everyone raised their shields and pointed whatever weapons they had out at the enemy. The Raishan crossbowmen shot pointblank, hitting their targets in their faces. The

Raishan lancers threw their spears, slaughtering more and breaking up the Arktorian formation, allowing them to land.

All around Sory soldiers were fighting and slashing at each other. Blood drenched the deck in seconds. The screams of the dying and the ringing of steel blades filled his skull. He waived his sword, just trying to not die when a dead archer fell on him. Sory tried to stand when another soldier fell on them, pinning him to the floor.

The rain was pouring onto Sory's head, then stopped for a moment as something flew over him. He somehow knew who it was. Ramous landed at the bow of the frigate, cutting away at Arktorians as he searched for his sons. An axe was thrown at his head. He dodged it and looked to see Ruby standing there, her eyes locked on him.

Sory's heart sank as Ruby jumped up and thrust her sword at Ramous' face. He smacked her out of the air with his shield. She stood back up and started stabbing and slashing at the general who blocked every blow. He slammed her with his shield again and cut her across the ribs.

Ruby's infuriation exploded and she jumped up screaming. She hovered over Ramous and stabbed toward his face and neck but still could not penetrate his defenses. He knocked her out of the air again. On the wooden deck, she could taste her own blood in her beak.

Ramous down-swung, she leapt onto a beam holding up one of the sails. Ruby pointed her body at the general, then sprung forward screaming.

Ramous froze, waiting. An instant later he swung his shield into her face. Her voice cracked, her body went limp and fell against his before falling onto the floor, motionless. Sory sprung onto his feet, the weight of two dead bodies on top of his seeming to vanish with his rage.

His father spotted him, "Tysorious! Come!" Sory stood without reaction, "Tysorious!" Sory picked up his sword and shield, holding them out in front of him as his father walked over, "what do you think you are doing, boy?" Sory stood still as a statue. Then he thrust his sword at Ramous' gut who blocked, "Tysorious!"

"AHHH!" Sory jumped and swung. Ramous slapped him down with his shield. Sory's head spun as he laid on the floor. He grabbed his sword but Ramous planted his foot on the blade.

Sory looked up and found his father's saber in his face, "you have gone mad, boy. They have gotten to you haven't they?" They locked eyes, "look around, you have lost." Sory did look around, all the other Arktorians were either dead, dying, or surrendering. "Enough of this nonsense. Stand up, and we will return to Hyleeda where you will fulfill your destiny." Sory looked back to his father, confused as to what he meant by 'fulfilling his destiny.' Then he noticed that his father's feet were naked. "Tysorious, what are waiting for?" Sory grabbed the sword, turned its edge up and sliced Ramous' foot. "AHHH!"

Sory stood, blood on his blade. Ramous gave him a deathly glare. Then he put his shield over his head which was hit by an arrow, more streamed down. Everyone looked to see thousands of Arktorian soldiers flying in. "RETREAT!" yelled Colonel Zarfis.

"NO! Do not retreat! Stand your ground!" yelled back Ramous, but most of his soldiers were already in the air. Ramous went to grab Sory who swung his sword as dozens of Arktorians rushed at the general. He charged into the air, following his soldiers.

Sory ran over to Ruby and kneeled down next to her. As he held her head a sword was pointed at his face, it was Bahren. "Stand!" he ordered and Sory did as told, "drop your weapons." Sory did and Bahren turned to a private, "go and find his two companions." Bahren turned back to Sory, "get away from her." Sory didn't move, "I said – get away from her!" Bahren pushed Sory away, "who are you? How did that Raishan general know your name?" Sory said nothing when Ayro and Dyricio were dragged up, swords at their necks, "who are the three of you?" they remained silent. Bahren was growing impatient.

"I am Tysorious Trajetton," Sory announced, "son of Ramous Trajetton."

Bahren's eyes widened, "put them in the brig!" he commanded. The three of them were escorted below deck. Bahren bent over and felt Ruby's pulse, "she's alive. Bring her to the medical bay and fetch the surgeon." She was carried off as Bahren followed his prisoners downstairs.

The trio was brought to the bottom floor by a half dozen soldiers, then shoved into a small cell. Bahren came down, Sory's sword in his hand, the ship continuing to rock with the growing waves. Bahren stood at the bars of the cell door which Sory then leaned against, "how is Ruby?"

Bahren squinted before answering, "she's fine," Sory sighed in relief, "what do you want with her?" Bahren inquired suspiciously.

"Nothing," answered Sory.

"Really? Did you see her fighting your father?"

"Yes."

"Did you help?"

"I was stuck."

"You were stuck? On what?" Bahren's eyes scanned Sory's.

"Under someone."

"And who might that have been?"

"What's the difference anyway?! You don't believe me!"

"Who were you stuck under?"

"I don't know, a dead soldier."

"On whose side?"

"Arktorian, I think."

"Oh," Bahren backed up, put his hand to his beak as if thinking hard about something, "did you kill him?"

Sory slammed the cell door, "NO I DID NOT!"

"Whose side are you on?"

"What's the difference, you won't believe-"

"Answer the question-!"

"I AM ON YOURS!"

Bahren scowled at him for another second, "we'll see," he went upstairs. Two of the soldiers that had escorted the trio down there remained and stood at attention on either side of the cell door.

Chapter 7

By nightfall, the fleet had found itself in the midst of a raging hurricane. Lightning flashed every couple of seconds, splitting the black sky above as the ocean writhed and swelled and crashed onto the deck. The bobbling of the ship and the roaring of the wind kept anyone from sleeping. "This storm is endless," complained Ayro.

"Quiet in there!" one of the guards yelled.

Bahren was sitting next to a still unconscious Ruby in the medical bay when a wave smacked the ship and knocked him off his chair. Ruby opened her eyes as he got back up, "Ruby!"

She rubbed her bandaged head, "ugh, what happened?"

"A Raishan."

"Did I head-butt him or something?" she complained as she sat up.

"The nurse said not to get up." Bahren cautioned.

"I'm fine," she kept rubbing her head as Bahren dabbed a wet cloth on it. "What did you mean by 'a Raishan?'" she asked. Bahren stopped dabbing, "Bahren?"

"That wasn't any Raishan," said Bahren.

"Who was it?"

"Trajetton," Bahren answered.

"No!"

"Yes, congratulations Ruby, you went toe-to-toe with Raishany's greatest soldier and survived," said Bahren.

"I don't feel that great."

"And that's not the half of it," he added.

"What?"

"You know that Sory character and his two friends?" he asked and she nodded, "Sory and Dyricio are Trajetton's sons! Sory actually fought Trajetton after you were knocked out." Ruby's face became blank, "Ruby?"

"Where are they?!" she anxiously asked.

"Where they belong, in the brig." Ruby then sped outside with Bahren following, "no! Ruby! You're not supposed to be standing!"

"Let them out, Bahren!"

"Are you insane? Release the sons of one of Raishany's top generals?! Ruby!" he grabbed her shoulder, "Ruby we could ransom them to end this war before it even begins."

"Where's Captain Zat?"

"Manning the wheel. Why?" they emerged onto the deck where the hurricane was still raging. They dug their talons into the deck so as not to get blown away by the wind or washed away by the waves. Soon enough though, they made it to Zat at the wheel, fighting the storm with his bare hands, straining with all of his might to keep his frigate under control.

"Captain Zat!" Ruby yelled over the gusts.

"We've lost the fleet!" he replied.

"What?!"

"I can't see the rest of the fleet – I've lost them!"

"Captain, I need to ask you something!" He was staring ahead at something – petrified. "Captain Zat?" Ruby turned to see what he was looking at – and her eyes widened. Bahren turned too. A gargantuan wave was rumbling toward them. As its white cap scraped the tops of the masts the ship tipped backwards, groaning as it did. The wave broke, thrusting the upside-down vessel into the ocean. The masts snapped like twigs and impaled the ship as hundreds of tons of wood, water, and steel thundered into the sea.

Water flooded into every room. Sory, Dyricio, Ayro, and their guards struggled to keep their heads above the rapidly rising water. "Help!" Sory yelled at the guards, "get us out!" One of them handed him the key then swam off with the other. Sory submerged himself and searched for the keyhole in the watery blackness. He soon found it and opened the door. With mere inches of air left, Sory turned to his brother and friend, "take a deep breath."

The trio dove into the water and frenziedly felt for the stairs. Once they found them, the trio clawed their way to the entrance of the next floor. Lightning flashed and they could see a hole where a piece of a mast had gone through. When they arrived at the hole, they could see that the mast hadn't pierced all the way through the bottom of the ship so they charged down toward the deck with their air beginning to run out. Every second stretched into a minute then and hour then a week as the water pressure built up and compressed their heads and ears before the trio could finally see the deck just as their lungs started lurching for oxygen. Now outside they swam for the edge of the ship and then for the surface as it teased them by convulsing closer then farther and closer then farther. They reached it. They gasped for air.

Some of the surviving sailors dragged them atop the capsized ship, a few others had survived as well including the captain, Ruby, and

Gyric, but Bahren was nowhere to be seen, "Where's Bahren?" Sory asked Ruby.

She hesitated before replying, "he's somewhere on the deck."

Ayro had heard her too as Sory pondered what to do, "Sory – Sory what are thinking?" he asked. Sory dove into the raging waters, "Sory!" Sory filled his lungs before reaching the deck. In his rush earlier, he hadn't noticed all of the debris that was floating just under the ship, sails, countless ropes and bits of wood. Sory knew that it wouldn't be too difficult to become tangled in this mess and drown down there so he moved guardedly, using the flashes of lightning to his advantage. With one flash he thought he saw an arm so he moved toward it as his air began to run low and his trachea started tingling and all of the debris only made him more apprehensive.

Sory eventually reached where he'd seen the arm, when a current pushed a nearby sail away and the wide open eyes of a sailor met Sory's who's heart lurched as the body floated away and allowed him to see Bahren as he floated there unconscious and Sory grabbed him and pulled him out from under the ship with the endlessness of the dark abyss below them and finally to the surface. Sory gasped for air as he and Bahren were dragged up onto the ship.

Bahren was laid down on his back as the sailors tried to figure out what to do. Ruby held his head in her lap and sobbed. Ayro punched Sory in the shoulder, "ouch!" Sory yelled.

"What the hell was that?!" Sory didn't answer as he watched the helpless sailors argue with each other. Sory suddenly got an impulse and knelt down next to Bahren. He put his hand on Bahren's chest and moved it towards his head, when Sory's hand reached Bahren's throat he heard a gargling, but it was as if he was hearing it through his hand. Sory balled his hand into a fist and struck Bahren's throat. Water burst out of his beak and he came to life.

"Bahren!" Ruby hugged him.

"What happened?" he dazedly asked.

"Sory saved you!" she exclaimed. Bahren looked at Sory as he went back to Ayro.

Ayro couldn't believe his eyes, "how did you know to do that?!"

"I don't know," said Sory when a wave came and nearly washed them all off.

"We haven't much time before this ship slips below the waves!" warned Captain Zat.

Lightning flashed and Sory could see ships in the distance, "there's the fleet!" he pointed.

"Why aren't they coming for us?" asked Ayro.

"They can't see us." Sory thought for a moment, *we can't fly over, the wind's too strong.* he went over to Ruby, "Ruby, did the crew salvage anything that we could use to draw attention?" he yelled over the wind.

"I don't know." Another wave washed over and brought a sail with it. Then Sory noticed a few archers. He grabbed one of their bows and a quiver that still had a few arrows in it. He clawed his way over to the sail with Ruby following him, "what are you doing?"

Sory tore off a piece of the sail, wrapped it around the arrow, then pointed it straight into the air, "Come on! Come on!" he said to himself, then lightning struck. He released the arrow only for it to be sucked away by the wind long before it reached the clouds. He ripped off another piece and stuck it onto another arrow. Ruby and the archers each grabbed a bow and arrow and did the same, only this time they aimed against the wind. Lightning struck again, they fired. The arrows reached the lightning just as it disappeared. A few flames sparked in the sky. They repeated this a couple more times before the fleet finally started to turn.

"It's working!" Dyricio cheered.

Just before the frigate slipped below the waves the fleet reached it. The survivors were brought aboard and were given blankets. They went below deck where Commodore Pdosvine greeted them, "it's a good thing the wounded from the fortress and the battle were brought onto ours ships before this storm hit," he told Bahren.

"Yes, sir," Bahren responded.

"What about your prisoners? We weren't able to find any and are worried that they're disguising themselves as our own."

Bahren opened his beak, staring blankly, "we have no prisoners, sir."

"I see, well then, best get you poor boys off to bed. You have had one hell of a night after all." They saluted and the commodore went off as Bahren approached Sory. The storm had calmed some by then, yet the rain was still pouring. The waves were beginning to shrink, the ships only bobbed in the sea instead of being tossed about like toys.

"Sory, I just wanted to thank you for saving our lives. And I would also like to apologize for assuming that you and your friends were spies. Obviously you wouldn't have done all that you did for us – and me, if you were working for the enemy."

Sory stared at him for one last second before saying, "thank you."
Outside, the sky had lightened, the pure black of the night had been
replaced by gray as the sun rose. Silence overwhelmed the senses
before Sory yawned, "well I guess I should get some shut-eye," he said,
and started toward the nearby bunks.

"Oh wait," said Bahren and gave Sory his sword back, "this is
yours."

Sory put it in his belt, "thanks," and he went to bed.

Ruby, who was watching all of this, came over to Bahren smiling,
"see Bahren, I told you you were paranoid."

"Yeah, I don't know."

"We should get some sleep," and so they did, the hurricane
calming.

Chapter 8

Raishan Fortress Red Shield on the southern coast of Hyleeda.

The sun was setting the day after the raid on the Ark fleet. All around and within Fort Red Shield soldiers went about their business, which created a sort of hum. Meanwhile at the harbor, adjacent to the fort, workers were busy unloading cargo for the war off supply ships. At the fort's center stood its command post where General Trajetton paced in the officer's private sleeping quarters. He paced with a limp because of the wound his own son had given him.

There was a knock on the door, "enter," said the general. A rather nervous looking courier entered, then handed the general a piece of parchment with the Royal Seal on it, it was a message from the King. The general read the message within.

To: General Ramous Trajetton.

From: King Sairus Raish.

Order: Return to Rathimus immediately.

"The King sent his private yacht, sir," said the courier. "He wishes for you to use it." The general said nothing as he hastily collected his things and went downstairs then outside. When he arrived at the docks, he eyed the magnificent Royal Yacht, which had an intricate engraving going along its entire side from bow to aft. Once he was onboard, they set sail, heading out over many miles of endless ocean.

A couple weeks later, they had arrived at the port city of Dalsizar. The dreary metropolis housed hundreds of thousands of citizens and stretched nearly to the horizon. The general wasted no time and headed straight for the Royal Chariot waiting for him at the edge of the docks. Twelve griffins, six in the front and rear, stood at attention and waited to lift the chariot into the air, yet another example of royal Raishan decadence with its intricate designs similar to those of the yacht, adding a dash of color to an otherwise gray world.

The general sat down inside, only to discover someone was already in there with him. Sitting across from him was Prince Saitick Raish, the King's son, a young griffin about Sory's age. He wore a military uniform, although he had never served, and his face had a rather smug look on it. Ramous worried about the future with this hatchling potentially succeeding the throne should his father die. The Prince was tapping his index finger as if he were waiting for an apology, Ramous did owe someone an apology, but not him, "hello, Ramous."

"Prince Saitick, Your Majesty, how are you?"

"Fine," he said as the chariot lifted off the ground. The Prince peered out the window, "look at them down there. I've always wanted to spit on someone's head from up here but by the time I work up my spittle we are always too high for me to aim."

Ramous struggled to keep his composure, "how is your father?"

Saitick gave an annoyed sigh, "he's fine, he's pretty upset with you, Ramous. I don't know why though, he won't tell me. I don't think he has any confidence in me, but he sent me here to meet you on his behalf." He faced Ramous, "so tell me, General, how was Hyleeda?"

"Haven't seen much action, yet."

"What about that raid on that Ark fortress? What was that like?"

"Short," Ramous answered bluntly. Saitick nodded and looked down at his feet.

They spoke no more until the following night when they reached the capitol city of Rathimus where it was raining, a vast city even larger than Dalsizar with a rather grandiose center. The center of the city was a series of conjoined castles orbiting the tallest, the Monolith, which stretched far above them and scraped the clouds.

The chariot landed at the foot of the Monolith and two Royal Guards opened its doors. Prince Saitick, who outranked Ramous, stepped out first. The general had not seen the Monolith ever since he had left the city for Hyleeda, before his sons were born. It brought back memories. He stood and stared up at it as the main entrance opened, its two towering wood and iron doors sent vibrations through the stone floor and up the legs of all who were nearby.

Prince Saitick stepped inside, then faced the general and to himself said, "old fool is losing his mind." Ramous felt the Prince's eyes on him and stepped inside where they entered an elevator. They could hear distant cranking as wingless-griffin slaves yanked the chains attached to the elevator's top up.

The elevator jolted when it arrived at the top floor. Saitick once again stepped out first with Ramous following. In front of them extended a hall with an arched ceiling one hundred feet above their heads, with great columns holding it up on either side, and Royal Guards standing at attention in between each. They each wore red steel uniforms and had two sabers that they held in an X over their chests.

When the Prince and general reached the entrance to the Throne Room they both froze before daring to peek inside. They leaned inside, and then looked to their right. The expected to see the King sitting on the Throne only to find it empty. Velvet covered its seat and back, its golden headpiece stretched to the ceiling, and its armrests too were solid gold. A small, gnarly looking little beast with big buggy eyes and horns running down its back hissed at them from the Throne as the Prince and general stepped inside.

"General," said a deep, raspy, ancient, and piercing voice from their left. The King stood hunched over a window, staring out onto the city, the tips of his extended talons lightly touching the windowsill. All the two of them could see was his soaring silhouette against the rainy sky.

The two of them snapped to attention. Saitick spoke first, "father," he managed to get out, then swallowed deeply. Ramous could see Saitick's shaking hand. The Prince closed into a fist in an attempt to steady it.

"Saitick, how was your trip?" asked the King.

"Fine, Your Greatness," Saitick replied.

"Ramous, I have not seen you in a very long time," said the King.

"Yes, Your Greatness. I think it has been seventeen or eighteen years since last we met."

A tense minute went by before the King asked, "how are your sons?"

Ramous knew that the King had heard about his sons already, he also knew that the King wanted him to say what happened to them himself, "they have been lost, Your Greatness."

The King's head was slowly lifted by his giraffe-like neck, a neck three times normal length. Ramous had forgotten about how his neck seemed to allow the King to peer over all like some great monster from ancient mythology.

The King calmly passed the two as he walked to his throne, their beaks not even reaching the height of his elbow. As he sat on his throne, the little creature jumped off. Ramous and Saitick stood at attention in front of the gold covered cathedra, then kneeled and bowed their heads. The King spoke, "And how, Ramous, did this happen?"

"Arks, sir. Arks stole them."

There was a pause, "which was the eldest?"

"Tysorious, Your Greatness."

"How were they taken?"

"My sons happened to be in the stockades of my captured fortress when Ark commandos stormed it and took them. However, I take full responsibility for not being ready for the attack, sir."

"I see, and why were your sons down there?"

Ramous took a deep breath, "my eldest had befriended a blue-backed whom I believed to be a spy."

The King's talons slowly extended from his fingers then scraped the golden armrests. A shattering screeching resonated through the room. Red hot lines gleamed out from where the armrests had been scratched. "How did your eldest befriend a Lesser?"

"I don't know, Your Greatness."

"You were supposed to be training him. He has a rather important future."

"I know, Your Greatness. He was being trained, but he was rebellious. I think he snuck out at night, I think that's how he found the Lesser. It was he who put ideas into my son's head. However, sir, I take full responsibility in not being able to remove those ideas."

"I hope you know how important your eldest is," warned the King.

"Your Greatness will have him back soon," Ramous reassured him.

"Did he go of his own volition?"

"Your Greatness?"

"You say he befriended a Lesser. Could the Lesser have convinced your son to come with him? Or perhaps, your son may have even chosen to go without any persuasion."

The very thought sickened Ramous, "Your Greatness, I cannot begin to convey how much I hate the thought of some Lesser befriending, then mind washing my son so well that he chose to betray Raishany."

The King closed his eyes and held his palm out, "I can feel your anger, Ramous."

"Tysorious will fulfill his destiny to Raishany," Ramous declared.

"He is irreplaceably necessary," the King said.

Saitick looked up, "father, what about me?"

The King's head shifted gradually to his son, "what about you?"

"I – I could be of great service to my kingdom – if Your Greatness would give me the chance."

"Saitick, you have a different destiny."

"Yes, Your Greatness."

"Now leave us." The King waved his hand as if Saitick were a servant, "General Trajetton and I have to talk in private." Saitick stood, saluted, and bowed, then marched out the door in a soldierly fashion.

The fires in the torches above suddenly grew as the King walked back to the window, "how do you plan to retrieve your sons, Ramous?"

"Both, sir?" asked Ramous.

"Yes, if the mind of one has been poisoned we will need the other."

"Of course, Your Greatness. I'll be on my way immediately." Ramous saluted.

"Where are you going, General?"

"To retrieve my sons, Your Greatness."

"There will be no need to do so."

"Sir?"

"There are other ways, ways that will show your sons the true power of Raishany in this world, as well as in the Underworld."

"Who do you plan to summon, Your Greatness?"

"Not who, what. Whence last we met, when you left for Hyleeda, I thought my powers to be at their maximum. Soon after though they strengthened greatly, around the time your eldest was hatched. I believe that it was his birth that widened the door between our world and the others, and so strengthened my abilities."

"I did not know this, Your Greatness."

"Your sons will be at awe by what I have planned for them." King Sairus removed a small pouch from within his pocket. It contained black ash which he poured onto the floor. He blew on the ash and it twitched. Then he held his open palm over it and began to chant some otherworldly spell, his talons extending. The pile started to twitch and shift about as the King's voice echoed within Ramous' mind. He cringed and covered his ears as the chanting grew louder. The feathers on his neck stood erect as a jolt of icy water leaked down through his spine. Meanwhile, the torches above them dimmed.

Then the pile of ash began to shimmer with red light as it swirled up towards the King's hand. When the ash-cloud touched the King's hand it burst into red and white flame. Where the cloud and King's palm met a shape appeared. It quickly solidified into red-hot ember in the form of a creature's snout. The rest of this thing's head soon coalesced. When it did, it let loose a distant scream. The torches above them began convulsing and changing color.

Ramous could soon see that it was the head of a serpent. The rest of its body, with a hood on either side of its neck and two arms, soon formed. It floated toward the ceiling, its body longer than the King was tall. King Sairus prayed one final verse, the creature then raked itself about the air, screeching and thrashing. Then the embers covering it peeled off and fell to the floor like flaming snow as the creature fell silent. It floated back to the floor and stuck its face in Ramous', sticking out its tongue. "General Trajetton – I give you – the Slithus!" It leaned forward and roared into Ramous' face, revealing its hundreds of curved, serrated, and razor sharp fangs.

Chapter 9

It had been a couple weeks since the attack and hurricane as the Arktorian fleet neared the city of Vallce, Arktorion. Ruby sat on a bunk in the sleeping quarters reading a message from her father, a response to one of her letters, one she had written the morning after their ship sank in the hurricane.

Dear Ruby,

My heart almost stopped when I heard that you had been in a battle, and then that a hurricane had sunken your ship, but I am grateful that you are alive. However, there's something else that I wanted to ask you about, in your letter you said someone saved you in the battle, then during the hurricane. I would surely like to meet this fellow, when you come to visit I want you to bring him along. I'll get you a pass to take a temporary leave of absence.

Love, father.

Ruby was confused, she had never thought about Sory meeting her father, though it did make sense. Bahren walked in, "what's that?" he asked.

"A letter from my father," she said as she folded it up and put it in her pocket.

"What did he say?"

"Just how he was scared for me and he's glad that now I'm okay. He can't wait to see me and Sory-"

"Sory? Why does he want to meet Sory?"

"He saved my life."

Bahren nodded, "we'll be in Vallce soon. We should eat before we arrive."

Sory, Dyricio, and Ayro were already down there. They had finished their lunch when Ruby and Bahren came down. The place was full of griffins talking and filling the room with noise. "Sory," started Ayro, "perhaps you should say something." The three of them looked to Ruby.

"Perhaps I shouldn't, Ayro."

"All you must do is figure out her type."

Sory decided that Ayro was never going to let this go so he stood and slowly approached her, his heart pounding ever more with each step. He was a pace's distance away when a sailor ran down from the deck, "land-ho!"

Everyone ran upstairs as Dyricio and Ayro came up to Sory, "maybe next time." said Ayro as he patted Sory on the shoulder, then followed everyone else upstairs.

Up on deck, Sory could see the coast as hundreds of griffins took off from the ships to land, eager to see their families. It was late afternoon and the sun was just beginning to turn orange, illuminating the vast city under it. Vallce was a centuries old center of culture and finance. Towers and monuments, ancient and modern alike, shaped the skyline. Warmed by the glowing sun almost all year round and with its dynamic structures, it attracted many poets and writers as well.

Soon the ship had docked and Sory was glad to have made it all the way to Arktorion. He had been through so much in so little time. Yet he also felt sadness because now he had nothing left to do, nothing else to look forward to.

The trio began to help the crew unload the supplies when Ruby came over, "Sory, my father wants to meet you."

All three of them looked at her, "he does?" Sory asked and she nodded, "why?"

"It's a bit unusual, I know, but you saved his daughter twice and he wants to thank you in person."

"Alright, well Dyricio and Ayro can come too right?"

"Fine, and Bahren's coming along as well." she added.

"Why?" asked Dyricio.

She smiled at him, "he knows the way better than anyone."

Bahren landed with a pack on his back and another in his hand which he handed to Ruby, "well, are we going or what?" he asked.

"Can't we sleep first?" complained Dyricio.

"We'll sleep when it's night," Bahren replied before taking off with Ruby following.

Ayro then teasingly whispered to Sory, "you're already meeting her parents."

Soon they had put Vallce behind them. Ahead of them was a mountain range, the snow-covered peaks shimmered in the red-orange light. They flew in between these peaks before rising through the clouds above. Up there, they could follow the wispy clouds as they snaked around the mighty mountains, while the billowing ones seemed to sprout into space. They flew through the billowing ones and by the time they'd reached the other side night had just about fallen.

With the mountain range just to their tails, they landed on the bank of a river with dense forest on either side. Bahren laid out a blanket on the sandy bank, the light of the full moons above not being able to penetrate the pitch-black forest surrounding them. Soon they were all asleep, the babbling river and the singing of the crickets helped.

*

Sory jumped up, his talons extended, adrenalin surging through him. A tremendous fear had awoken him, a feeling that something sinister was nearby, he also noticed that the crickets had gone silent. He scanned the trees, a breeze rustling them. Sory approached the forest one step at a time, just waiting for something to jump out at him, he knew something was there.

Sory tip-toed through the trees, dashing his eyes about. He heard rustling in the branches above, whatever it was it had taken the high ground and was keeping just out of his sight. Sory couldn't stand it anymore, his nerves were getting to him as he trembled. He dove into the hollow trunk of a tree, waiting for this thing to go away. But he could feel it closing in. He clawed his way up to the top of the tree and was about to take off when an arm with long claws grabbed him. Sory pulled away but lost his balance and fell, hitting every branch on the way down before hitting the ground unconscious.

Sory's head was spinning as he rose to his feet. It was daytime and he could hear Ruby calling him. He saw her flying and once his head stopped spinning he climbed a tree and took off, "Ruby!"

"Sory! Where have you been?!"

"I went out for a walk and must have fallen asleep."

"Well don't wander off like that again. You had us all worried."

The other three were eating breakfast when Ruby and Sory returned, "where have you been?" Bahren demanded.

"I had taken a walk and fell asleep in the woods," answered Sory.

"And I went looking for him myself thank you very much," added Ruby.

"Well, now that we're all together we should continue on." They finished breakfast and washed up before setting out.

By the time they had landed again it was sunset, "how much farther to Arktorion City?" asked Dyricio.

"Not far, just over the horizon," answered Bahren. Sory went and stood at the forest's edge, "what's he looking at?" Bahren asked Ayro and Dyricio who both shrugged. Once night had fallen, they made a fire and roasted their dinner. After that, Bahren, Dyricio, and Ayro went to sleep.

Ruby had stayed next to the fire as Sory kept his eyes on the forest. She was still hungry but didn't want to enter the trees alone, "Sory, do you want to go into the woods?"

"What?"

"I want to get something to eat."

"Sure," he answered, taking his sword just in case. He didn't think they'd go that far, but before he knew it they were way out over the forest. He looked back every couple of seconds toward the riverbank and when he couldn't see it anymore he decided that they had gone far enough, "I think it's time we turn back." Ruby ignored him, "where are we going?"

"Oh Sory, you sound just like your brother." Sory watched her eyes as they tracked something. He looked to see if he could find it. Something was moving through the treetops. At first, he thought it was the creature from the night before, if it existed, but he wasn't feeling the same adrenalin filled exhilaration he had had.

The little animal went for a cave and Ruby dove down and caught it. Sory came down a minute later and the instant his feet touched the ground that surge of adrenalin then coursed through his body as his senses heightened, and the feathers on his spine stood. He could hear it in his head, hissing, a hissing that seemed to follow a pattern. It was more like a hellish language. He could feel it getting closer. He could feel it as it clawed its way through the trees.

"Ruby we have to get out of here," he whispered, trying to be as quiet as possible, she was oblivious.

"Do you want some, Sory?" Sory knew that whatever was after them could smell the blood spilling out of the kill. He grabbed it and threw it as far as he could, "hey!" she punched him in the shoulder,

"Ah!"

"Do you know how much time I spent tracking that thing?!" she punched him again.

"Ouch! Would you stop punching me?! We have to get out of here!" There was a flash of lightning, followed by torrential rain. Sory was ready to fly back to the river, but Ruby ran inside the cave. Sory called for her, "come on, we have to get back to the others!"

"Why?" she asked, "it's pouring out there and dry in here. We can go back when it stops."

Sory could feel this thing closing in. He ran inside, "come on, we have to go!"

"Why?" she asked.

Sory's spine jolted and he felt something breathe in his ear. Through the waterfall created by the rain at the cave's entrance he could see something moving. Ruby could see he was frightened but couldn't understand why. She started toward the cave's entrance.

"Ruby!" Sory loudly whispered, "get away from there!"

Ruby stood at the waterfall and looked up. Then she turned back to him, "what are you so fearful of?" WHOOSH! A giant snakehead ripped Ruby out of the cave with her screaming.

"RUBY!" Sory bounded to the waterfall. A scaly tail then whipped him into the cave's wall. He moaned in pain with his eyes closed. He opened them and could see something in the corner of his vision. He moved his head to see but this thing stayed just out of sight. A tingling licked at the back of his neck. Soon this thing was right over Sory, and he could finally see it. Its monster sized, black scaly head with searing yellow eyes that glowed in the night pointed straight at him as a red tongue flicked out.

Tysorious Trajetton? A voice whispered in Sory's head. It was this beast, only it wasn't talking to him – it was thinking to him.

"Y – yes?"

I am the Slithus. I have been sent here to return you to Raishany.

Sory didn't know what to do when he heard a cry, "AHHH!" Ruby flew in, her sword pointed at the Slithus' head.

"Ruby, no!" The Slithus' tail whacked her. She was flung into the cave wall like a bug. She got back to her feet and the beast lunged at her. She jumped back and its head missed but it punched her outside. Sory ran after her but the Slithus blocked his path so he unsheathed his sword.

Drop your weapon, mortal. Sory swung his sword and missed. The Slithus tried to grab Sory but he jumped to the cave's wall. The Slithus tried to bite him, but he jumped aside at the last moment and the beast's head went right into the rocky wall.

Sory ran outside, "Ruby!" he shook her, "Ruby! Wake up!" The Slithus burst out of the cave. It wrapped its jaws around him and tossed him back inside the cave.

Sory tumbled but managed to land on his feet as the Slithus approached him. *I will give you one last chance, mortal, come with me, or die.* Sory covered his wounds as he clinched his beak in pain. He couldn't fight this thing, its head alone was half the size of his own body, its claws as long as his forearms. The beast's tail wrapped around his ankles and yanked him into the air, then towards the cave's opening. Sory cut off its tail just before he passed through the waterfall. He could hear it screaming.

Fear froze Sory for a minute, but when the Slithus stopped screaming, he remembered that Ruby was still out there. He ran outside and both of them were gone, "Ruby!" he was walloped and sent flying into a tree. He was about to stand when the beast pinned him against the tree's trunk.

You had your chance, mortal. Now you will perish as only inevitable.

"What did you do to her?" he managed to utter under the crushing force squishing his torso.

Who? Ruby screamed as she dove down and stabbed the Slithus' neck. It roared and writhed around, rushing into the cave with Ruby and her weapon still attached.

"Ruby!" yelled Sory. Inside, the animal flung her off, her sword still in its neck. The Slithus coiled its neck as it readied to strike at her when Sory threw a rock at its head. It turned around, "Slithus! I'm the one you want!" It flung itself at Sory who jumped outside and into the air. The Slithus' tongue then wrapped around his leg and pulled him to its jaws. Sory sliced off the tongue. The beast hissed as Sory fell. His wing hit the ground first and a sharp pain then pulsed through it. He grabbed his wing just as the beast turned its attention back to him. Sory opened his wings but the pain in the injured one was too great. The serpent's jaws ripped through the air. Sory dodged them and sought shelter in the forest.

Sprinting through the forest, jumping over logs and shrubs, Sory could feel this thing pursuing him. He leapt toward a tree to climb up it and take the high ground – only to be smacked down and pinned against the muddy ground. His arm with his sword also pinned. *Now you die.* Sory grabbed Ruby's sword still in its neck and twisted. Its head lurched up in noisy agony, bringing Sory with it. He then stabbed it where he hoped the heart would be, right in between the arms. Yet that only made it writhe about more. The Slithus ripped out Ruby's sword, flinging Sory away. When it did, the scar burst into flame as rainwater fell into it. The Slithus flinched and took cover under the branches of a tree.

It spotted Sory, a hellish ferocity in its eyes. It growled, bearing its fangs. Sory could see Ruby's sword glimmering in the corner of his eye. He ran in the weapon's opposite direction, the beast following. He ran in a circle before leaping for Ruby's sword. With both in hand, he charged up a tree with the Slithus snapping at his ankles. its syrupy saliva splashing onto him.

Sory swung the swords behind him, not slowing the Slithus one bit. He made it to the top of the tree, his wing still in too much pain to fly. *You have run out of room.* Sory pointed his swords, the Slithus grabbed them and ignored its own pain as tried to pull them away. It lunged forward as Sory pushed his swords into its hand. The beast stopped with its jaws around Sory, its longest fangs scratching his skin. It yelped and Sory twisted the blades out, then stabbed them through its eyes, both entering one side and exiting through the other.

The Slithus lurched backwards. The bit of rain that made it through the canopy drizzled into its wounds, which flamed up. Sory then cut away at the branches, letting the rainfall. Its bleeding eyes exploded and it cried yet louder. The rest of its scars also lit up. It fell into the mud and started wriggling around. Yellow fire erupted out of its mouth. Sory watched as its wholly black body turned red as embers. The flame in its eyes then devoured the rest of its body with its screeching sounding more and more distant until it too evaporated.

Sory collapsed, gasping for his breath, staring at the scorch mark burnt into the ground in the shape of the beast, his sword with a burnt mark on it. He heaved heavily as the blood from his wounds poured out. Ruby came down from the sky, "Sory, are you alright?!" He did not answer. Ruby saw her sword in the middle of the scorched ground and picked it up. "Come, we should return to the others."

Chapter 10

By the time Ruby and Sory had returned to their camp the rain had stopped falling. There the other three were huddled under a blanket they had propped up to protect themselves from the weather. They were all anxious to know where Sory and Ruby had been. The two told them that they had been out hunting. They did their best to conceal their wounds.

Neither Sory nor Ruby slept a wink that night, their hearts never stopped thumping. Sory replayed the entire battle over and over in his head. *What was that thing?! More could follow, if the King wants me back so badly who knows what lengths he will go to. Did father know about this? Is he capable of sending this thing after me? Or was he incapable of stopping it?* When morning came he and Ruby watched the sunrise. Sory washed his face in the river, his wounds still stinging as he washed them too. When the others woke up, they packed everything back up, then continued on their way. Sory's wing was still sore but not so much that he couldn't fly.

By midday, they could finally see Arktorion City, the capitol, just on the horizon. Ruby couldn't stop looking at Sory as his head slumped down and watched the forest underneath him pass by. The question of how much his own father had to do with the Slithus attack persisting in his mind. *Could he have done such a thing? Could my own father have done this?* He wasn't concentrating on his flying and so was nearly knocked into Ayro when a breeze blew by.

"Watch it!" Ayro exclaimed.

"Sorry," Sory apologized groggily.

"Hey Bahren," Dyricio yelled from the back of the formation, "how much longer?"

"Not much."

Ayro flew up next to Sory, "what's the matter?"

"Nothing."

"You sure?"

"Yeah, yeah I'm sure."

Sory turned back to say something when Bahren yelled from in front, "we have arrived!" Sory faced forward. A fifty foot stonewall surrounded the inner city and separated it from the surrounding suburbs. On top of this wall stood or marched thousands of soldiers in either direction. The group ascended as they flew over the inner city, a hand full of the towers soaring as high as they were, though most of the edifices were only a few stories high. Below and around the group countless griffins milled about on the streets and in the air, resembling a swarm of insects.

The group dove under an archway between two twin towers. When they re-ascended on the other side, they could see the Imperial Obelisk just a small distance away. It stood on a small island where three great rivers met, these rivers divided the city and flowed off into the distance. The Obelisk was a complex and great castle that spired into the atmosphere as a seven-sided pyramid, its silhouette resembling a sword's blade. They were all transfixed, except Ruby for some reason.

The five of them landed at the entrance at the base of the Obelisk. The entrance was a white marble floor laid out in front of two open doors made of black iron and shaped into a pointed arch at the top, the doors were ten times their height. The walls surrounding the doorway were white marble that glimmered in the sun. On either side of the entrance stood two black, iron statues that were the same height as the doors. They stood at attention with oval shields on their sides facing the doorway and spears on the other.

Inside, they all gawked at the vast main hall, which spanned the entire base of the castle, except Ruby. Sunlight poured in from the hundreds of arch shaped windows that dotted the walls and the white marble floor made it look all so heavenly. Thick blue stone columns also stood around the perimeter of the room. The five of them walked to the center of the hall where a fountain was. One covered in dozens of life sized, intricate statues of griffins praying, fighting in battle, crawling on the ground and flying. Spotted around the room where all sorts of griffins in fine clothes, in small groups whispering to each other.

Sory noticed the dome-shaped ceiling where the painting of a battle was. At the center of it was a young red griffin with gleaming steel armor. His eyes and sword glowed like stars against a black night. At his feet, a city lay in ruins with rubble all around. Behind him, an army with the same armor as his charged toward an enemy force. The enemy wore red armor, brandished weapons in their hands and ferocity in their eyes. Below the enemy crept the underworld as it erupted with all its beasts and creatures, with fire and blood streaming out in a river of hell. Above it all, hovered a giant griffin in red flame. Yet fire did not engulf this griffin, rather it was made of fire. It was a phoenix. Its demonic eyes glared straight out of the painting and through whoever dared peer into them. Sory did just this – and became locked in them. It felt as if they were looking right back. Whispers crawled into his ears from bodiless voices, a chill dripped down his spine, and a tingling feeling brushed his neck.

"Beautiful isn't it?" Ruby broke Sory out of his hypnotism when she spoke.

"W – what?" he stuttered.

"I said beautiful isn't it?"

"I don't like it."

"Many have been driven mad by looking into that fiery monster's eyes," she said as she eyed the phoenix.

"So it's not just me then," he said as he turned his attention to the underworld. There he saw a Slithus emerging from it with glowering eyes and an outstretched arm reaching for the younger figure with the silver armor and glowing eyes.

"So Ruby," said Ayro, "what are we doing here?"

"My father works here," she said as she led them to one of the many elevators in the main hall. This one had two Imperial Praetorian Guards on either side of it. As Sory looked around, he realized that it was the only elevator with guards. They wore round, blue helmets with golden edges and small wings coming out of the tops. Their armor was also blue and their oval shields were black with gold around the edges. All together a very regal appearance as they remained at perfect attention.

When the five of them arrived at the elevator, the Praetorians crossed their spears over it, "silver shield," said Ruby and the

Praetorians uncrossed their spears. The other four were confused. Together they rode the elevator all the way to the top of the Obelisk, chains cranking far above as they were pulled up.

Finally, the elevator stopped and opened into a rather glamorous looking hall, where a rather glamorous looking small crowd stood and made small talk. Ruby confidently strolled right through the small crowd while her counterparts shyly followed.

Ruby sauntered right on through the archway at the far side of this hall. It led into another glamorous room where a rather depressed looking, middle-aged magnus griffin was slumping down on a throne. Twelve Praetorian Guards stood beside the throne.

The magnus griffin's face lit up as the five of them came in, "the emperor!" said Bahren who immediately stood at attention, Sory, Ayro, and Dyricio all copied.

"Ruby!" exclaimed the emperor.

The four of them all looked to Ruby, "father!" The emperor stood just as Ruby jumped up and hugged him, "it's been so long."

They released each other, "how have you been?" asked the emperor.

"Can't complain," she turned to her befuddled friends, "it's alright, he doesn't bite." The four of them cautiously stepped forward, "father this is Bahren, Dyricio, Ayro, and Sory."

"Sory. You're the one I've wanted to talk to," he extended his hand to Sory.

Sory nervously shook the emperor's hand, "I know, Your Highness."

"Please, just call me Emperor Mecila."

"Yes, Emperor Mecila." The emperor smiled, and then turned to the others, "Bahren, Ruby's told me much about you, but I don't know you two," he said to Ayro and Dyricio.

"These are Sory's friend and brother," said Ruby.

"Oh, well, nice to meet you, Dyricio," he extended his hand to Ayro.

Ayro excitedly shook his hand, "nice to meet you too, sir, although my friends call me—" Sory slapped him on the back of the head.

"That is Ayro," said Sory, "this is Dyricio, my brother."

"Oh yes, of course." The four of them were all still staring at Emperor Mecila, "you still seem to be in shock," he said.

"Well sir," started Sory, "I think you can understand. We never knew Ruby was your daughter."

"Yes, it is unusual for someone of her-" Emperor Mecila struggled for the right word, "placement in society to join the army, but she was persistent. Of course, I had to make sure that my little girl was safe, so I had an old friend train her," he smiled at her. "Now, please, everyone, make yourselves at home. Except you Sory, I want to talk to you." Ayro, Bahren, and Dyricio started meandering about the room as the Emperor put his arm around Sory's shoulder. He brought Sory next to Ruby who was sitting in her father's throne, "so Sory, tell me, where are you from?"

"Hyleeda, sir."

"And what did you say your last name was?" Ruby looked to Sory.

"I don't have a last name, sir. I'm an orphan."

"I see. Well Sory, since you seem to be so good at protecting my daughter I'm officially giving you the task of being her personal guard."

Something shattered behind them. They turned to see Ayro standing over a broken vase. "Sorry, sorry," he said with his hands in the air.

Emperor Mecila continued, "the rest of you, as personal friends of the emperor, will have your own personal guards. Captain," called the emperor, signaling for one of the guards to come over. A short, middle-aged griffin marched over to the emperor and stood at attention.

"Yes, Your Highness."

"Bring me four guards."

"Yes, Your Highness," and the guard marched out.

The emperor turned back to Sory, "my boy, you have brought much relief to my heart, more than you could ever know. So tonight – we shall celebrate!" he said rather melodramatically.

"Celebrate, sir?"

"Uh-huh, Ruby how'd you like to see Fusna?"

Her face lit up and she jumped off the throne, "he's back?!"

"Yep."

"Yes! I haven't seen him in ages."

Emperor Mecila chuckled, "yes, I suppose it hasn't been since he finished preparing you for war."

Ruby turned to Sory, "he was the old friend that father had me train with."

"He performs magic shows now that he's retired," added the emperor. "He's performing one tonight, and you are all my guests of honor." He put his hand back on Sory's shoulder, "how does that sound, my boy?"

"Alright, sir," Sory replied.

"I told you, call me Emperor Mecila." He turned to Ruby, "Ruby, come."

Ruby leaned into Sory's ear and whispered, "I don't need a personal guard," before following her father out of the room.

What did that mean? Sory thought.

Then the captain returned with four guards who lined up at attention, "sirs, these will be your guards for the foreseeable future." They were Praetorians, same as the others, except Dyricio's wasn't wearing a helmet. A mountain griffin, he was short and covered in golden feathers, his eyebrows and the area around his eyes were black and the top of his head had a cluster of bright red feathers in the shape of a diamond. He had a very nonchalant expression, the only noteworthy thing about him was a long and deep scar that went from his right eyebrow across the entire left of his face.

This one is rather peculiar, decided Dyricio.

Bahren walked off with his guard following him. Sory, Dyricio, and Ayro and their three guards started over to the throne. Ayro started, "I cannot believe that you have been courting the princess for all this time and hadn't even known it."

"I don't know if you could say I was courting her."

"Well, you will be able to tonight."

They reached the throne and stopped, "yes, I suppose I will."

*

The four of them were shone their rooms a bit later on. Then they were measured for the formalwear they'd have on for that night. A couple hours after sunset, they were summoned back to the Throne Room. From there they followed the Emperor down to the main entrance and then out to a large carriage pulled by large, flightless bird like creatures.

The carriage rode through the teeming city streets, which were lit by thousands of candles and lanterns. Vendors yelled from either side, trying to sell their products, while soldiers marched in front of, beside, and behind the carriage. Within a half hour, they arrived at an ancient coliseum, one constructed thousands of years ago by a civilization that had long since fallen. Ivy and cracks covered this coliseum as thousands of griffins flooded inside.

Emperor Mecila stepped out of the carriage first, followed by Ruby. As the entourage passed inside, Sory couldn't help but notice all the high-ranking generals and admirals there. *Shouldn't they be off fighting this war? The Raishans will tear the Arks apart without these officers.* Sory tried not to step on Emperor Mecila's cape. The emperor was making small talk with a half dozen senators, "Emperor Mecila." said Sory, the emperor didn't answer. "Emperor!"

"Yes?"

"Why are all these generals and admirals here?"

"What do you mean?"

"We were just attacked by Raishany–"

"Oh that, Arktorion and Raishany have been in tension since before I was born, we've been in a quasi-war with them forever."

"A quasi-war, sir?"

"It's when they raid one of our cargo ships, then we raid theirs. It's much like a little dance."

"But they attacked a fortress."

Emperor Mecila turned to a senator who had stolen his attention, "my boy, why don't you go and just enjoy yourself," he commented before turning away.

Emperor Mecila had his own private booth just at the edge of the arena. He sat in front with Ruby on his right and Sory on his left, the other three behind them, as well as a few high-ranking military griffins and senators. They were fed chocolate and wine, which Sory indulged in, but he was still worried about the state of the war. *This is a waste.* He thought to himself.

The roar of tens of thousands voices echoed across those ancient walls as everyone settled down to their seats. The emperor was telling a joke to the senators when the great torches lighting the arena dimmed and the stadium quieted. Then a sudden electric sensation jolted Sory and Dyricio. The torches reignited, revealing a wingless figure at the center. The rather tall and lean figure stood with a bowed head as the crowd gave a low clap. Emperor Mecial stood, "Arktorians, males and females, young and old," his voice echoed off the walls, "I present...Fusna!"

Drums sounded out in a thunderous chorus. Fusna levitated until about forty feet off of the ground, his head still bowed as another surge of energy coursed through Sory and Dyricio. Fusna reached out his arms, his hands cupped and the fire from one of the torches rushed down to them. He then flung the fire about, the crowd in awe, shrinking into their seats when the flames were thrown at them. Fusna threw a flame at the emperor's booth and everyone in it shrunk away. Except for Sory and Dyricio, who somehow felt no danger. The fires shot into the air then dissolved. Fusna slowly floated back to the ground, his arms back at his sides, his head still bowed.

He touched down on the sand of the arena before facing the crowd. "Good evening," echoed his deep voice, "I am Fusna, and I have a grand show for you tonight." He walked toward the booth, "for my first performance I-" he saw the brothers, "will need a volunteer." Half of everyone in the crowd raised their hands, but Fusna never took his eyes off of Sory and Dyricio, "how about you?" he pointed at Sory, who looked left and right in disbelief.

Ayro pushed Sory's shoulder from across the booth, "go on, then!" he urged.

"Do not be shy, Tysorious," assured Fusna. Sory climbed over the booth's edge and into the arena, approaching Fusna slowly, cautiously. This character was different, in such a way that Sory had more fear of him then the Slithus, "do not worry, I will not bite. I may set you on fire but I do not bite," a muffled laugh came from the crowd. Sory was now standing just in front of Fusna, his eyes only as high as the performer's shoulders. He peered up at this stranger with a defiant gaze, much the same as the one he once given his father. "You do not like me," Fusna turned back to the audience, "I am going to find out why he does not like me," he began to circle Sory, "now Tysorious–"

"It's Sory."

"What is your name?"

"Sory."

"You do not like the name 'Tysorious?'"

"No," Sory mumbled.

"Louder!" he whispered in Sory's ear.

"No!"

"I think I have my answer. You do not like me because I call you by a name you despise, yes?"

"Yes," Sory mumbled again.

"I still cannot hear you, Tysorious."

"Yes!"

"Then why have a name you do not like?"

Sory barely waited for Fusna to finish when he started to answer, "my father g–"

"Yes?" Sory realized his mistake, "what about your father, you are an orphan, remember?"

How did he know that? "There was a note," Fusna raised his brow, "they found me still in the egg outside of an orphanage with only my name on a piece of parchment."

"Really?"

Sory looked at the ground, "yes."

"Ladies and gentlemen – Sory!" They clapped for the agitated Sory who glared into Fusna's eyes one last time. He knew Fusna did not believe the lie. With his head bowed shamefully, Sory went back to the booth, Fusna watching him.

The show went on, a spectacular one, but Sory did not enjoy any of it. He was still wondering how Fusna seemed to know everything about him. The others wondered the same at first, but soon became lost in the performance.

That night Sory's mind spiraled with thoughts of that Fusna, but his exhaustion soon outweighed them and soon he was asleep. The next morning Dyricio came into Sory's room, "how did you sleep?" asked Dyricio.

"Fine," Sory groggily answered.

"Were you still thinking about last night?"

"How did he know all of that?!"

"He does seem to be magic."

"But it was as if he were staring into my soul."

"I thought that bit about our father abandoning us was good."

"He saw right through it."

"How do you know?" asked Dyricio.

"Trust me, I felt it. There's something about him."

"Speaking of feelings, did you get that – that – rush when he appeared on the arena."

"Yeah!" exclaimed Sory.

"And then when he floated into the air and–"

"And when he did that trick with the fire!" Sory exclaimed again.

"Yes, and all throughout the show!"

"I'm just glad I wasn't the only one. I thought I was going mad, ever since that Slithus–"

"Slithus?"

Sory's guard, with one of those winged helmets, opened the bedroom door and said, "Sory and Dyricio, the emperor has summoned you." With fear, they looked to each other. They got dressed into some of their new casualwear, courtesy of the emperor. Then they were escorted, by their personal guards, to the Throne Room. The brothers took baby steps, as if walking to their deaths.

Dyricio leaned into Sory's ear, "why are we being escorted by soldiers? Do you think that Fusna told Mecila who we are?"

"Sh!" When they reached the Throne Room, the emperor was sitting on his throne with Fusna standing to his right. The guards made the brothers stand directly in front of Emperor Mecila and Fusna before leaving, the doors closing behind them.

Emperor Mecila spoke, "Fusna tells me that there's something important you two have been keeping from me. He hasn't said what it is, but he assures me that you two will give me the answer," neither answered. A long, silent tension passed, "what is it you're hiding from me? Speak up!" still nothing. "He has told me that you aren't orphans...why did you lie to me?"

Sory spoke, "perhaps it is your friend who lies to you."

"Oh I doubt that."

Fusna responded, "if you think me untrustworthy, Sory, then perhaps his highness would like to examine the scar on your cheek, given to you by your father." Sory's look of scorn turned to shock. Dyricio became a bit more fearful.

Sory wanted to ask Fusna how he knew all of this. Yet he also knew that if he did ask he'd give himself away. Still, the interest was overwhelming, "how did you know about that?"

"Your curiosity overpowers your will."

"Shut up!"

"Sory!" yelled the emperor, "what have you been hiding from me?"

Sory turned to Fusna, "you know everything. Why don't you tell him?"

"Because it must be you."

"Why?"

"It is your lie."

Sory's face twisted into a terrible scowl. His beak cracked open, ready to speak while he worked up the words, "my father–" Dyricio shook his head, "is Ramous Trajetton."

Instantly, the emperor stood, "spies! Both of you! Spies! Guards! Guards!"

"Now emperor," started Fusna, "if they were a threat I would have killed them myself by now, but they have much good in them."

"How can you know for sure?" insisted Emperor Mecila.

"I know."

"How do you know it's not some trick?"

"I have seen every trick the enemy has, trust me."

"Well perhaps this is a new one!"

"No," Fusna smiled, "they are good, more than good actually," he intently fixed his eyes on Sory, "they…are Fyzars."

"Them, Fyzars? How can you be so sure?"

Fusna kept his eyes on the brothers, "do you two know the story of the Fyzar?"

They both shook their heads. The emperor cut in, "how do we know they're not lying about all this?"

"They are not," assured Fusna. The emperor sat back down as Fusna started the story, "the origin of the Fyzar goes back to a time centuries before civilization. To a time when beings descended from the heavens and gave supernatural powers to a selected family of griffins, the Fyzar. It was a lineage that would persist through the ages, through countless wars, and the collapses and rises of kingdoms and empires alike. The Fyzar persisted through all of this. That changed with the Raishan Invasion. The invaders attempted to befriend the Fyzar, only to fail, until a Raishan Queen seduced one of the family members over two and a half centuries after the invasion, about three hundred years ago. They were soon married and had a son, a son who eventually became King. This young King then imposed a harsh rule over his Arktorian subjects, and calls for revolution began. Many of these calls came from his resentful Fyzar cousins. In what appeared to be an attempt to make peace, the Raishan King invited his rebellious relatives to his home in Rathimus, but it was a trap. In a desperate attempt to stop the rebellion, the King slayed his Fyzar brethren, sparing only one young hatchling. This betrayal only spread the Revolution which Raishany eventually lost. But Arktorion had still lost their beloved Fyzar, and Raishany was still the only nation to possess them, until now. For centuries later would come a prophecy, one that proclaimed the birth of a Fyzar just prior to the war. This Fyzar would choose his side of it, and bring victory with him." Fusna paused, "of the six Fyzar alive today there have only been three hatched in recent year, Prince Saitick, Dyricio, and you Sory. You are the Fyzar that the prophecy speaks of."

Sory's eyebrows rose, his body froze, but not out of shock. Instead, it was out of how right this felt. Now he was aware of his destiny, that he was meant for something better than anyone else, that his fate was important above all others. Though not in an arrogant way, in a way that he had this destiny to help everyone else, to save them, to serve them, to lead them. "I know. As if some distant memory, I know. I've always known."

"You would not be a Fyzar if you did not," said Fusna. "Now Sory, time is of the essence so you will have to learn quickly. You must absorb all that I say. You must do all that I say. And you must fight until you are fighting the urge for the sweet release of death, understand?"

"Yes, sir."

"Wait," interjected Dyricio, "how do you know Sory is the Fyzar? Why couldn't it be me or Prince Saitick?"

"If Prince Saitick were the prophecy's Fyzar than his father would not have tried to retrieve Sory. However, dear Dyricio, you cannot be the prophecy's Fyzar because, as the younger of two siblings, the powers you inherited from your father are not as strong as those in your elder brother." Dyricio hung his head.

"Sir, who are the other Fyzars still alive?" asked Sory.

"Just Ramous and King Sairus."

"What about you?"

"I was not born a Fyzar."

"Yet you are?"

"Yes."

"How did you become one then?"

"That is not important right now. All that matters is that you begin your training as soon as possible. And that your true identities, and Sory's training, be kept secret, even from your own guards."

"Now Fusna," started the emperor, "isn't that a bit paranoid?"

"No, no one can be trusted. Sairus will have his spies everywhere." Looking back to Sory, Fusna could tell he was terrified, "do not fret, my boy. I will teach you to wield your abilities, to hone your skills, to fight, to kill, and to stand back up when you are knocked down – like a true knight." Fusna held his fist up. Sory now seemed intent on what he needed to do, "so Tysorious Trajetton, will you fight?" Determination filled Sory's eyes for but a moment –until fear reared its ugly head. And the assuredness that had once sparked – drained.

Chapter 11

That night, Sory wasn't able to fall asleep until well after midnight. Eventually though his exhaustion from the long journey got the better of him. By the time the first gray light of the predawn hour was covering the city Sory was still asleep when there was a crash. He jumped up in time to see his door fly across the room. He grabbed his sword and pointed it at the darkness, all he could see was a silhouette standing in the doorway. The most horrible of feelings overcame him, "father?"

The figure unsheathed his sword. Sory raised his blade, but it was knocked out of his hands. A hand wrapped around his throat and forced him against the floor, "count yourself lucky that I am not your father."

Sory could see the figure's face now in the light, "Fusna, what the hell are doing?!"

"Would you have given your life up that easily?" Sory was bewildered, "would you have given your life up that easily?! As easily as you did – just now?!"

"N – no, of course not."

Fusna let Sory stand, "then why did you?"

"W – well I thought that if you were my father–"

"That what? That he would spare you because you are his son? You must disregard that fact, Sory. If he is ordered to kill you, he will and will not lose a minute of sleep over it. You must expect anything, and that is where we will begin." Fusna slapped Sory in the face.

"AH!"

"Did that hurt?"

"Yes!"

"Good, the pain will make it easier for you to remember." Fusna went into the hall, "come," he ordered, and Sory followed. Fusna walked to the end of the hall where there was an open window. He stepped onto its frame and peered out onto the city. Then this wingless griffin stepped off into thin air.

Sory jumped to the window only to see Fusna levitating just outside of it. "Will I be like this someday?" he asked.

"I hope so." Fusna flew off and Sory followed. Arktorion and the sky were still painted gray, the three rivers that met at the city's center resembled three great stone roads.

Within a few minutes, they were over the outskirts of the city, a bit later on and they were over grassy fields. Sory had been watching

Fusna flying, so mesmerized was he by this supernatural ability he did not notice how far they had flown until now. "Fusna-"

"From now on you will address me as sir."

"Where are we going, sir?"

"To where I am to teach you." Sory spotted a building off in the distance in the middle of a field surrounded by thick forest. One not very extraordinary in appearance, it was grey and had an arched roof and doorway where they landed. When they did, Fusna reached out his hands, and without touching the doors, they opened.

Inside, Sory's eyes wandered about the room, which seemed longer on the inside. Perhaps because there was nothing inside except for eleven white stone columns on either side and a humble door on the far end of the room. "What is this place?"

"This is where I teach all of my students. I call it the Iron Structure. But before we begin, Sory, I have to explain why you are here."

"I know, sir. I am the Fyzar from the prophecy."

"Everything is not as simple as that. Do you know why the Raishans are attacking? Why now?" Sory shook his head. "It is because Ramous was about to commence your final training."

"My final training, sir?"

"The Raishans seized that fortress and started this war because you had come of age to begin your final training to be a Fyzar."

"And now that they don't have me?"

"The war has already commenced. All that the enemy can do now is retrieve you."

"The Slithus."

"Yes. However, that was a failure, and believe me, King Sairus will try again. Only his next scheme will be far less overt."

"What will he try?"

Fusna sighed, "even I do not know that, Sory. Do not worry though, by the time he strikes again I will have you well prepared." Just when Sory was beginning to feel a sliver of confidence, Fusna said something that shook it, "there is one more thing I must tell, my boy. Even though the prophecy says you will not lose the war, it does not say what else you might not lose. This victory will require sacrifice, it may even require the ultimate sacrifice. So you must be ready, are you?" Sory thought about it. Fusna shook his head, "you are not ready."

Sory was offended, "how do you know?"

"Because you had to think about it." Fusna walked further into the building with Sory following, "What I must first explain to you is about the ability to utilize extra cerebral energy, or qi. What qi is – is an ability. Your body functions by taking in the energy from the food you eat. Yet it is the Fyzar, and the Fyzar alone, who possesses the ability to bring this energy into his mind and channel it with such great force that you can lift an object without your hands ever touching it. This concept is what you must first understand. You will not be learning it yet though. You are not ready. Before we train your mind, we must train your body. For this endeavor, Sory, your body must be sharp – so that your *mind* is sharp, and that is the first step."

"Sharpen my body, sir?"

"To use qi, you need the utmost of concentration, to a level that you cannot even comprehend yet, for it is this concentration that allows a Fyzar to bring the energy of his body into his mind. To achieve this level of concentration you will need a mind that is clear and fast. To develop this we need to erase all the fear and doubt within. For a distracted soldier is a dead one. And the best method to clear your mind is to sharpen your reflexes, in other words to develop mind-muscle memory. And that will be done by working on your body."

"How long will that take, sir?"

Fusna smiled, "so many questions. Come here." Sory stood with Fusna in the center of the room. "For as long as Fyzars have existed, they have always been great soldiers. So from here on out, that is how I will treat you so that you may become one. Now, ATTENTION!" Sory flinched. "I said – ATTENTION! Put your knobby little knees and heels together! Straighten your spine! Have your scrawny arms at your sides!"

Why is he yelling at me?! Sory wondered.

"Because you need to be a soldier to fight a war, boy." said Fusna.

How did he know that? Sory thought.

"Because I can read minds, boy. Back to the topic at hand, though. You are a soft piece of dough which I have the pleasure of somehow molding into a rock!" Fusna put his beak in Sory's ear, "let me ask you something, do you think this is loud?! Is this scaring you, soldier, is this disturbing you?! Well guess what, this should be nothing for you! What will scare you is Sairus' saber coming down on you like a great steel monster. That, and nothing less is what you are allowed to fear! DO YOU UNDERSTAND?!" Sory began to open his beak, "from here on out, you will not speak unless spoken to. You will not blink unless given permission. You will not lay a brown egg unless I say so. Do I make myself clear?"

Sory looked Fusna in the eye, "y-"

"Did I give you permission to look me in the eye?!"

Fusna's voice rung in Sory's head, "no, sir."

"Unsheathe your weapon." Sory did. Fusna snatched it and held it to his eye, "this is a very well made weapon. Where did you find it?"

"I stole it from my father, sir."

Fusna nodded, "this is not just any weapon you know, this is one made for an officer, an exceptional officer at that. You have not earned this yet." Fusna placed it in his belt, then he reached his hand out to a large pair of wooden doors on the opposite side of the room from where they entered. The doors swung open and a sword flew out and into Fusna's hand, which he handed to Sory. "At ease." Sory did not know what that meant so he stood naturally and took the sword. "For the foreseeable future, this will be your weapon, and from here on out your weapon is your god, the deity to which you pray to save your skin in war, understand?"

"Yes sir."

Fusna unsheathed his sword, "we will start with the basics." They fenced slowly for a while, before speeding up. They continued until noon when Fusna used his qi to bring out two circular shields. He handed one to Sory, "now Sory, all I want you to do is block." Swoosh! Fusna smacked Sory's shield with his sword, then body slammed him with his shield. As they continued, the student did his best to block the blows but quickly grew exhausted. Fusna made one last powerful shield-swing. Sory tried to block but was knocked to the floor.

"Ow!"

"It only hurts if you let it, Sory." Sory got back to his feet only to be knocked down again. They continued for what seemed to Sory as an eternity. An eternity of Fusna stabbing, thrashing, and swinging from every angle possible, each blow more potent than the last. Fusna never tired while Sory felt his energy drain with each strike. He attempted to hide it, but Fusna could see it anyway and only came at him with an ever-mounting ferocity. After about an hour, Fusna floored Sory one last time, only this time Sory couldn't get up. "Stand!"

Sory tried to reply but he was gasping uncontrollably. *This is ludicrous! How does he expect me to fight him?*

"You question the point of this exercise," said Fusna, Sory hesitated but then nodded. "The only way that you will become evenly matched with Sairus is if you are evenly matched with me, at the very least." Sory stood, "attention! Sory, you have it in your head that this training will take far longer than it actually will. However you are closer to the end than you think, and I will demonstrate why." Fusna stabbed at Sory's face who blocked with his shield, then Fusna commenced a torrent of cutting and slamming until Sory had been backed into one of the columns. Sory's adrenalin climbing, instinct took over and he pushed Fusna off and jumped away. Fusna stabbed once more. Sory bent backwards and put his right hand on the ground as he hoisted his body up, then kicked Fusna in the navel. Sory stood back up, his fists raised. Gasping, the student's rush soon subsided. After a few seconds, he began to grasp what he had just done. "How did I do that?"

Fusna smiled, "instinct, these are identical for all and that is where equality in any fight is. All you have to do – is let go. We still have a great long trek to complete though, come." He walked Sory outside where the sun was just beginning to turn into its late afternoon orange. "To master even the basics of qi you must let go. Unhinge your mind. Only then will you be able to wield your body's energy outwardly. To unhinge your mind you must empty it first, and for a novice like you an effective way to do this is to distract your consciousness until your subconscious is released as I just showed you how to do. However, there is another way, a way which I find most effective." Fusna suddenly shot across the ground like an arrow, dust spattering behind him. A moment later, he disappeared behind the tree line. Sory blinked, he couldn't believe what he just saw, Fusna had disappeared after running at what looked like the speed of sound.

Sory heard a rush of air behind him and turned to see Fusna heading right for him. Sory hurdled himself out of the way just as Fusna came to a halt. "How did you do that?!"

"I freed my mind. Once you accept the fact that your body and mind are capable of incredible things, things that no one else can do, you will be able to practice qi. If you cannot free your mind, you will fail. And the Run is how all training Fyzars realize this."

"The Run, sir?"

"Sory, what I want you to do is run, run as fast as you can, as fast as you *actually* can." Sory looked over the valley, over nothing but flat grassland as far the horizon. He crouched, then ran.

The first bit was downhill, but when the ground leveled out as he went further out into the valley his exhaustion caught up. With every step his exhaustion grew, grew into a weight on his back as his joints turned to stone, his mouth dried, and his lungs lurched for air. *This is pointless. I can't take another step!*

Sory's jog ended with a gradual halt, huffing and puffing as Fusna came up next to him, "what was that?"

"I have-huh-huh-huh-no-huh-energy." Sory panted, his head hanging.

"You can keep going, Sory. All that is holding you back is your doubt."

"No, sir, I'm too tired."

"Exhaustion is only a state of mind. You have to let go of what you feel."

Sory took a couple last deep breathes, then raised his face into the gleaming sun. His eyes glowed with new determination. He cracked his neck and extended and retracted his talons, then ran. At first it was barely a jog, again his mouth grew dry and his joints felt as if they were going fall apart. After only a few seconds, his jog became a fast walk. Just as he was about give up again Fusna's words reverberated in his head. "It's only a state of mind." Sory said to himself, and he pressed on. At that instant in time the field and grass in front of him warped into a funnel, as if the fabric of the universe was bending as Sory tapped into the edge of the abyss of his mind. A new part of his mind, which he never felt before, caught on fire and a small white light glowed from out of his brain and could be seen just barely piercing through his pupils. Adrenalin exploded out of his heart, his joints became liquid, as if they had no limit to their speed or flexibility as his body lost all feeling, as if it had become air. He could feel everything around and in him, every bug flapping its wings, every eye floater squirming across his vision as everything went into slow motion. To him though, he was still moving at a normal speed. Behind him, Fusna watched Sory as he suddenly darted off, freeing himself, streaming in a circle around the field and back to the Iron Structure where he stopped. Sory's eyes were wide with excitement, "I think I know now, sir."

"Good." Fusna pulled out a blue shirt and blue pants that had been tightly folded in his pants pocket.

"What's this, sir?" Sory asked as he took the clothes.

"It is your uniform, whenever you come to the Iron Structure you are to be wearing these, understand?"

"Yes, sir."

"Good, now go home Sory, rest. Return here at dawn."

"Thank you, sir." Sory flew off to the Obelisk with Fusna watching him. A feeling of hope filling the teacher, a feeling he had not known in a long time.

Back at the Obelisk, Sory stumbled into his room hoping to catch some sleep when he opened the door and saw Ayro, Dyricio, Ruby, and Bahren all in there. "Sory!" exclaimed Ruby, "where have you been?"

"What are you all doing in here?"

"Waiting for you! Dyricio has been going on about you being a Fyzar-" Ruby pressed.

"Dyricio!" exclaimed Sory.

"I'm sorry. They forced it out of me."

"Is he right?" she asked, "I mean are you really a Fyzar?"

Sory sighed, "yes."

There was a pause before Ruby broke it, "how is that possible?"

"Because my father is one too."

"Why isn't Dyricio being taught too?" she asked.

"Because I'm the Fyzar from the prophecy."

There was another pause, this time Bahren broke it. "The Fyzar from *the* prophecy?" Sory nodded, "how do you know?"

"Fusna knows." Sory responded.

"How does he know?" asked Bahren.

Ruby cut in, "he knows." she turned back to Sory, "so, what will happen now? Are you going to – to confront King Sairus?"

"I don't know." Sory mumbled.

"Are you going to have to confront your own father?" she continued.

"I don't know!" Silence. "Sorry. I just don't want to talk about it." Sory sat on his bed next to Ruby and put his head in his hands, "I'm very – petrified about all of this right now. I don't feel like talking."

"What do you feel like doing?" asked Ruby.

"I don't know."

"Well," Ayro cut in, "you cannot traverse into this alone."

"What are you saying?" asked Sory.

"Sory, we've know each other for years. And you cannot fight a war without a friend by your side." Sory looked at him inquisitively. "I shall join the army tomorrow."

"If Sory is the Fyzar," said Bahren, "then he would be fighting alongside Ruby and I in the Knight Corps."

"The Knight Corps?" asked Ayro.

"The Knight Corps always has to be on the front lines. This is where the Fyzar would always be as well and so would be a member of the Corps."

"Then I shall join the Knight Corps."

Bahren smirked, "you cannot simply join. We are the elite of the elite. Half of all recruits drop out within the first month."

Ayro gave him a stern look, "nevertheless," he turned back to Sory, "Sory needs an old friend." Ayro turned to Dyricio, "Dyricio, why don't you join as well?"

Dyricio was taken by surprise, "me?"

"Yes, why not?"

"I – I wouldn't make it."

"Not with that attitude."

Sory cut in, "Ayro, trust me, it would not be a good idea."

"Why not? Ramous is his father too, so he is a Fyzar, right?"

"That's not the problem." said Sory.

"What is?" Sory didn't answer. Ayro turned to Dyricio, "Dyricio. Do you still want to return to Hyleeda?" Dyricio looked at the floor. "I cannot believe it!" said Ayro.

Dyricio shot to his feet, "Well believe it! That island was my home. I liked it there. And you all stole it from me!"

"Is that what you think?" asked Ayro. "Is that what you think? We didn't steal anything from you. You chose to come along."

"I chose nothing! I wanted to stay!"

"Then why did you come?!"

"I – I don't know!" he sat down and buried his face in his hands.

Sory answered, "because a Raishan threw a spear at him."

Dyricio shot up, "no! No that's not it! I could have easily snuck back into the forest and all the way back home."

"So why didn't you?" pressed Sory.

"I don't know! I was scared! I was – I was – I don't know!" and Dyricio stormed out.

A moment later and his personal guard, the one with the scar, peaked inside, "curfew has begun, the emperor has asked that all within the castle go to bed."

Bahren and Ayro started out as Ruby put her hand on Sory's shoulder, don't be afraid, just fight this war one battle at a time." she smiled, then left with the others.

*

An orange glow shown in Sory's eyes, it bothered him for a minute before he realized it was dawn, "blast, I'm late!" He leapt out of bed, put on the blue uniform Fusna had given him the day before, and burst down the hall to the window. *Gods know what he's going to do. I barely survived yesterday, what will he do now that I'm late?*

Within a few minutes, Sory had arrived at the Iron Structure. He charged through the doors and stood at the center of the room, "Sir! I'm here, sir!" After a minute of silence and stillness, he started looking around for his instructor. He looked at the columns and followed them up to the ceiling which sat shrouded in blackness. Sory squinted to see if anything was up there, he had the creepiest feeling that Fusna was. *Perhaps this is a test.* He thought to himself.

"You assume much, Sory," he heard Fusna say from behind.

Sory whipped around, "sir, I apologize-" but Fusna wasn't there. "Sir?"

"Did you really think that I would hide in such an obvious place?" The voice now circled behind Sory.

"I don't know why you would hide, sir," Sory said, spinning as he followed the disembodied words.

"All part of the training."

"And what part of the training is this, sir?"

"It is a few things," the voice continued to circle, by now Sory had turned all the way around, "but more than anything…it is reflexes." Fusna's immense chest appeared in front of him. WHAM went the air when Fusna upper-cut Sory.

Sory collapsed, a ferocious stinging engulfed his head all the way to the brain, "ahhh-ooww!" he yelled as he rubbed his beak.

"You were not ready." Sory stood and put his fists up, "always be ready."

"I am, sir." Fusna kicked Sory in the belly. "Ohhh!" Sory exclaimed as he doubled over, his blood boiling.

"Drop all previously conceived notions. You cannot win this fight in this manner."

"And what the hell is kicking my ass getting accomplished?!"

"The best and only way to learn is to feel it when you fail."

"Then I guess I have."

"Stand up straight." Sory did. "To strengthen your body we will start with your arms." He turned to the arsenal and one hundred foot-long iron bars flew out and connected into one long bar, its ends each connecting to a column on opposite sides of the room. "Grab it," ordered Fusna, and Sory did. "One!" belted Fusna. Sory thought he knew what his teacher wanted him to do so he pulled himself up and brought his beak up over the bar. "Two!" Sory had never done pull-ups before and so by the time he had made it to fifteen his arms felt as though they were about to fall off. "Another!" screamed Fusna as Sory hung there, "come on!" Sory started to lift himself, his arms quivering, an audible strain coming from deep within his throat, "I have seen starving war refugees who have flown across oceans do more pull-ups – and faster!" The tip of Sory's beak was mere inches from the bar, but he could go on no further, his arms strained, his voice groaned, "come on!" Sory released his grip and fell to the floor.

Sory jumped back to his feet as fast as he could. Fusna was in his face immediately. With a glowing intensity, Fusna's eyes speared through Sory's for a full minute before he spoke, "now your wings." Fusna had Sory hover at the center of the room, just out of arm's reach of the floor. "The task at hand is simple, no matter what, you are to stay in the same spot above the floor," Sory nodded, "and the weights are not to touch the ground." *Weights?* Sory thought. Fusna reached toward the arsenal and two spherical metal weights, each about the size of his fist, flew into his grasp, which he handed to Sory.

With every flap, Sory's body bobbed up and down, the weights nearly touching the floor every time he went down. After a minute Fusna attached another two weights to the ones Sory was already holding. Sory reared up and forced himself into the air a few more feet. In his arms, he could feel the beginning of the immense pain soon to come, while his wings flapped furiously. Another minute passed and Fusna attached an additional pair, Sory reared up again but this time bent his arms to keep the weights as high as possible. "That is an excellent idea, boy." Sory didn't know what he was talking about. "You can do two things at the same time, start pumping." With an internal groan Sory straightened his arms, then lifted them back up. The weights combined with the fatigue earlier made his biceps sting as he brought those iron spheres up and down.

Sory began wobbling about so much that he had to synchronize his pumps with his flaps, it helped, but then Fusna added another pair. Sory's wings now stung as much as his arms. He was bobbing and wobbling so much it looked as if he were flying through a hurricane. Ding! rang a metallic noise. Sory closed his eyes, one of the weights had touched the floor. Still hovering, he waited, waited for Fusna to admonish him, or worse. What seemed an eternity lasted only a second as Sory opened his eyes, then dared look to where Fusna had been just a moment before, but he was gone.

Sory looked about. "Sir?" Nothing. *Now what? I can't simply drop these weights, Fusna's probably watching – somewhere.* "Sir?" Still nothing, so Sory continued on, an ever anxious agony growing within.

With every pump and flap he could feel the fibers that made up his muscles splitting like a strained rope. Every second was a year, every strain was a heart attack and stroke in one. *Where is he?!* Sory pushed on, a thread of anger snaked through his head. He had to ignore the pain, he concentrated on his breathing, then on the war, then about whatever popped into his head, but every flap and pump broke his concentration. "AHHH!" he finally let out. "This is ridiculous! Fusna damn it, where are you?!" *How could he make me suffer through this?*

Despite this dissention Sory pressed on. All the while, despite what he said out loud, in the back of his mind the feeling of who he should really blame for this was struggling its way forward. For as long as he could, he denied it to himself, continuing to fault Fusna, but the throbbing of his body soon forced the thought in the back of his mind to the front. To himself Sory admitted, "this is my fault." It was just barely a whisper, he pulled his arms up one more time but this time the weights – were weightless.

As they floated back to the arsenal, Sory let himself fall to the stone floor where he began to massage his arms and wings. Fusna thudded down in front of him, "you are making progress." Sory smiled. Fusna then yelled, "attention!" Sory leapt to his feet. "Now we practice your fencing," and Fusna raked his sword out and across Sory's neck.

"Ah!" Sory put his hand to the wound, blood trickling out.

"You were not ready," reminded Fusna. Sory glowered back, yet his body ached too much to retaliate. Fusna waited, "I know you are sore, Sory, but in battle the enemy will cease for nothing but his own demise." Sory then whirled his sword at Fusna who blocked it. And so, they began, began a sort of fighting that Sory had never witnessed nor knew existed, one that was as much martial arts as it was fencing. Fusna went slowly, pulling his punches just enough for Sory to learn.

Midafternoon, Sory gasped desperately as he raised his sword one last time, only to have Fusna smack it down and point his own at Sory's throat. Sory hung his head, appearing as though he were about to drop dead. He could feel Fusna's white-hot eyes on him and did not dare look up, "meet my gaze, boy." Sory kept at the floor, "meet it!" Reluctantly he looked up, "the war will be over by time you are ready to fight in it." Sory turned longingly to the windows, thinking of escaping from that stone prison, "do not look out there!" With his blade, Fusna forced Sory's face forward, "there is only now, Sory, the present.

Yesterday? There was no yesterday, and there is no tomorrow either! And right now is all that you are to concern yourself with!" Fusna reached toward the arsenal where a log, as tall and thick around as Sory, came out and crashed to the floor. "Now Sory, your final task for today is to lift this log up and carry it on your shoulders until the sun sets." Sory eyed the log, hesitating, before finally giving in and dragging it upon his back. The weight crushed his neck, his tired body lost balance and he stumbled forward. "Now walk the perimeter," ordered Fusna.

Sory put one foot in front of the other, his knees and ankles buckling with each step. He grappled for air, even more than before. The weight of the immense wood stabbed into his shoulders, squashing and pinching the flesh between it and his bone. Not long after that, the pain spread to his legs and knees, and he started to limp with both legs. Sory groaned in agony, he could walk no more. The moment he stopped, the log also rolled off his back. He dug his talons into it but to no avail. Sory wanted to prove that he could accomplish what Fusna asked for both of them. Alas though, he had failed.

Once relieved of the source of his misery, Sory collapsed with a sort of profound fatigue that he was sure no one had ever felt before. He no longer had a will, whatever happens happens, he didn't care. He hit the cold, dusty stone floor and didn't move, he just kept his eyes on the log. He blinked, and when he opened his eyes again, they barely opened at all. The next time he opened them they only opened a squint, but it was just enough to see Fusna's shadow passing over him as he fell asleep.

*

Darkness filled the space around Sory, yet as a dim light peaked in he could see three figures. The one closest was facing away, with fear in his heart. In front of them were two much taller figures, one standing while the other sat on a great throne, a long neck above his shoulders. The longed necked figure was speaking, all Sory could hear though were whispers as the strangest feeling crept into his mind, that he knew who this griffin was, that this was King Sairus. When Sory looked at the figure standing next to the King, he knew who that was too, his father. However, this was not the case with the third figure standing in front of him, still just a silent silhouette.

Sory attempted to escape Sairus and Ramous, only to find himself stuck as if in tar. He struggled ever more, the King's whispers only growing louder, escalating into a squall within his head. Sory could not think, the voices clouding him, he covered his ears and nearly ripped them off as he thrashed about. Hate filled him, and as it did the whispers became clearer, and he could understand a word, "Tysorious." Sory froze, soon realizing though that Sairus was still talking to the third figure. Sory leaned forward, struggling to see this griffin's face, he managed to see his beak, and the edge of his eye. Sory thought he knew who this griffin was, but he had to know for sure.

A mere moment before Sory would be able to see this mysterious griffin's face, the whispers then screamed in head. Sory lunged backwards, thrashing himself about, his head burning as if about to explode. He fixed his eyes on the King, begging for mercy – screeching. The King ignored him, sitting there coolly, calmly. Then, he eerily slowly shifted his gaze toward Sory. Sory's heart raced, then it stopped, he could feel himself die.

Sory's eyes tore open and he jumped practically out of bed, terrifying Ruby, "Ruby!"

"Sory! Are you alright?"

"I'm fine." It was dawn, blue-gray light shone into his bedroom through the window over his head.

Ruby handed him a cup of tea, "here."

"Thanks," he said taking a sip. It burned his mouth and he coughed.

"Sorry, I never was the best cook. How bad does it taste?"

"No, no, it's fine," he took another cautious sip, "mmm," he said when he noticed that it was after dawn. "I have to get to the Iron Structure." Sory put on his blue uniform.

"Actually that's what I came here about," she paused. "You know how Fusna taught me too? Well when he did I barely survived, and I didn't have anyone to talk to about it. So I was wondering if, when you returned–"

"Sure, I'd love to talk." She gave a look of gratitude as he sped out the door and ran into Ayro. "What are you doing here? Shouldn't you be at your barracks or something?" Sory asked.

"They gave me a permanent pass because I'm a friend of the emperor." Sory ran to the window, "where are you off to?"

When Sory arrived at the Structure, he flew through the entrance and ran to the center of the room where he stood at attention, "where have you been, Sory?" Fusna asked from behind.

"I slept in, sir."

"Do you know why?"

Sory hesitated. Guessing the query was rhetorical he finally said, "I don't know, sir."

Fusna stepped in front of him, "it is because you are weak! So far, you have not been on time once! Where were you this morning?"

"I – in bed, sir."

"You miserable little swine. Though, perhaps your extra time asleep has allowed you to have retained more energy. Shall we see then?" Fusna forced his student to push himself twice as far as the day before through endless exercises and practice fights. Sory was just as fatigued by that noon as he had been by sunset the day before. "Something the matter?" asked Fusna.

"No-hih-huh-hih-huh-sir."

"You seem tired," Fusna raised an eyebrow.

Sory knew this was a test, "I can go on-hih-huh-all day."

"Do you remember the Run, Sory?"

"Yes, sir," still winded.

"When you did the Run you were able to achieve an extreme form of concentration, like a trance. Do you remember how tired you were before entering this trance?"

"Yes-hih-huh-sir."

"And do you remember how tired you felt *after* you entered trance?"

Sory tried to remember, "I wasn't tired, sir."

"Precisely. Being in trance disconnects one from feeling their exhaustion."

"Really, sir?"

"Yes, but be mindful, stay in trance too long and you could expend all of your energy without even knowing it, which could kill you."

"Kill me, sir? Has this happened before?"

"In the past, when there were more of the Fyzar."

"How do I prevent this?"

"It is simple, you must occasionally exit this heightened state of mind. There is a downside to this though, as you become more tired, it will be more difficult for you to concentrate enough to re-enter trance. For that you cannot be faint of mind, you cannot doubt yourself, now follow me." Fusna led Sory out onto the grassy field, "I want you to do the Run again."

Sory was visibly nervous, "yes sir." Even though he had overcome this already, doubt filled his mind. *Will I be able to do this? Does Fusna think I can't? Is that why he brought me out here?* Sory jogged as far as he could but his exhaustion was overwhelming, as was this doubt that had crept into his mind. He collapsed only a minute later. Fusna poured water from a canteen of water into his mouth, "foolish boy, you will never learn that all that is holding you back is yourself." Fusna pulled the canteen away, "now rise." Sory gradually stood, "I am not finished with you yet," he glared down at his student as if glaring down at an insect he was about to squash.

Sory closed his eyes, thinking of how easy it would be to give in. Surrendering would feel like finally being able to rest in a bed after flying around the world. It would be so easy, just to lie down, rest, and surrender. All he had to do was say *I give up* and that would be it. Like standing at the edge of a precipice, it would be so easy to just fall, to fall into the abyss and everything would be easy from there, even though he'd be a slave to his own doubt. Yet in his mind swirled a sweet temptation for this because he'd never have to fight his doubt, he could simply let it be and he'd never have to feel pain or fear again.

Fusna could sense this in Sory. He frowned then slapped him in the back of the head, "we will practice until sunrise if we must." Sory tried the Run until sunset, failing each time. Yet when darkness came, he was not allowed to go to bed, instead they remained outside. Fusna showed Sory the proper form for fighting and his student attempted to emulate as best he could. Every few minutes he would slouch over and his teacher would whack the back of his head or spine. Eventually this pain had permeated enough to keep him awake, counter-balancing his tiredness. Sory's mind went numb, and like he was sleep-walking, everything just passed in front of him, he couldn't feel his body, he just commanded it and went through the motions. It was a state he had never experienced, it was weird, he couldn't feel himself, he couldn't feel anything, he just forced himself on, becoming a part of nature.

A dim blue light shined over the horizon, and dew had coalesced all over him. "The sun has risen, Sory. You have made it through the night." Sory, with glazed eyes and heavy eyelids, fell to all four feet as Fusna continued, "go now, rest." Sory was about to fly off when Fusna asked a question, "how is your brother, Sory?"

Sory paused before answering, he remembered the conversation he and Dyricio had had on the ship just after the raid on the fortress. He knew his brother did not want to be in Arktorion. Sory answered, purposefully not facing Fusna when he did, "he's fine."

*

The next morning, when Sory arrived at the Iron Structure the doors were wide open. He knew better then to simply saunter on in so he landed next to the doorway and peeked inside. Because he had arrived on time, it was still too dark to see most of the way in. He eyed the rafters above, still shrouded in blackness, thinking Fusna could be hiding up there. *This is what I get for arriving on time. I can't see a thing.* He looked forward, knowing that the arsenal was somewhere in there. *I need a weapon.* He flew into the rafters, darted to the opposite side of the room, then glided to the arsenal's entrance. Sory warily opened the door, which creaked. When he stepped inside, he could barely identify a tall white figure standing in the darkness. His heart skipped a beat, and then he realized he was standing in the light and stepped aside. The white figure was just a towel atop a broomstick. Sory sighed in relief before wondering; *who put that there?*

Something snarled above him. It tackled Sory who struggled. This thing then picked him up and threw him outside. Sory attempted to right himself midair only to fall on his back. He jumped to his feet, a spear flew at him, he ducked. Then another, he jumped away, two more streaked at him just as he ducked behind a column. The adrenalin surged and he couldn't think, but he knew what to do; *the spears,* he thought. He peaked around the column, then bolted across the open room and grabbed a spear. Another flew out and Sory slapped it away with his.

"Your reflexes are improving," said Fusna from inside the arsenal, "but they are still terrible." The spear that Sory had just blocked flew into Fusna's hand as he came out. "At least you came mentally prepared, in time you may be able to defend yourself, or perhaps, even defeat me."

Sory stood at attention, "I hope to one day, sir."

Fusna smiled, "would you like to do the Run again?"

Sory hesitated, "yes sir."

"You are a horrible liar, boy. You have yourself convinced that you will fail. You have allowed your doubt to overtake your mind. Today it is this doubt which we will commence erasing." The floor opened underneath of them, Sory backed away as Fusna levitated, "if this does not succeed, nothing will." A fire then spontaneously ignited at the bottom of this pit, and then thirty bars flew out and formed a pole across it. Fusna bound Sory's wings together and blindfolded him, "whenever you are ready."

Sory tentatively searched for the pole with his foot. When he found it he wrapped his toes around it and extended his claws. He did the same with his other foot and so on. "Come on! Stop taking hatchling steps and reach the other side!" Sory tried to speed up but every time he took a step he lost balance which made his heart jump and his body tighten. Fusna had had enough and made the flames grow. They brushed over Sory's feet who froze, "move! Or I shall burn your feathers off!" Sory felt as if he were about to fall and grabbed onto the pole with his hands. A flame singed his face, "get back to your feet!"

Sory did as ordered. He could hear the flames roaring, "sir-"

"Embrace the fire!" Sory pushed on, each step was an eternity, every time he faltered Fusna would stream a flame past his face. Sory could see the yellow light leak through the blindfold and halted and Fusna screamed, "move!" A flame seared his wings. Sory darted forward, and within a few steps had found the floor where he removed his blindfold. Fusna yelled at him, "what are you doing? Again!" They continued for hours with Sory making little but some progress, beating his previous time with each crossing. After a few hours, he was almost walking at a normal speed. Satisfied for the day, Fusna moved on.

The next day, after exercises and practice fighting, Fusna stood Sory by the door. "Time for another test." he announced before snapping his fingers. There was a pause, but then a rumble came from below the floor, which then opened up. Sory watched as twenty-two giant iron poles, each with huge wooden spheres at their tops, rose from below the floor. Each of these spheres were wider than Sory's wingspan and had a few dozen sharpened metal spikes, each almost as long as Sory was tall, covering them. These jagged, crooked, and sharp spikes gleamed in the afternoon sun. Once all the way raised, the poles bent in half so that the spheres themselves formed a maze through the air, "this will be the ultimate test for your confidence," yelled Fusna from the other end of the Structure, "this is the Gauntlet,"

Sory mumbled to himself, "you have a name for everything don't you?"

"Yes, I do. Every day that you come here you will be blindfolded and fly through the Gauntlet. So I urge you now, look at it, memorize it, because every day the maze will be laid out the same. Hopefully, eventually, you will be able to fly this on memory alone, to do this you cannot have any doubt or a cluttered mind. If you do not have faith in yourself, if you let your nerves reach you, if you cannot make a decision, you will be cut. If you can arrive at the opposite end unharmed you would have developed the confidence in yourself to move forward."

"Right."

"You may begin when ready." Sory pulled the blindfold over his eyes and took flight, but he could feel the gleaming metal shards, he could feel the light twinkling off them. He reached out and began feeling his way about, the shards snipping at his fingertips. "Do not use your hands!" but Sory couldn't help it as he felt his way about the first sphere, his wing clipping it. He stretched his arms out for the next only for his wing to scrape it, he winced, but forced himself on.

One sphere after the next shredded his body, bit by bit. For the first half his hands and wings had the worst of it until he reached the spheres that were positioned one over the other, spreading the carnage to his back and chest. He could contain his nerves no longer. Sory ripped off the blindfold and scrambled out of the Gauntlet, enraging Fusna, "what are you doing?!"

"I can't – I can't do it, sir."

"Get back in there!" Sory just hovered there, staring down at this oversized deathtrap. Fusna sighed, then snapped his fingers, lowering the Gauntlet back below the floor.

The next afternoon, Sory stood at the doorway with his blindfold on. He could almost smell his dried blood from the previous day. Fusna whispered in his ear, "today you are to reach the other end, understand?"

"Yes sir." Sory lunged up at those spheres with his arms out and his heart racing. He made contact with the first and pushed away from it to give his wings room only to fly right into the next one. One spear cut an inch into his arm and out came the blood. Another stabbed a bit through the skin just below his ribs, he yelled and flapped his wings furiously to get away but his left wing was sliced up as it scraped the spikes, "ah!"

"Embrace the pain! It will make you stronger," called Fusna.

Sory flew away from those shards of metal only to fly into another cluster, his right wing scraping through it, "ah!"

"Stop crying or I will give you something to cry about!" Sory hovered, the long feathers at the ends of his wings scraping spikes on either side. He groaned, no longer fearful but infuriated. After a few seconds, he continued two seconds before another spike scraped his cheek, digging into where his skin met his beak. Sory flung his head back and could hear his skin tear as he did.

Sory hovered, gasping as if he had just flown across an ocean. However, he wasn't gasping out of exhaustion – anger, fear, and humiliation all swelled and boiled in his chest, "Come on boy! FLY!" Sory charged the spikes, his arms out in front. He skirted around one sphere but his right wing was scraped again. He flew too close to the next and his left wing was caught in the shards. He fell and hung by that wing, screaming from the incredible blinding pain. Fusna swiftly lifted him out of the snag and back to the floor.

The Gauntlet vanished into the floor as Fusna kneeled over Sory, "get up." Sory did nothing, "I said get UP!" Sory took in a deep breath, then rolled onto his elbows and knees, kneeled, and finally stood all the way up. "Wait here." Fusna went into the arsenal and when he came out he handed Sory a jar with a green liquid in it. "This salve is for the scars. Now you may go home." Fusna clicked his heels together and saluted Sory who did the same. Sory then walked back to the Obelisk instead of flying.

The next morning, Sory was walking to the window at the end of the hall, whilst the yellow-orange light of the morning sun shown into the castle, when Bahren came up, "Sory? Where are you going in such a rush?"

"I can't talk, I have to get to the Iron Structure."

A few minutes later he arrived there. The doors were open as he entered, "where have you been?" asked Fusna from behind.

Sory immediately went into attention, "I have no excuse, sir."

Fusna stepped in front of him, "no excuse?"

"No, sir."

"Would you like to begin then, soldier?"

"Yes, sir."

"I can't hear you!"

"Yes sir!" so they began, Fusna working Sory until he could go on no more. When afternoon came, Sory was aloud a brief respite before he had to face what he now considered his mortal enemy. When ready, he approached the Gauntlet slowly. He had invented a plan to finally reach the other side, he would count the wing flaps between each sphere. As he neared the first one though his adrenalin mounted, his hands trembled, he just wanted to fly into the spikes and get it over with. He felt as if he had no control over his body, a feather's width from panicking he forced himself on.

When Sory finally felt the first spikes he noted the number of flaps, then cautiously traversed around. When he made contact with the second he remembered how long that took as well. Then he climbed around it, each shard pricking his palms, and flew to the next, "stop using your hands! You have to *fly* around them!" Sory kept using them though, ignoring the scars that multiplied across them.

Soon Sory was approaching the fifth speared sphere with his hands out when he was scraped on the top of the head. He felt above him, he had found the fifth sphere. Now he didn't know where to feel, the sixth scratched at his chest. He didn't know what do, he lost track of his wing flaps as shear, uncontrollable fear mounted and swirled in his mind. He flailed his arms and legs about, the spheres seemed to be at every angle, he had become lost within the labyrinth. He had to remove the blindfold, "calm yourself, boy!" ordered Fusna.

Sory paused, then he flew in the direction he thought was forward. He tentatively felt his way through the next few spheres until he felt the wall. Sory ecstatically ripped off his blindfold and eyed his defeated foe, "horrible! Again!" yelled Fusna. Sory did run the Gauntlet again, but failed to reach the other end, it was the same for the rest of the day until sunset. "Enough!" Sory took off the blood-soaked blindfold then stood at attention, "you may go home now."

Back at the Obelisk, Sory walked into his room where Dyricio, Ruby, and Ayro were all sitting. They saw the scars. Ruby stood, "Sory, what happened to you?!" she screamed as she ran over to him and grabbed his hands.

"I'm fine," she touched one scar, "ow!"

"What happened?!" she cried.

"Nothing – training."

"Does that training entail your body being sliced up?" asked Dyricio as he and Ayro crowded around. Sory shot Dyricio a look.

Ruby answered, still inspecting Sory's hands, "you don't understand. Fusna's instructing is…different. It's harsher."

"Really, I'm fine," insisted Sory.

"You should have your hands examined," suggested Ruby.

"No, Fusna told me not to use my hands. I should have listened."

Ayro spoke, "use your hands on what? Giant balls of spikes?"

"Yes." Sory pulled his hands away, "Ruby, really, I'll be alright," he sat on the bed. "How are you?"

"Concerned about you. Fusna isn't making things too difficult, right?" persisted Ruby.

"No, he's not." Sory paused, "you never answered me." Ruby tipped her head, "how are you?"

She sat down next to him, "there's nothing much to talk about. We're all here just waiting to be sent back to war. If I know my father though, he will keep me here for as long as possible."

"How do you feel about that?" asked Sory.

Ruby thought, "it is nice being home, not having to fight a war, but–"

"But?"

"But I feel guilty. Just because I am the emperor's daughter what right do I have to be here while there's a war on?" Sory looked down at the floor as he rubbed his hands, "please let me get the surgeon," she begged.

"Alright," said Sory.

"I'll go," said Ayro.

"You'll need bandages for these wounds," Ruby said.

"It's not that bad. You were once taught by Fusna, you know what it's like."

"He never did anything like this with me."

"Perhaps he thought you couldn't handle it," Sory said jokingly.

She squeezed his hand and Sory cried out, "OWWW!"

She leaned in close, "who can't handle it now?"

Ayro came back in with a surgeon. An old bearded griffin, so named for their white beards and mustaches hanging down around their beaks, "where is the patient?" he asked.

"Right here," said Ruby.

The surgeon sat on the bed, "let me see your hands, son," he said, Sory put his on the surgeon's who's eyes nearly popped out of his head. "What in heaven's name happened to your hands?!"

Sory tipped his head and looked to the side, "I can't tell you."

The surgeon appeared confused and turned to Dyricio, "go get some warm water and a cloth." Dyricio nodded and left. The surgeon turned back to Sory, "this will take a while to heal."

Ruby became more concerned, "how long?"

The surgeon sighed, "it's too early to tell now." He turned to the door, "where's that water?!" He turned back to Sory, "do your hands hurt?"

"No, not really."

Dyricio ran in, "I don't know where to get hot water."

"How do you not know where the water is?" bellowed the surgeon.

"Doctor, really I'm fine."

"You're sure?" the surgeon asked.

"Yes."

"Alright," he said and got up, the rest started leaving and saying good night.

Sory went over to his brother, "Wait, Dyricio, how are you?"

"Fine."

"You're sure?"

"Yes, I am fine," with that, Dyricio left.

That night, Sory was in so much pain he didn't even bother to sleep. He put some more salve on and went to the dining hall where he drank tea to keep him awake. He looked forward to tomorrow's night sleep.

The next day was the same, the exercises soon waking him up from his sluggish state. Mid-afternoon, the Gauntlet arose once more, luckily though Sory's hands had somewhat healed. Yet lap after lap of the Gauntlet quickly laid waste to his body once more, not as much as it used to however. By the end of the day, with his self-confidence rising, he barely even needed to use his hands anymore, probably because he had already gone through the worst of what the Gauntlet had to offer. Every day he became slightly better than the last.

The next month grinded by, by the end of it, Sory's muscles protruded from every part of his body and he was able to endure all of the exercises with ease, even the Gauntlet. Fusna had also began teaching aerial combat to his student. Barely anything was the same about it. Sory had to concentrate on his teacher and make sure he stayed airborne at the same time as they fought in three dimensions, both inside and out.

Fusna often forced Sory to fight high into the atmosphere, then dive to the ground at full speed, the air sometimes bursting around them. Their blood would rush to their feet and make them feel as if they were about to explode, while their heads felt as if they were about to implode. Other times they would fight midair, tumbling about, spinning the blood in Sory's head like a whirlpool. Fusna made him endure this every day to prepare him.

Meanwhile, it had been a month since Sory had done the Run, until one day at sunset, "do you think you are ready for the Run, now?" asked Fusna and Sory nodded. Fusna nodded, "alright then," Fusna extended his hand toward the field. Sory eyed the grass, illuminated red and orange by the setting sun. He then crouched, closed his eyes tight, shut out all things, blanked his mind, then, there was nothing. His mind collapsed in on itself like a great star at its death, and an electricity sparked out of nothing in the center of his brain and then burst forth. Just as before, Sory could sense all that surrounded him. His body had no feeling as he opened his eyes. His pupils glowed white as he shot off, becoming a blur. He came back to Fusna and stood at attention, his eyes still glowing as the dust he kicked up caught up and clouded around them. Fusna smiled, "very good, you have conquered the first phase, Sory. Now that you have though there is something you must know about being in trance. It is that you can only do so in the presence of another Fyzar. Outside of that vicinity, which is different for each Fyzar, you risk great damage to your brain and body, not to mention how much faster your energy would drain." He paused, "now, on to phase two."

Chapter 12

The next day, Sory stood at the center of the Iron Structure as his teacher spoke, "the next phase of your training will be far different than the previous, different because it is far more mental than physical. In due time you will experience phenomena that most have not dared dream about. Phenomena that will warp your mind into a state where it may utilize these gifts given to you by your ancestors, understand?"

"Yes, sir."

"Let us commence then." One thousand bars flew out of the arsenal and assembled themselves into a vast web between the twenty-two columns. "Stand at the doorway." Sory did. "Now, attempt to reach the opposite end." Just as Sory prepared to start, one dozen ballistae, giant crossbows that fire spears, assembled on either side of the Structure. "You will need to enter trance." Sory did. Once his eyes glowed, he bounded into the metal web. Spears zipped all around as Sory maneuvered every which way, getting scraped every few seconds. Some spears would miss him but hit a bar and ricochet back at him. "Always be mindful of your surroundings." Sory leapt for the wall once close enough. Fusna saw his opportunity and fired. Sory could sense what was incoming and rolled in midair, dropping to the floor. Sory put his feet out just in time. "Terrible! You could not even reach the wall! Again!" Trance heightened Sory's senses to the umpteenth degree, he took advantage of this as best as possible. He listened for the spears while watching where he was going. Over the proceeding hours he was able to reach the opposite wall from time to time. "We will not stop until you can reach the other end without so much as a scratch!" Sory was never able to achieve this and so again went home covered in scars.

Reports from the war flooded in. Hyleeda had nearly been overrun by the Raishans. Arktorion, with its small and inexperienced military simply could not stand toe to toe with their oldest enemy. This retreat consumed Sory, though he seldom showed it. Fusna constantly reminded him of many things, that the threat of spies finding him only grew as the war deteriorated, that Sairus would not cease until the world itself was within his control. Yet most of all, that Arktorion, as well the rest of the world, would need Sory now more than ever.

One night a week later, Sory, Ruby, Ayro, Dyricio, and Bahren all went to the dining hall of the Obelisk. After getting their meals, they chose a spot near one of the soaring windows that overlooked the luminescent city. Soon Gyric had joined them as well, "can I sit down?" he asked with his deep voice.

"Of course," said Ruby. Awkward silence persisted for a minute before Ruby broke it, "Sory, how is training?"

"It's fine."

She saw a couple cuts on his arms, "are you alright?"

"I'm fine."

"Come on, Sory. You can tell us."

Sory hesitated, "we're going to lose Hyleeda."

"It will be alright in the end," said Ayro, "we have the Fyzar on our side."

"Yeah, yeah we do," said Sory.

"Sory?" asked Ruby, "are you alright?"

"No, no I'm not alright! I am afraid. Afraid I might lose this war. If entire armies cannot stand up against the Raishans then what chance do I, a single griffin, have?"

"Fusna will teach you well," reassured Ruby. That just made Sory more tense, "he will teach all sorts of things-"

"And every time he teaches me something new I know it's a bit closer before he's finished teaching me, and I have to face the enemy myself." Sory took a minute, "I mean, where am I even going to be sent? To Hyleeda?"

Gyric cut in, "if you ask me, we shouldn't even be fighting there."

Bahren took offence to this, "how dare you?! Arktorian military honor dictates that we shall never give ground!"

"I'm just sayin' that the indigenous do not want to be in a war between two far away nations. If we should have a war it should be in the countries that started it, not our colonies."

"So you'd rather have a war here, in Arktorion?"

"Better here than in some colony, because either way, this war has to be fought on someone's homeland, why is ours so much better than theirs?" Bahren was speechless, his beak wide open and ready to say something but nothing came out.

Ruby interrupted, "I think what Bahren's trying to say is that the Arktorian Empire colonizes those lands to help advance the undeveloped griffins that are in those areas."

"The Raishans think they're doing the same thing."

"It doesn't matter!" yelled Sory. "None of this arguing matters. It will not decide who wins this war."

"You will," said Gyric.

Sory shot him a look, "yes, I will."

"How can you be afraid when you know that there's no chance of failure. When there are thousands, perhaps even millions of griffins out there scared for their lives?" questioned Gyric.

"Do I not have the right to be afraid?"

"I meant your self-centeredness," shot back Gyric.

"You would be afraid if you were me."

"If I were you I'd let these two empires decide the victor by themselves. That is how I would decide the outcome."

"So you're a coward?" asked Sory.

"No, fighting for Arktorion would simply be choosing one empire over another."

"The Raishans are worse!" barked Sory.

"Is that your philosophy? If society followed that way of thinking it would collapse within a century."

"What would you do?"

"I told you, I would let the two decide for themselves and let civilization run its course. And even if Raishany won, it wouldn't be able to run the world for long. For all we know its army would be stretched so thin that those in its homeland would be able to rise up and overthrow the tyranny over them."

Sory looked away for a moment, then turned back, "I'm just afraid," he took a minute, "and besides, Raishany still has slavery. They still enslave the natives of their colonies. They don't try to improve, they destroy."

Gyric replied, "how do you know?"

Sory's rage and frustration swelled, "because I'm one of them."

Gyric turned to Ruby, "what is he on about?" She turned to Sory and shook her head. Gyric turned back to Sory, "what do you mean 'you're one of them?'"

"I meant what I said, that I'm a Raishan. I grew up on Hyleeda and my father is the general-"

Ruby cut in, "Sory-"

"Ramous Trajetton." Ruby and Bahren tensed up.

Gyric leaned in, "your father...is Ramous Trajetton?"

"Yes," answered Sory. Gyric glowered at him with a burning hatred. A few seconds later he stormed off.

Ruby leaned in as if she were telling a secret, "his family was captured and enslaved by Ramous. Gyric managed to escape."

Sory's face broke with guilt, "what happened to the rest of his family?"

Ruby sighed, "worked to death."

Sory's and Dyricio's eyes grew saddened, they looked at each other and Sory said, "do you still want to go back?"

Meanwhile, a summit of the heads of the military had been called in the Throne Room. Fusna was the last to arrive, all the other generals and admirals and even a few economists had already gathered around a large table with a map of the world on it while Emperor Mecila sat on his throne. Those around the table were all too busy arguing to notice him entering until Emperor Mecila greeted him, "General Fusna."

"Good evening," he replied.

"We've missed you at our assemblies," said the emperor as he shook Fusna's hand, "how are you?"

"I am fine, thank you sir."

"Good, good, oh and how are things going with the uh-" he leaned in close, "the project?"

"Very well, sir."

"Great! Why don't you join the others?"

"Very good, sir."

Emperor Mecila started back to his throne when he mumbled with a grimly depressing tone, "goodness knows, we need all the help we can muster."

Fusna found a spot at the table and began to speak, "so, what have you decided so far?"

General Meethvayd, a tall, obese general who commanded several legions and wore a blue and silver uniform replied with a shaky sigh, "nothing. We cannot decide where to launch a counterattack."

Admiral Ailzwushva, a short, old, and exhausted looking admiral in gray and light blue uniform responded, "we haven't even decided if we should counterattack."

General Meethvayd shot back, "wars are not won by retreating, Admiral Ailzwushva."

"What I mean is that we lack the materiel and troops to do so," explained Admiral Ailzwushva.

"Perhaps we should issue a draft," suggested another general.

"Pheh! A draft," scoffed General Meethvayd, "morale is low enough as it is and you want to issue a draft? Not only will that make the population resent the state, it will show weakness."

"Well what do you suggest?" pressed the Admiral Ailzwushva.

"One well planned attack that will buy us time to get the military back into shape," said Meethvayd.

"We cannot do that. We would have to cease all combat operations on all other fronts to launch an attack of that scale – wherever you prescribe."

"We need to strike at Hyleeda," said General Meethvayd, a couple other officers nodded their heads, a few others shook theirs, Fusna just stood still. "If we don't do something to stop the Raishan advance there we'll lose the island and they'll gain a secure base from which to launch an invasion of the Arktorian Homeland!"

"Hyleeda is a lost cause. We'll only be wasting resources by holding there any longer!" called another officer.

General Meethvayd replied, "those soldiers are not resources, they are lives!"

"So you admit that Hyleeda would cause us great casualties?!" said the admiral.

"I admit nothing! Every single military campaign has had casualties!"

Fusna simply observed all the infuriated griffins surrounding him. Then he took in a deep breath, and the torches lighting the room exploded in huge roaring flames. The generals all suddenly crouched down in fear, "we should counter attack," announced Fusna, "and we should do so on Platu."

"Platu?" said Admiral Ailzwushva. "Why would we want to counter in Platu?"

"For a few reasons, the first of which is that we can afford to lose Hyleeda."

"How?!" General Meethvayd yelled out. "There will be an invasion of our homeland if that happens."

Fusna replied, "while Hyleeda is close to our shores, it is very far from Raishany. If we construct another forty or fifty ships, we will have a large enough fleet to sever the vastly long and vulnerable supply routes from Raishany to that island. From there we can starve their Hyleedian forces without even having to invade. We'll be setting a trap for them."

"Forty or fifty ships?" asked an admiral. "Do you know how many coin and time it would take to create such a fleet?"

"Our only alternative would be to rebuild the entire army and Knight Corps to invade the island, which would be far more costly both in time and coin."

General Meethvayd cut in, "so we should not rebuild our forces?"

"We should do so later."

"How much later?"

"We will have to choose an ideal time when it comes." Fusna paused and drew a deep breath. "We will have to play it by year."

"Play it by year?" groaned General Meethvayd. "We have no more available forces, meanwhile the Raishans out number us two, maybe even three to one, and wherever they attack next they'll be able to take it, and you want to wait to expand our army?"

"And attack on Platu."

"And–" General Meethvayd threw his hand into the air, "and attack on Platu! How do you expect to do that?! Did you not just hear what I said about us not having enough troops?!"

"As it happens," started Fusna, "we do have some available soldiers, the First Knight Division." A breathtakingly awkward silence took the room as those gathered around cautiously turned their fearful gaze toward the emperor. "Sir, it is the only division that is both fit for battle and not already in one. If we are going to make a stand it must be with that division." Emperor Mecila said nothing. "Sir," Fusna stood in front of him, "we cannot just let the Raishans keep taking land. Now I know Ruby's in the First Division, but it is our only hope." A dreadful anticipation filled the room.

The emperor loudly exhaled as he faced forward. He rubbed his forehead and eventually responded, "fine."

"Sir-" said one general in disbelief.

"No! Fusna is right," snapped Emperor Mecila.

Fusna walked back to the table as General Meethvayd spoke, "I still do not like your play it by year strategy."

"I know. I don't like it either."

"We need a better plan."

"General, when has a military operation ever gone completely to plan, even mostly to plan?"

The general scoffed and mumbled to himself. Admiral Ailzwushva spoke, "Fusna, how can we guarantee that the Raishans won't cut off our supply lines to the place you suggested we attack, Platu. That continent is as far from here as Hyleeda is from Raishany."

"We must act before they know what is happening," said Fusna.

*

The next morning, Sory entered the Iron Structure as Fusna stood at the center, his eyes locked on a piece of creased paper in his hands. "Sory," he said without not looking up.

"Sir," Sory tried to get a peek at the paper Fusna was holding. It was a map of Platu, a continent far south of Arktorion and colonized by a few empires including Arktorion and Raishany. Each side had a color to represent itself, the Arktorian colony was represented by blue, Raishany by red, the neutral nations in green. There were about a half dozen white squares on the blue side going down the length of the border with Raishany, forming a front. Sory guessed they represented armies of soldiers since he had seen something similar when he lived with Ramous. Going down the length of these boxes it had written *"First Knight Division."* There were ink lines and arrows drawn and squiggled all about, showing where the armies were supposed to be stationed. After a minute of staring at the map in a deep state of thought, Fusna folded it up and put it in his pocket. "First Knight Division, sir?"

"Yes."

"I've heard about the Knight Corps, sir. Ramous used to mention them from time to time. He seemed to have a certain respect for them. He said they were 'the elite soldiers of Arktorion.'"

"Indeed they are, and right now they are all we have left."

"What are you talking about, sir?"

Fusna took a deep breath, "nothing, attention!" Sory snapped into attention. "I have a new exercise for you today. How do you feel about that?"

"It makes me feel good, sir."

"Excellent." The floor opened up into the fire pit, which lit up. Fusna hovered over it when a couple dozen iron bars flew out of the arsenal and formed two vertical poles, then two circular pieces of wood landed onto, then screwed themselves to their tops. Fusna then bound Sory's wings before they each stepped onto one of the poles.

Sory's pole wobbled, he regained his balance when two swords came out of the arsenal, one into each of their hands. The roaring fire caused a scorching wind that never ceased to remind Sory of its existence. Fusna spoke over the fire's roar, "Sory, this is the next part of your training. It is different this time though, this time, if you fall, if you stumble, you will die. You may begin when ready." Sory swung his sword, Fusna leaned back and a wall of fire streamed up in between them. Sory wrenched backwards, the heat seeming to push him back and he lost his balance.

Sory fell, thrashing about, reaching his talons out to the walls to end his descent, all he could think was that Fusna surely wouldn't let him die, he was to save the world. Sory peered up at Fusna as he fell, only able to see his face over the flames as they commenced searing his back and wings, slithering in between his feathers.

When Sory slammed into the ground, the heat literally stabbed into his back and wings like yellow hot knives. Nothing but flashing as giant white and blue flames danced around and above him. The roar of the fire deafened him as his ears rung, he couldn't even hear himself scream as the cinders burned through his feathers and skin like small animals burrowing into the ground. They scorched all the way to his bones, and then kept going. Sory clambered up a pole, it burning his hands and feet as he went, yet he knew the far worse fate that awaited him if he let go.

Sparks flew off the pole as Sory's talons scratched into it. He grasped the wooden platform and pulled himself atop, a crazed look in his eyes. His back and wings were on fire when a blast of wind vanquished the flames. After taking a respite and putting salve on the burns they returned to the wooden platforms. "Let us try that again," said Fusna who then swung his weapon, Sory dodged, his pole starting to tip over. He put his arms out to his sides to regain balance, leaving himself open. Fusna jabbed into his chest, "stop worrying about falling, boy!"

"Yes sir," Fusna swung again and Sory lost balance and stuck out his arms.

"Sory, you are going to have to become accustomed to your fear." Fusna wobbled Sory's pole with his mind. Sory put his arms out again, his eyes locked on the flames below. "You must become used to your life being in danger if you are to stand any hope of entering trance whilst in a real duel." But Sory didn't seem to hear a word of it. Fusna kicked Sory off the platform, knocking the air out of him. Sory dropped his sword as he clawed at the pit's wall, refusing to let go or even move. "Embrace the fear, Sory! It is the only way you shall defeat it!" Sory remained petrified as bits of pebbles fell out from under his feet, causing him to slide. Fusna floated over to him and grabbed his head, "LOOK!" he forced Sory to see the blaze below, "Look at the fire! Accept it, accept it for what it is!"

"What is it, sir?"

"What is it?! It is what is holding you back, your fear, you must defeat it, to defeat it you must accept it, and to accept it you must become accustomed to it." Fusna ripped Sory off the wall and held him just above the fire, the flames licking his face. "Now," Fusna whispered, "are you scared?"

"Y – yes, sir," his nod like a tremble.

"Good," Fusna released his grip. Sory could feel his heart stop as terror exploded from it and ripped through his veins into the entirety of his physical being. However, this time, he didn't think Fusna would save him. Sory watched the flames as they grappled upward. He put his arms across his face and closed his eyes.

A tingling took hold throughout Sory's body, moving upward from his front to his back. He opened his eyes and took his arms away. He was levitating as he peered amidst the depths of the fire, able to see the bottom from where he was. He tried to grab the wall, extending his talons, straining just for a touch, a touch that would allow him to escape this nightmare, but he couldn't as he floundered about. "Sory!" yelled Fusna from above, "stop struggling!" Sory stopped, "calm yourself, concentrate, if you can enter trance – I will let you back up."

Sory closed his eyes and forced himself to concentrate, but the more he tried the more afraid he became. Meanwhile the flames continued to singe his body as the heat scorched him and the air screamed in his ears. He opened his eyes, he could not concentrate, but he must to escape. He closed them again, squeezing them tight, figuring that attempting to ignore the danger around him only makes him fear it. Therefore, he would accept it, only then realizing that Fusna had already said this. Time slowed, he could feel every arm of every flame as it scratched the air, he opened his eyes, and they were glowing.

Fusna breathed a sigh of relief and returned to his platform. "Good, now do you think you are ready to fight?" Sory nodded. "Spectacular." Fusna brought him back onto his platform, returning his sword from the bottom of the pit as well.

And so they fought, Sory's platform persistent in its wobbling with every swing, duck, and dodge. However, this did not affect him now. Sory soon figured that he could use the wobbling to strike at odd and hard to defend angles. They continued all day, and the next day Sory took on the fire-pit again, this time getting into trance immediately.

That night the six of them, Dyricio, Ayro, Ruby, Bahren, Sory, and Gyric all gathered for dinner in the dining hall. No one was talking at all and the air was tense. Sory and Dyricio were at a loss as to why, "Ayro, how is training?" asked Sory.

Ruby appeared distraught, "excuse me," her voice choked as she stumbled out the door.

"Is she alright?" asked Sory.

Bahren reluctantly answered, "they're sending us back in."

"Into what?"

"The war!"

"Where?" asked Dyricio.

Gyric leaned in, in the same manner that one would tell a child that their parent had died, "we're being sent to Platu."

Sory nodded, Bahren seemed unsure though. "No, I don't think that's it. When we were sent to Hyleeda she was fine, almost kind of excited. Excited in a way that you could run around the world, but at the same time, you are also afraid enough to run around the world." Bahren paused. "She was not like this though. I don't know what's different this time."

"Is Platu a dangerous place to be sent?" asked Sory.

"No. She seems sad, almost like she's leaving something behind," said Bahren.

*

The next day, Sory went to training distracted with Ruby's leaving for the battlefield once more. He wasn't able to enter trance and towards the end of the day Fusna had had enough, "Sory, where has your head been?"

"It's nothing, sir."

"A distracted soldier is a dead one, now what is it?"

"Ruby's leaving for Platu, sir."

"Yes, I know."

"Well sir, I mean I don't want her to get hurt."

Fusna drew in a deep breath, "Sory, there is no way Ruby would get hurt."

"If it were up to me I wouldn't even let her go." Fusna slapped him in the face, "OW!"

"It is a soldier's duty to serve his or her nation. A soldier must go where they are required despite all they are leaving behind."

"I know that sir-"

"Do you?! If you did understand, you would not have any objections to Ruby's departure! Now I have known and loved her for years, almost as a daughter, yet I had no trouble in making the decision to send her into battle."

Sory beamed up at Fusna, "you decided to send her?!"

"It was a grim decision-" Sory trampled out the door and into the sunset, the field and sky lit red as if on fire. "SORY!" screamed Fusna as he pursued him, "Sory!" he grabbed Sory's arm.

"Let me go!"

"Listen to me!" he shook Sory's shoulders, "she is a soldier, and as a soldier she has a duty. She volunteered to lay down her life. Understand?" Sory had never thought about that. A rock fell into his heart. "They fight and die so that those of their nation do not have to. And I know she did not want to go, but her division was the only one available. And sometimes you just have to do things that you do not want to. And sometimes, even if you may not know why you have to, you cannot whine and moan about it! Now I do not care that I am ruining your life, so you are just going to have to suck it up, soldier on, and realize that my decision was for the greater good, understand?!" Sory's anger grew with the humiliation of being yelled at like a child. In some way though he knew Fusna was right, but he did not want to admit it to himself. They locked eyes for a couple more seconds, neither wanting to back down. Finally though Fusna released Sory, "it matures you, Sory. You learn to live with having something taken from you. I love Ruby too, but I did not let that get in my way, you should not either."

Sory charged back to the Obelisk, back to his room where he slammed his door and paced the floor, grumbling to himself. He couldn't believe Fusna would scold him like that. The fresh embarrassment made him relive the whole scene, and the more he thought about it the more he realized that Fusna was right. Soon Sory began to think about himself, sitting there on that bed while thousands of other griffins fight, their lives on the line. He knew they fought for two reasons, they wanted to, and because their empire asked them to while he simmered about not getting his way with Ruby.

*

The next morning in the Iron Structure, the rays of the sun had just begun to streak over the horizon as Fusna landed at the doors. He scanned the field and the sky above, searching. He sighed and then went inside where he saw Sory standing at the center. "I thought you would come back," said Fusna.

"I never thought that I'd arrive here before you did," said Sory. Once more, they stepped into the fire pit each on their poles in trance when Fusna started looking at something behind Sory who turned around. "Ruby?" She saw his glowing eyes. She stepped back and gasped. He jumped out of the pit. "Ruby," his eyes dimmed but she kept staring at them.

She blinked, "wow."

"What are you doing here?" Sory asked.

"Well I was leaving tomorrow and I just wanted to say good-bye."

There was a short silence before Fusna interrupted it, "Sory, go be with your friends. You do not know the next time you will all be together."

"Thank you, sir."

"Come on," said Ruby, "let's go find the others." She grabbed his hand and they went off to the Obelisk where they all gathered in the dining hall in the spot overlooking the city.

Ayro raised a toast, "to our last meal together!" he took a drink.

Bahren corrected him, "we'll still have supper together. It's our second-to-last."

Ayro raised his glass again, "to our second-to-last meal together!" Sory laughed and they raised their glasses together and said, "live miserably or die happy!" and they all drank.

The next day there was to be a parade for the departure of First Division. So, when Sory awoke the next morning he did not go to the Iron Structure but instead got dressed into his formalwear which was given to him and the others when they first arrived in Arktorion. When he was fully dressed, he stood in the mirror of his dresser when there was a knock on his door. "Come in," Ruby entered, "hey," he said surprised.

"Hey," she looked him up and down, "you look nice."

"Thanks, you too," said Sory as Ruby went over and gazed out the window. An eerie silence grasped the air outside. No bugs or birds stirred, no wind blew, nothing. As if nature itself knew what was to come. "What is it?" Sory asked.

"Nothing, just, wanted to talk," her eyes still pointing out the window, "just need someone to talk to right now."

Sory stood next to her, "what is it?"

"Just – I can't believe I'm leaving. It just feels so different this time."

"Why do you think that is?"

"I don't know," she slumped down on the bed, "I just can't get over it."

"Maybe you need to know what's different before you can get over it." She stared off distantly as Sory sat next to her. "What changed since the last time you went off to war?"

Ruby thought for a moment, "I should probably return to my barracks."

Sory put his hand on her back and moved it up and down. He didn't know what to say. "There-there," she laughed, "what?" he asked.

"Oh nothing, you're just so good to me." She hugged him then went to the door. "Bye." Before he knew it she was gone.

Sory laid on his bed, nodding off into space, "'good to me?'"

Ruby sprang down the hall and out the window to her barracks just outside the city. Across the city, tens of thousands of other soldiers said their good-byes to their families, their children, their wives, their parents, their siblings as they hugged and cried before flying off for what they all knew could have been the last time.

Back at Ruby's barracks, everyone else was already putting their battle armor on for the parade. Each barrack was long and full of nothing but bunk-beds, leaning up against the head of each bunk-bed was a pike. These weapons were the symbols of bravery and tenacity for the Knight Corps. They were each about one and a half times the height of Ruby with a spear and axe at one end. Just underneath of the axe was the symbol of the Knight Corps, a long triangular flag outlined in yellow with a red field on the inside. In the center of this field was a globe on which a griffin perched.

Once all of the Knights had their armor uniforms on they lined up into formation outside along with the rest of the division, their pikes rising high over their heads and their flags flying proudly in the wind. Once the entire division was in formation the commander of it began leading it toward the city, his immediate subordinates following. All of the commanders rode atop giant flightless bird like creatures. Behind them flew the flag of the Nation as well the flags of all the Provinces, followed by the Knights. They all marched in perfect synchronization, making the ground rumble.

Back at the Obelisk, Sory, Dyricio, and Ayro had gone to the Throne Room where they had been summoned as guests of the emperor. The emperor was dressed in a cascading blue cape and wearing his black ceremonial tights that were tucked into his black leather boots. He also wore chest armor while a team of make-up artists poked and prodded at his face. Around the perimeter of the room stood the Praetorians at arms' length of each other, senators and governors and a few generals and admirals stood around getting themselves poked and prodded as well. Ayro, Dyricio, and Sory all stood in the doorway, awestruck at this odd site. After a minute the emperor noticed them. "Ah, boys," he waved them over and signaled the make-up artists to leave. They all took a couple steps back, bowed, then walked away. "How are you?" He turned to Sory, "nervous?"

"Nervousness was trained out of me, sir."

Emperor Mecila laughed, "indeed, indeed. Say, Fusna's here if you want to talk to him."

"Yes, sir, if that's alright."

"Hah-ha-ha! 'Is that alright?' I see Fusna trained some manners into you too." He put his hand on Sory's shoulder who furled his brow because of this last comment. The emperor turned to the guard on his right and said, "find General Fusna," then waved his hand, the guard clicked his heels and went off. The emperor turned back to Sory, "so how is it otherwise?"

"Fine, sir."

"Well, Fusna really did make a soldier out of you. You really have changed since the last time we met. Seems like such a long time ago, huh?"

"More than you could know, sir," Sory said, when Fusna entered.

A guard spoke, "Your Highness, General Fusna."

"Ah, my dear old friend, come and join us. I was just talking to your newest student here, and I was just saying how different he is from last we spoke."

"Oh yes, Your Highness, I trained him just as well as I trained your daughter. And I must say, sir, it was different teaching a Fyzar. I had not done so for a while."

Who else had he taught? Sory thought, when one of the staff approached the emperor.

"Your Highness," he bowed, "the Knights are about to reach the city."

"Ah, good." He turned and faced the door. "Boys, if you would please," they all stepped out of the emperor's way as he started walking, everyone following. The three of them fell in at the end of the entourage while half of the guards marched in front of it, and the other half in the rear.

Dyricio leaned into Sory, "why do you think the emperor asked us if we were nervous?"

"I don't know. What other Fyzars do you think Fusna has taught? He said that he hadn't trained one in a while. Who else could there have been?" Dyricio shrugged his shoulders.

They eventually arrived at a great balcony over a hundred feet above the ground and big enough to fit all four dozen of the entourage. It overlooked the city, and the crowds gathering around. The admirals and generals all stood regally with their heads up and their chests out, their capes shifting in the breeze.

Sory, Dyricio, and Ayro stood at the railing on the north side of the balcony. Meanwhile small crowds began to gather, and grow, conjugating on roofs and the sidewalks below. Soon there were tens of thousands of cheering citizens waiving the national flag. Sory looked north, waiting for the Knights to come. "Where are they?" asked Dyricio.

"I don't know," answered Sory. It was a cloudy, gray day. The sky itself, sad. A low rumble started like some distant titan trampling the ground, which vibrated. All those in the audience and on the balcony could feel it in their feet. Soon the vibrations grew stronger and rose up into their bodies, into their joints, into their muscles, and finally into their lungs. The crowd began to scream and wave their hands as the generals of the First Division came into view who then waved back. As the generals approached the balcony, they stopped waving and faced it, the sternest of expressions on their faces. When they passed under it, they saluted in unison, banging their right hands on their hearts then raising their fists with their arms in an L-shape. The emperor and everyone else on the balcony saluted back. The generals' silver, shining armor covered their entire bodies, even their heads, only their wings and faces could be seen.

Behind them came the Knights, marching with a tremendous zeal, each company saluting the emperor one at a time, who would then salute back. Sory spotted Ruby and Bahren beside each other at the very front, he raised his hand and caught a glimpse of Ruby winking at him. The noise and feeling from their marching made the ground tremble as if it were afraid. Their flags flew in the wind and their pikes moved back and forth with each step.

Soon the parade had ended. The Knights now off in the distance and the crowds dispersing into the sky while everyone on the balcony filed back inside. "Where are they all going?" asked Dyricio.

"I don't know," said Sory. He turned to Fusna, "sir, where is everyone going?"

"To the Field of Tears, Sory."

"Field of Tears, sir?" Emperor Mecila and his entourage had soon taken off, following the crowds out of the city and over a vast grassy field. Here, the soldiers fell out of formation and gave their final farewells to their loved ones. In all directions, a sea of griffins hugged and cried, fathers pulling their children close and telling them to be brave, then hugging their sobbing wives, telling them they'll be fine.

Ayro, Dyricio, and Sory just stood in the midst of this horrid scene. Ayro leaned in close to Sory, "I guess this is why they call it the Field of Tears."

A near intolerable somberness blanketed this small patch of land, a somberness which Sory could not help but absorb as his eyes scanned the masses. He soon found Fusna as he took it all in as well, his eyes raked with a pain too powerful for words. A pain so powerful that Sory became hypnotized by it, before he broke himself out of the spell. "Sir…sir," said Sory, "Fusna!"

Fusna blinked. "Sory," he said.

"Are you alright, sir?"

"I'm fine." He couldn't take his eyes away. "For centuries soldiers have begun their journey into warfare from this field," he paused, "it is the only purpose of this field." His eyes on the ground, "all are forbidden to be on or fly over it, unless you are on it for," he looked back up, "for this reason."

"Father, father!" yelled Ruby who hugged the emperor.

"Ruby!"

"Are you going to be alright?" she asked.

"Who me? Phh! I'll be fine, it's you who has to be worried."

"You never have to worry about me, father." They smiled at each other, then the emperor turned to Fusna and Sory, Emperor Mecila brushing a tear from his eye.

"Sweetheart, why don't you say good-bye to them, too."

"Yes, father," she went to Fusna and saluted him, and he back, "sir," she said.

"Ruby, you will remember everything I taught you, yes?"

"Yes, sir."

"And you will be a good and loyal soldier of the Empire and of the Corps, yes?"

"Yes, sir."

"Good," he put his hand on her shoulder, "I have trained you well, and I am sure you will make me proud." She smiled and they hugged.

Then she walked over to Sory. "So," she said.

He took a deep breath, "good luck out there."

"Thank you."

"You'll give them nightmares, Ruby."

Ruby was about to say something when the commanding general called. "Form up!" Signaling the end of good-byes. From there on out, the very existence of these soldiers was doomed to an uncertain fate as their final chance to bid farewell came to a close. For they were traversing into that dark abyss of fear, death, and war. Solemnly, and reluctantly, thousands of Knights ended the warm grasp of their families as they reformed into their ranks, some sobbing like hatchlings, longingly peering back at what which they were leaving, from all that they knew, all that was good, all that was safe, all that was warm, into an unknown and terrifying fate. Wives cried madly, some dropping to the ground on their knees, the mere thought of what could happen to their husbands knocking them to the ground, more powerful than any other force.

Ruby grabbed Sory's hand, "I must go now," and with that, she turned away, turned away from him. That was it, he couldn't do anything about it, she could be dead tomorrow, her cold, hard, lifeless body lying on some far away battlefield.

Like black powder this exploded inside his mind, he couldn't handle the thought of her dead. "Ruby! Wait!" He grabbed her arm and hugged her, nuzzling her neck, "I'll be there as soon as I can. I won't let you die," he whispered in her ear.

The general yelled again. "Form up!" Ruby embraced Sory for one last second, her head on his shoulder, before pulling back and looking into his eyes one last time with tears rolling out of her's. She had a certain tragic and spirit-crushed disbelief on her face. And with that she ran off, ran off like so many other countless others have. Sory watched her leave, not in sadness, but in fear. Soon she was becoming lost in the crowd, she waved to him, still moving further and further into the formation. Sory waved back, but by the time he did, she had already disappeared.

"She didn't see me wave," he said to himself.

Once the soldiers were all in their ranks the generals took flight, those companies in the front rising first, and eventually those in the rear rising last. Tens of thousands of wings flapped, creating a kaleidoscope of color against the background of the sky. Those they left behind watched this great armored, silver cloud as it gradually, almost torturously slowly, disappeared over the horizon. Eventually the crowds dispersed, except for Sory who stayed, waiting until the formation could be seen no more, only then did he leave.

Three days later, just as the sun fell under the horizon, the First Knight Division reached the coast. They loaded themselves and their belongings onto the dozens of ships in the Vallce harbor, the water shimmering a blood red from the setting sun's light. Ruby landed on the aft of Captain Zat's ship. From there she watched the coastline shrink as the fleet set sail, her fellow soldiers going below and sleeping. Behind the coast, the sun disappeared, leaving but a near feather thin line of red on the horizon. Soon both the light and the coast had disappeared, as did the sanctuary of home. Ruby remained for one last second before turning to go below deck, only managing a step before peering back one last time, hoping that she could still see the coast, only to witness the dead of night.

*

Nighttime, the Obelisk, Dyricio gazed out over the city, which resembled a second sky as millions of torches illuminated it through one of the huge windows in the dining hall. He stood alone in there when Fusna walked by and spotted him. The old soldier went to Dyricio, his eyes on the city as well. "What are you searching for?"

"Huh?"

"One does not simply gaze out a window, looking out onto all of creation if he is not searching for something, unless he has lost something, or perhaps feels lonely, like he is too far from home." Dyricio clinched his beak and looked down at the floor, "ah, I hit it didn't I, there is something isn't there, or maybe, some one, Dyricio. Your father, perhaps."

"My father, he-"

"Do not hide your feelings from me boy, I can read minds and I know you miss him despite all that you know about him. I have known for a *long* time." Dyricio was ready to punch Fusna. "Dyricio," Fusna exhaled, "I understand this, your will to return to what you knew your whole life, that big tree out in the middle of nowhere. But sooner or later you are going to have to accept the fact that you cannot go back to that again." Dyricio shot Fusna a deadly look. "I am sorry, and I can feel your anger, but you will not be able function – unless you let go."

"I – don't need – to let go of anything!" and he stormed off, stomping the entire way out.

Fusna knew something had to be done about Dyricio, but he didn't know what. He went to the throne room. "Your Highness," Fusna said as he came in, the emperor looking out one of the windows distantly, much like Dyricio.

"General," he said, "what brings you here in the middle of the night?"

"I see the guards are not outside of the door, sir."

"Yes, given the mood of things I decided to give them the night off. Now what can I help you with, old friend?"

"Your Highness, what brings me here is my worrying about a certain young griffin."

"Sory?"

"No, Highness, his brother," Dyricio, who had followed Fusna, put his ear up against the door, "Dyricio." Dyricio's heart jumped and he pulled his head away, staying frozen, he waited for Fusna to come to the door.

"What about him?" asked Emperor Mecila.

"I fear his loyalties are not with us." Dyricio cautiously put his ear back to the door. "Dyricio, I believe, is good in his heart, he is just homesick, but in this homesickness there may still be a threat." said Fusna.

"That's it, that is all you're worried about?" asked Emperor Mecila.

"He knows things, Highness."

"So do Sory's friends and my daughter."

"Yes, but we know where *their* loyalties rest, Highness."

The emperor inhaled, "homesickness does not equate to disloyalty."

"Perhaps that was not the best word. He still feels a connection toward his father. He has been resentful toward everything around him ever since I first met him," said Fusna.

"Has he been?"

"Oh yes."

"Did you read his mind?"

"I did, but anyone could see his longing to return to the arms of Ramous."

"Why would he hate everything here, we've treated him well enough," Emperor Mecila said.

"I think he is jealous of his brother." Dyricio frowned, looking towards where Fusna's voice was coming from.

Emperor Mecila chuckled, "oh jealousy, fickle beast." He thought for a second. "What do you say we do?"

"For now, we just keep our eye on him, I have faith in him yet, and we may even be able to earn his loyalty,"

"Good chance," Dyricio whispered to himself.

"And once we have, we will probably not lose it."

"How good a griffin do you think he is?"

"I believe that given the right chance he may be able to prove himself," said Fusna.

"Given a chance? What are the odds of him failing that chance?"

Fusna hesitated, "Fair, I would estimate." Again, Dyricio pulled his head from the door, his talons scratching it as he clinched his fists.

"And if given said chance he fails, how would we proceed?" pondered the emperor.

Fusna breathed heavily, "I do not know." Dyricio had heard enough. He grimaced, his talons all the way out, his hands in fists. He backed away from the door a few steps, then ran down the hall. Fusna sensed someone outside and went to see. He saw the tail of Dyricio as he disappeared down one of the staircases. In the shadows stood Dyricio's guard, the one with the scarred face, smiling a devious grin.

Chapter 13

It was morning in the Iron Structure as Fusna paced in front of Sory, "today my student, we advance to the next phase of your training. All that you have experienced so far has been but a warm up."

What else could there be? Sory wondered.

Fusna went into the arsenal and reemerged with a bowl of grapes. "One of the Fyzar's greatest weapons is using his qi to see." he held out a grape, " *This* is the next step beyond the Run, and just like the Run you must first go into trance." Fusna paused as Sory closed his eyes, held them, then opened them glowing. "What you must do is concentrate on this grape." Fusna slowly moved it in a circle and Sory followed it with his eyes. "Now close your eyes," Sory did, "and sense the grape as it moves. Do not go from memory, I want you to actually sense it, to feel it move, to feel it in the air." Fusna levitated backwards a few feet before gently touching back down. Then he threw the grape at Sory's face who flinched and opened his eyes. Fusna sighed. "Come," they flew out over the nearby forest, "close your eyes, Sory, feel the wind, see it, but see it with your mind." Sory crumpled his brow, he didn't know what to make of 'seeing with his mind,' but he did his best. "Focus on what you can feel, focus on the wind brushing on your face and body." Sory did, paying attention to every nerve ending, every cell of skin, feeling the brushing of the moving air. Then he began to see it, only the wind touching his skin appeared as thousands of white snakes slithering through his feathers. Fusna smiled, he knew Sory was starting to understand as his student began to move his arms around in the air, extending his talons out to cut it.

Back in the Structure, they sat with their legs folded, the bowl full of grapes back in Fusna's hands. "Seeing what is in contact with you is child's play compared to what you must do to complete this skill. You must be able to see that which is not in contact with you. Now close your eyes again." Sory did. All Sory saw were blurry lines and blotches with black in the background, the normal thing one sees behind their eyelids. After a couple seconds, Sory felt a tap on his beak as a grape fell on it. Then another tap. "Come on Sory, sense the air splitting as the grape falls through it."

Another tap, Sory tried focusing on the air above him yet still saw nothing. However, when the next grape fell it made his brain begin to slowly have a deep, heavy feeling in its core as he concentrated ever more. Another bounced off his beak just above the left nostril, a flash like lightning beamed out from that very point, as well as a series of blue vibrations that spread across his beak and face, vanishing as fast as they had appeared. Yet the vibrations also went into the air in the form of sound. He saw the sound, he didn't hear it, he saw it. That too vanished into space. Sory opened his eyes. Fusna smiled, "you could see something couldn't you?" Sory blinked then closed them again. Another grape bopped him and created the same flash and lines as before. Yet in the center of all the blurry lines, blotches, and black of the inside of his eyelids was a blue spot that soon shrank away.

Another grape hit and the blue spot jumped outward with the flash, then shrank away. "I am definitely seeing something, sir." Another came down just as he finished his sentence, the blue spot came back, then shrank again. The next caused the same occurrence, only now the blue was remaining longer, so long that it was still there when the next grape came. When it did it entered the blue area and Sory could see it before it touched him. Sory realized that the blue was three-dimensional. He jumped back. "Whoa!"

Fusna smiled, "very good, the part of your brain meant for this has finally been awoken after being dormant your entire life." Sory put his hand on his head, smiling with the utmost excitement in his eyes. "What does it feel like, Sory? Discovering this new part of your brain?"

Sory had to think about it. "Well, sir, I suppose it's like moving your leg after it falls asleep. You can move it but it hurts in a way when you do."

"Good, let us move on." Fusna leaned a black and white wooden target from the arsenal against the wall. Sory, with his eyes closed, was standing with his back up against it as Fusna spoke, "I am going to throw spears at you, Sory."

"And I have to dodge them, right sir?"

"No, you must catch them." Sory raised his eyebrows as his palms started to sweat. "Ready?"

"Re-" WOOH! A spear tore the air. Sory ducked. "Whoa!" He opened his eyes.

"Concentrate! Keep your eyes closed!"

"Yes, sir."

"And be ready!"

"Yes, s-" WOOH-WIH! Another spear as Sory ducked.

"SOLDIER!"

Sory straightened his spine. His eyes still closed as he concentrated on that pins and needles sensation somewhere in the depths of his brain, focusing on the now barely visible blue. Another spear zipped past and he flinched again, still not able to see it. Yet he did get a glimpse of the moving air from the sound. He kept focusing on the blue, trying to keep it at the size it was, squeezing his eyelids so hard it started to hurt his eyes underneath.

WOOH! And a white flash exploded in his face, and one-thousand white lines dashed across his vision. Sory jumped back and opened his eyes. A spear was floating mid-air mere inches from his face. Fusna was shaking his head. "Sir, I think I'm beginning to understand this," said Sory.

"No, you will need your energy, you should rest your mind."

"I feel fine, sir."

"At this early stage this kind of mental exercise drains your energy faster than you may think. Exit trance and you will see." Sory did, and like a fist flying through his brain a sweeping dizziness flooded his skull like water. He lost his balance as his knees became loose. Sory stumbled to his side before regaining his balance. "You see? We will stop for today. Take a bit of time to regain your second wind."

Fusna started walking away when Sory said something, "sir, can I ask you something?"

"Yes?"

"I don't know if you've ever heard of this before but — there's this dream that I keep having. I — I'm in Raishany, inside a castle I think, and Ramous was there, and so was Sairus."

Fusna turned all the way around, "how do you know it was Sairus? Have you seen him before?"

"No – but I could sense that it was him."

"And what happened in this – dream?"

"There was this third griffin. I couldn't tell who it was."

"Did you see his face?"

"No, he was facing away from me, but I couldn't see Sairus's face either and I still knew who he was."

"Sory, what is your question?"

"What does this dream mean, sir?"

Fusna drew in a deep breath, "I am not sure. Tell me more."

"There really isn't much else, sir. Just this griffin, who I didn't know, standing in front of Sairus and Ramous."

Fusna nodded, "it was probably just a nightmare," he said and walked away.

"I was frozen in the dream,"

Fusna stopped dead, "frozen?"

"Yes, I tried to move but couldn't, then I leaned forward to see who the third griffin was and when I did I think I got too close or something and Sairus…" Sory paused, his hands balled up in tense, fearful fists.

Fusna waited, "yes?"

"It was like he – attacked me, but – it was like he was attacking my mind – with his." Fusna's eyes burst with alarm which Sory noticed, "sir, does this mean something?"

Fusna kept looking away for another couple of seconds, thinking intensely. "No. It means nothing." Sory looked down, almost disappointed. "Now let us go home, I shall escort you."

"Why, sir?"

"To make sure that you do not pass out midair." When they arrived at Sory's room, he sat down on his bed as Fusna leaned against his dresser, "do not become accustomed to this Sory. This ending of the day so early will end when your mind is stronger."

Then Dyricio walked in, "Sory?" he saw Fusna and froze.

"Dyricio," greeted Fusna.

"Dyricio?" interjected Sory, "what is it?"

"I suppose that I shall take my leave now," said Fusna as he walked out the door.

Dyricio stood next to Sory's bed, "Sory do you truly think you should be spending such great time with that one?"

"We've been over this, Dyricio."

"Your body's never received this amount of injury before you met this Fusna."

"Dyricio, please," said Sory as he stood.

"No, you should stay lying down, who knows the harm done to you."

"Dyricio, I'm fine. I'm actually much stronger now."

Dyricio spoke with his hands waving about as his frustration built, "Sory you have to listen to me! All that stuff about the war, about the brutality of the Raishans, all of it, he could have just made it all up!"

"Did he make this up?" Sory closed his eyes, and when they opened, they were glowing.

"What the-?!" Dyricio jumped back and fell onto the floor.

"Dyricio-"

"He's turned you into a demon!" Dyricio pointed his finger.

Sory had had enough. He tried to grab his brother who staggered backward, trying to reach the door. He managed to open it and was about to run out when Sory grabbed his arm and pulled him back inside. "Dyricio!" Sory yelled as his brother struggled. Sory tightened his now iron grip. "Calm down!"

"You're hurting me!" Dyricio scraped Sory's arms with his talons.

"Ah!" Sory, not knowing his own strength, threw Dyricio headfirst into the wall on the other side of the hallway.

"Ah-ouch!" screamed Dyricio, rubbing his head then looking at his bloodstained hand.

Terrified, his eyes wide with the comprehension of what he had just done, Sory didn't know what to say. "Dyricio, I – I didn't mean to-"

Dyricio sprung up, hatred and tears in his eyes. "No! If you don't want my help – I'll leave!" he stormed off.

"Dyricio wait!" but his brother did not listen.

*

The next day in the Iron Structure, Sory was once again standing at the center of the room while Fusna lectured him, "you are going to need to learn how to focus your qi's line of sight," Sory's thoughts remained elsewhere, "Sory," Sory blinked, "are you listening to me?"

"Y – yes, yes sir."

"You are going to need to learn how to focus your qi's line of sight. What that is is what you can see and right now you are seeing in all directions, yet if you focused your sight into one direction you would be able to see farther. Understand?"

"Yes sir."

"I expect that right now your sight can only extend to about an arm's length, correct?"

"Yes sir."

"Close your eyes and enter trance." Sory did, bringing that infant part of his brain to life, that blue spot soon reappearing. "Has the blue come back yet?"

"Yes sir." Sory could see the air vibrate as he spoke.

"Concentrate on that, think of nothing else, clear your mind of all thought. Concentrate…concentrate…concentrate…" Sory could tell where Fusna's beak was from the movement of the air. He centered on that, forcing his qi's sight forward. Every time Fusna spoke his vision stretched a little bit more.

Finally, after the fourth time Fusna said concentrate Sory could see his beak, by the fifth time he could see his face, then the rest of his head and soon even beyond that. "I can see you, sir." Sory's voice expressed his wonder.

"Good, now let us see how far you can see." Fusna began backing away as Sory strained to keep up, focusing on his instructor's breathing. Within a few seconds, Fusna was on the outer edge of Sory's sight and all that he could see was his instructor's beak. Sory leaned his head forward, then took a step. "No, stay where you are."

"I can't see you anymore, sir." No response. Sory waited, standing absolutely still. Nothing.

"RARRR!" came a deafening growl straight into Sory's ear.

Both the air and Sory jumped, "sir!"

"What made you think that I would remain directly in front of you? Never assume anything, Sory. If you were in battle you would have just learned that the hard way." Sory nodded. "Let us continue." A minute later Fusna had his bowl of grapes on his lap as the two of them sat on the floor. Sory focused his qi's sight upward. The first grape came and bounced off his beak. "You must catch the grapes, Sory." Sory saw the next an inch above his head. He moved his hand but the fruit had already hit him. But when the next came he saw it at a hand's length above his head and caught it. "Excellent, now for some more target practice."

Sory threw the grape into his mouth when a soldier burst through the door, "General Fusna, sir!" he yelled, out of breath.

"What is it?"

"Hyleeda's been taken, sir."

Sory opened his eyes as the glow went away, "what?"

The three of them rushed back to the Obelisk where a crowd of thousands had already swarmed around it, flooding the entrances and blocking the way in. Those in the throng screamed, yelled, and waved their arms, demanding to know how this had happened and if their sons were alive. Fusna, Sory, and the soldier landed on the outside of the mob, and shoved and pushed their way to the entrance. Those in the crowd recognized Fusna and began grabbing at him, begging him for any sort of information, a pitiful sight that struck Sory to his soul. The three of them made it to an entrance where the guards were struggling to keep the citizens out. Inside there was an anxious commotion as griffins huddled in groups talking in loud whispers about the news.

The soldier led Fusna and Sory to a small, ancient looking wooden door on the far side of the main hall. It was nearly hidden between two huge columns. The door was cracked and full of holes and was barely big enough to fit them one at a time. The soldier burst through it and led them into a dark, narrow, spiraling stair well. Fusna turned around to Sory, "close that door, Sory." He did and when he turned back, Fusna and the soldier had vanished into the darkness.

"Sir?" Sory took a step and strained to peer through the darkness. He reached his head around the bend of the spiral staircase and then followed it all the way down until he saw a light leaking through a door at the bottom of the staircase. Sory went through this door and into a room with soldiers and high-ranking officers scrambling all about it. They were all milling about between a series of tables with maps and intelligence on them. "This must be some sort of war-room," Sory said to himself. He heard a bang to his right and saw Fusna crouched over a table, his fist in the hole it had just made in the table.

"How could Hyleeda have been taken?!" Fusna growled.

"Fusna, it is actually worse," General Meethvayd paused, "Hyleeda was in actuality taken months ago, we just didn't know until now."

Fusna extended his talons and dug them into the table, "what?"

"Fusna-" started General Meethvayd.

"How long ago was Hyleeda taken? Exactly how long ago?" The generals around him recoiled, a couple exchanged unsure looks while Fusna grew impatient. "Well?!" he struck the table once more.

General Meethvayd answered, "about fifty days," he shamefully muttered.

Fusna glowered at the general who timidly kept his eyes on the table, the others doing the same. "Fifty days?" The general closed his eyes. Fusna hung his head for a moment, then flipped the table over. Those around it flung themselves against the wall. A thunderous boom struck everyone in the room. "How did it take fifty days?! It is supposed to take twenty to thirty!"

"Fusna, we-"

"What?!"

"Sir, we think Raishan agents may have slowed our intel," said General Meethvayd.

There was a pause, "this is unacceptable! Find the agents, kill them, and if there are traitors in our midst, kill them too!" With that he stormed through the door. "Come, Sory."

Just before Sory left he took one last glance at everyone in the war-room and said, "damn."

*

The next day, Sory stood at the center of the Iron Structure under hundreds of metal bars. The bars formed a web in between the columns in the same interweaving fashion as before. In front of Sory was a great sheet covering something square, and enormous. There was an eerie silence about whatever was underneath this sheet. "What do you know," Fusna began, "about the Azuta?"

Sory had never heard of an Azuta before. "Nothing, sir."

"I figured as such, you see, Sory," Fusna began to pace, "the Azuta is a beast from Ostrican legend. A terrible creature that lives in caves in the desert. They are extremely difficult to find, some say – it is because they are invisible. What is known is that they are lightning fast, have claws as long as your arm, eyes that pierce the heart like daggers, and a scream so loud and terrible that it is said to stun those who dare wander within earshot. They are hunters, Sory, but a different breed entirely. They prefer to play with their prey, to confuse them, to torture them. At night, they emerge from the shadows and grab at the ankles of their quarry, scratching them up, little by little, panicking them. All for the joy of watching them before these beasts eventually, and finally, kill them." Fusna looked down at the floor with regret in his eyes. "The Raishans are advancing faster than expected, and Arktorion is not ready for this war. It is truly unfair, but our nation's fate rests on your shoulders. Normally a Fyzar in training does not have to take this test until much later, but later belongs to the enemy." Fusna turned and faced the sheet. He moved his hand in a circle, whisking the sheet off and revealing the wooden crate underneath. Fusna unlocked its door then turned to Sory, "Sory, this thing feeds on fear, and your life will genuinely be in danger. So I want you to remember your training, as well as this advice," Fusna leaned in close, "fight like an animal, because animals," he smiled and shook his head, "their ferocity only grows with fear and pain." He stood back up. "Remember that advice, Sory, you will need it." With that, he took his leave outside and locked the doors.

Sory turned back to the crate and its door was all the way open. He froze and scanned the jungle of bars to see if this thing was above him. *Where is it? Could it have escaped and is watching me?* Then he started to approach the crate itself on all four feet, swiveling his eyes about with each step. He reached the crate. He strained to see through the pitch black inside. *I could use my qi's sight to see. But by the time I could see far enough this thing could have snuck up behind me and killed me.* He tentatively put one foot inside, then the other. Then he waited for something to happen. He wanted the Azuta to come to him, to reveal itself so he knew where it was. Even if that meant it attacking, but nothing happened. Then something scratched him on the head, "AH!" Sory ducked and heard a demonic cackle from on top of the crate.

Sory waited. Nothing. Silence. Blood dripping down his neck. He grabbed onto the top of the crate and hoisted himself up. He saw the Azuta. It saw him. It snarled, revealing its one hundred long, slender, gleaming fangs. Then it stabbed Sory's hands with its claws. "AH!" Sory fell to the floor. The Azuta screamed in a glass-shattering pitch as it jumped onto him, bit into his neck and held him down while raking its claws up and down him. "AHHH!" Sory flung it off him. The Azuta, a spindly animal with a long snout, bulging eyes, and bat-like ears, grabbed onto a bar and climbed up as its skin turned different colors, grey lines with a dark brown background, camouflaging itself.

Sory held his wounds for a moment before pursuing the Azuta to the top of the poles where he found nothing, so he scanned about in the stabbing silence. Then, the camouflaged animal shrieked and tackled him, it pinned Sory against the bar he had been standing on. It raked his wings and back with its claws. Sory rolled over and it grasped onto his wings, dangling as he hung from the bar. Then it started swinging and chanting, taunting him, its claws burrowing in. It swung one last time and let go its grip, causing Sory to lose his grip and fall. He cupped his wings to slow himself when the Azuta leapt down and kicked him out of the air. Sory bounced off the poles and tried to stop himself until finally he slammed into the ground. He clambered to his elbows and knees when the beast tackled him.

The animal stood to dive its claws back into Sory when he rolled over and knocked it off. He darted away as it scraped at his ankles until finally it grabbed his legs, stopping him. It sprung up to pancake Sory who kicked it up into the bars. The Azuta then scampered away, Sory not taking his eyes off of it for an instant as he followed close behind. It ducked into the darkness of the rafters. Sory poked his head into their midst and strained to see through the darkness.

Sory closed his eyes as he entered trance, the blue spot appearing as he focused forwardly. Yet he feared the Azuta sneaking up on him so he focused with greater and greater intensity, only to become more and more distracted by this fear. The fear grew and soon the blue shrank away, so he opened his eyes, the Azuta's face in his. It rammed Sory who fell and grabbed this monster, grappling with it through the jungle of bars before managing to stop.

The Azuta grabbed the thick of his neck and started smashing his head against the cold metal. Sory wrenched himself around and it jumped off of him and hung from a pole. Sory peered into its jaws as the beast snarled down back at him, bearing its shredding fangs.

Sory bounded down to the floor, his pursuer quickly catching up and scraping at his heels. When Sory reached the floor, the beast thudded down onto him. Sory raked his talons up and into his attacker. The Azuta then jumped away. Sory then rolled over just as the beast got to its feet. They stared each other down. The Azuta growled, bearing its teeth, arching its back. Sory shrunk back, but then, he heard something in his head. *Remember the fight of an animal, Sory.*

Sory raised the feathers along his spine, extended his talons, flattened his ears, and growled. His opponent opened its jaws and let out a throaty hiss, "hehhh!" Sory arched his back and hissed back, "hehhh!" The Azuta groaned, then launched itself with its arms outstretched. Sory punched its face and tackled it. It rolled him over and he bit its arm. The Azuta jumped back and Sory went after it, slashing with his talons as the beast clawed back at him, both of them biting at each other simultaneously.

Sory's training then reared its head. He grabbed the beast's arms and kicked it in the abdomen. The animal put its feet onto Sory's chest and pushed him away, then took a leap backwards. Sory went to tackle the Azuta but it jumped at the last moment and he hit the floor. It landed on top of him. Sory bucked and wheeled about but the creature stayed on top as it scraped and stabbed at his back. Sory rolled his body through the air and it fell off. He landed on all fours when the Azuta body-slammed him and tried to get him back to the ground but Sory grabbed its arms and tried biting off its fingers. The creature bit Sory on his neck and he pulled back, its teeth carving out some of his flesh. "Ahhh!" Sory screamed, then looked into the Azuta's blood-stained teeth. It saw him looking at its teeth and it grinned and laughed. Sory pushed it away, it lunged at him but he scampered into the bars. It ran off into them.

Sory didn't stop until he reached the rafters. From there he scanned the room, nothing. He crouched low and started stealthily walking forward. He heard something behind him but saw nothing. He started forward when the Azuta launched itself up from just below and chomped down on Sory's neck. "AH!" Sory wrenched himself backwards and kicked it off. The creature laughed as it wiped blood from its mouth.

Sory groaned, then wrapped his hands around the Azuta's throat and they fell. Sory slammed the thing's head into the first bar they came across, then the next, then the next. Then the beast got free as Sory continued to fall all the way to the floor. Above him the creature roared, its mouth wide open, its chest out, its arms in the air. Then it sprinted down to Sory who waited until it jumped from the lowest pole. When it did, Sory leapt away and it hit the ground. Then Sory rammed it into a column, hitting its head against the cold stone. It wriggled violently as it screamed and then managed to get free. Then it swung at Sory's throat, but he caught its arm and twisted it. A crack sounded and the beast screamed.

Sory flattened the Azuta against the floor and punched it in the face several times, then burrowed his talons into its throat. With its good arm, the animal reached for Sory's neck who pulled away, so it went after his arms. But as Sory closed his eyes and sank his talons in yet further, the Azuta's movements became more and more erratic. It flailed its arm about, giving Sory a thousand little scratches and slicing his feathers in half. Blood gushed out, the Azuta's legs scrambled through the air, its body convulsing. It grabbed his arm and dug in, yet as Sory's talons burrowed further in, its movements slowed, its legs calmed, its body subsided, and the torrent of blood became a trickle.

Sory opened his glowing eyes. The Azuta's eyes were freakishly wide-open. The tops of its eye-lids stretched so far it showed the white around its huge black pupils. Its mouth remained wide open as blood leaked out from the corners. Sory looked down at his talons deep inside its throat, his knuckles below the skin. He jumped off the beast, his eyes locked on it, his chest heaving when Fusna came in, "well done, Sory, well done." His student didn't answer. "Sory?"

Sory just kept panting, the glow beginning to leave his eyes. "What – the hell – was that thing?!"

"It was the Azuta." Sory just kept his eyes locked on it. "Go on Sory, go home."

"Yes, sir," he took a few steps before halting, "sir?"

"Yes, Sory?"

"When I was fighting that – thing, I swear I heard your voice in my head."

"It is called telepathy, something which you will learn in time." Fusna's eyes followed Sory's rivers of scars, "battle wounds," Fusna smiled, "better than any medal."

Chapter 14

Sory limped his way home and once in his room he slathered himself in the salve that Fusna had once given him. After his wounds had heeled a little, Sory went to Dyricio who was sitting in his room, staring into the night. "Dyricio?"

"What do you want?" Dyricio groaned.

"I wanted to see how you were doing." Sory paused, "how are you?"

"Fine."

Sory had had enough. He approached Dyricio like one would a dangerous animal, "we cannot go on like this."

Dyricio hesitated, "like what?"

"You know what."

Dyricio looked at Sory, the half-heeled scars covering his body brought Dyricio to his feet. "What has happened to you?!" Sory said nothing, "how did you get those wounds?"

"Dyricio…I know you're looking out for me, and I appreciate that, but pain is part of the process."

"Pheh! Did Fusna tell you that?" Sory said nothing. Dyricio turned back around. "Do you believe everything he tells you?"

"Alright–"

Dyricio faced Sory, "why don't you believe what I'm telling you? I'm your brother!"

"Because you're wrong!" silence, "Dyricio, that's not what I meant."

"Leave." Sory beamed back at his brother for a moment before turning and leaving, Dyricio watching every step.

*

The next day in the Iron Structure, Fusna was lecturing Sory on his progress. "Congratulations," he said, "you have made it to the final phase of your training." Sory then took in a deep breath of relief and jubilation. "This third and final phase, just as the previous one, has a greater focus on your mind than your body. Here and now, your mind will be totally and completely freed from the binding delusions that have so far restrained it. When I am finished with you, you will be ready for war. The easiest thing for your mind to control, Sory, is your body and so that is where we will begin. Now enter trance, close your eyes, and clear all thought." Sory obeyed and Fusna continued. "Just as you once focused your energy forward, you will now do so downward, into your body." Sory did, and a tingling, much like the one he had felt when Fusna had suspended him over the fire pit, tickled his insides as his weight vanished. It began in his neck, then his shoulders, and as it spread, it strengthened. Soon within every muscle, every feather, every vein he could feel that tingling as it lifted upwards. By the time this force had reached his heart, Sory was beginning to feel lighter. Eventually this tingling reached his feet, and when it did, it all coalesced like iron filings suddenly coalescing around a magnet. Sory levitated and Fusna grew a proud smile. "Open your eyes, Sory."

Sory did and was at eyelevel with Fusna for the first time. He looked around and realized why he was so high. Sory couldn't contain himself. "Whoa!" He fell to the floor. "Ouch. What happened? Why did I fall?" He asked as his eyes stopped glowing.

"You lost your concentration."

"I cannot believe – I didn't know I could do that!"

"Well let us try again then. But remember, Sory, always be mindful of your energy, because of all the things that one could do in trance, levitation is perhaps the most exhaustive. Do you understand?"

"Yes, sir."

"Good, then let us try again." On the second attempt, Sory levitated at only a couple feet again. After a few mores tries, Fusna decided that Sory was doing well enough to start the next step. "You have shown good progress with levitation, Sory. Now though we will start lifting materials outside of your body." Fusna magically produced the bowl of grapes from behind his back. "We are going to use the grapes again, only this time, you must stop and hold them in midair with your mind. Are you ready?"

"Yes sir." Fusna tossed a grape up. Sory summoned his energy, but before he was ready, the fruit landed on his face.

"Again!" Fusna tossed another with the same result. "Come on, Sory! If and when you fight Sairus, do you think he is going to be throwing grapes at you?!"

"No, sir."

"Well then, concentrate!" Fusna threw another grape, which also bounced off of Sory's face. However, his energy was returning. "FOCUS!" As another grape descended toward Sory, he could feel it as it fell through the field of energy above him. He converged his entire existence on it, and it was flung to the side. Sory smiled when another bopped down. "What are you doing?! Concentrate!" Sory recharged his mind and deflected the next one. "If I see this next grape hit the ground I will make you fight another Azuta!" This threat distracted Sory as the next came. Would he have to fight another Azuta? The thought broke his focus. With the grape fast approaching Sory panicked. It seemed to fall extra fast as it then bounced off the very tip of his beak.

Fusna scowled at Sory who's eyes stayed fixed on his target. Fusna looked down and saw the grape levitating mere inches off of the floor. "Excellent, now let us move on to something bigger."

From out of the arsenal, Fusna set up a long, wooden table with six glass jars on it. Each of the jars was a different size, color, and shape, some tall and thin, others short and fat. "Now Sory, do the same as with the grape." Sory picked a tall blue jar and squinted as a sort of tunnel vision took hold. A minute later, the jar began to shudder, then, Sory could feel he had it. He lifted it with his mind the same way one would tell their arm or leg to move.

It floated up a few inches, slowly spinning. "Good, now another." Sory started to lower the one he had. "No, two at the same time." Sory re-raised the first, then focused on the one next to it. But as soon as he did, the first one dropped a little. "Come on, if I lifted you, you can lift two little jars!" Sory focused yet harder, the other lowered a little as the one next to it shook for a minute, then fell over, rolled off the table and shattered on the floor. "Put that one down," ordered Fusna. Sory did, ashamed of himself as his teacher leaned into his ear. "The entire fate of the world rests on your shoulders. So the least you can do is lift a couple jars off of a bloody table! Now can you handle this?!"

"Yes sir!"

Fusna stood back up and thought. "Let us try levitation again." Sory could still only float a foot off the floor. "You will need to get much higher than that if you are to defeat Sairus! You need to be able to fly!" Sory pushed himself as hard as he could, clenching his fists and mashing his eyelids as he forced himself higher, but to no avail. He actually began to sink and soon touch down on the floor. "You will never be able to fight Sairus! You will never be able to fight your own grandmother at this rate! Now get back up there!"

Sory strained to rise any further for the rest of the day and for the next few proceeding days. His frustration built with each failure and was compounded by Fusna's incessant haranguing. Sory also began to learn to use his hands and feet to direct his qi. Either picking things up, knocking them down, or deflecting them. In his room, he would practice, sometimes until the sun came up, making little progress.

Yet Sory could feel his mind changing. It felt as if everything around him was changing as well. He could suddenly sense everything in his environment and now seemed to have near complete situational awareness constantly. However, this only served to overwhelm him even more. After a week and a half little progress had been made. Sory was so used to moving along in his teachings that now he felt stuck. Fusna's never ending tirades did not help either. The walls were closing in around Sory.

Meanwhile, reports of the war continued to flow in. The Raishan navy was relentlessly ambushing Arktorian cargo ships and transports because they had little to no protection. The over stretched Arktorian navy could not protect them. Simultaneously, the Raishans were shipping thousands of troops to the continent of Platu but not putting them on the frontlines. This troubled Fusna, the Raishan reserves were beginning to outnumber the Raishan troops on the front lines, something very unusual in warfare.

Fusna decided to go to the War Room one night. When he emerged from the spiral staircase and into the room, he went right over to the table with a map of Platu on it, the same table he had flipped over before. Around him were a hand full of generals, admirals, and analysts all drudging on through the night. Around the table, Fusna was at, laid or sat a few senior officers. "They are not bringing up their reserves." he commented.

"What?" asked a half-asleep Admiral Ailzwushva who was slumped in a chair. A general of the Knight Corps stood nearby.

"The Raishans have more divisions in reserve than on the front in Platu," repeated Fusna.

"What do you think that means?" asked the admiral.

"I do not know, though they seem to be bringing up all of these extra soldiers very rapidly, as if in a rush. Only to hold them in reserve far to the rear, farther than they need to be, almost out of range of our scouts."

"Perhaps they simply haven't had time to organize their forces," suggested the admiral.

"Yes but why now? And why so far to the rear?"

"I'd weigh-in but I know you've already made up your mind," said the admiral as he stared into space.

"They are moving to attack," said Fusna. The admiral seemed nonchalant. "And I do not think this will just be any attack. Judging by these reports it will be massive."

The Knight Corps general cut in, "why do you think they're planning an attack?"

"Besides the fact that they are hiding armies of troops, General Zlade, they are also spreading them across the continent, positioning them to fight across a vast area."

The general nervously sighed, "when do you think they'll strike?"

Fusna sighed, "I have no idea, their forces outnumber ours by a great degree already. They could take the remainder of the continent with one great sweep whenever they wanted."

"Well I hope you're wrong, general, because if you're right we lose First Knight Division, my division, the one you just sent to Platu."

"You are the commander of the First Knight Division?" asked Fusna. The general nodded.

*

The next morning, Sory rushed to the Iron Structure determined to advance in his training. "You have made little progress," groaned Fusna, "you are failing your training." He bowed in close to Sory's face. "Something may be about to happen. The Raishans are positioning themselves for their next attack and this time it will be on Platu. Once again we must accelerate your training."

Tentatively Sory asked, "sir, is that–?"

"Yes, that is where Ruby was sent," Fusna paused, "and do not ever interrupt me again."

"Yes sir," Sory said meekly.

Fusna stood back up, "we are going to need more soldiers down there, the First Knight Division especially. If the Raishans do strike the First Knights will suffer the heaviest casualties, for they would be the ones covering the retreat." A terribly crushing feeling of dread and gloom sunk into Sory's chest, "which is why I am asking you, Sory – to join the Knight Corps."

"Me, sir?"

"You have proven a good student, Sory, though perhaps not the fastest learner. Yet you have the potential to be a great soldier. That, and like I just said, First Division needs as many talons as possible." Sory pondered this. *I knew I would have to fight eventually, but now?* Fusna could sense his student's doubt, "well, Sory? Will you fight?"

Sory gave his teacher the answer he wanted to hear, "with my entirety, sir."

Fusna gave half of a smiled, "excellent, that is the spirit. I have already taken the liberty of enlisting you into First Knight Corps. And I told them that you would not need to attend basic training as you have already been trained by me. I knew you would say yes, I hope you understand."

Sory nodded, "I do, sir."

"Good, now onto what will probably be your final lesson, bolt fencing."

Intrigue grew on Sory's face as Fusna pulled out two swords from two sheaths in his belt, then tossed one to Sory. This particular weapon looked familiar to him, "this was the sword I had stolen from Ramous. I thought I was unworthy of it, sir."

"You still are, but alas time is not on our side." Sory's heart sunk a bit. "Bolt fencing, my boy, is the same as sword fighting, except," Fusna's sword then shined bright white as if the light of an entire star was focused onto it. A sparkling light that didn't seem to come from the metal, but instead seemed to reflect off of it as a faint ringing could also be heard.

Sory's eyes stretched wide open, "whoa!"

"A bolt sword cannot be any weapon, Sory. For it requires a specific type of steel to be made a specific way for this glow that you see to occur, and not destroy the blade. And it just so happens that the sword you stole from Ramous was just the right kind. Now this type of fighting is the universally recognized trademark of the Fyzar, and to create this glow is the mark of training completion." Sory eyed his blade. "The method to complete this is the same as with telekinesis and levitation, now try."

"Yes sir," he then fixed his gaze to his blade and entered trance. He could feel his energy surging into his head, tingling up through his body and into his skull, then moving down out of his head, through his neck, arm, and finally into his hand, then out and into the handle of the sword. As the amount of energy surging into his head and then into the sword increased, a slight glow could soon be seen. This glow grew more and more as an ever-greater amount of his energy was projected into it.

Within a few seconds, Sory's blade was glowing as much as his teacher's. Then Fusna knocked it out of his hands. The glow of Sory's sword vanished instantly. Then Fusna held his sword against his student's neck. "Rule number one, never lose contact with your weapon. If you do it will lose its glow, now retrieve it." Sory stepped to his side. "Never take your eyes off of your enemy, Sory!" Sory ducked, rolled, and grabbed his sword. "You must be able to achieve the bolt instantly!" Fusna then charged. He swung, Sory jumped back, Fusna's blade sliced through his feathers, which glowed, red.

Sory ran with Fusna in close pursuit. Sory redirected his energy into his weapon, and within a few seconds, the glow had returned. He then clambered up a column and into the rafters. Once up there he bounded to the corner of the room and waited. He peaked down, nothing. "I am always in the place you do not expect, Sory," said Fusna. He then tackled Sory and sent them both tumbling from the rafters.

Midair, Sory turned and slashed at Fusna who dodged the blow then flattened his student against a column. Fusna swiped his sword. Sory ducked and the blade left a great red-hot gash. Sory leapt to the next column when Fusna appeared on the other side of it. He smacked away Sory's armament, then grabbed him by the neck and tossed him to the ground. Sory reached for his sword, but Fusna flung it away with his mind. Sory turned around to find Fusna's blade in his face. Fusna groaned, then put his sword away. "Attention!" Sory then stood at attention. "You still need more training." Fusna's eyes beamed at Sory for a moment. "However, today is the final day of your training to become a Fyzar. Tomorrow morning, at sunrise, you are to report to the Knight's Head-Quarters. From there you and the graduates of the Knight Corps' basic training will travel to the eastern coast. From there you will all be shipped off to Platu, understand?"

"Yes sir."

"Good, and Sory, I want you to remember that if you ever need me I will always be able to help you. Now go home, say your goodbyes to your brother and friends, for you will not see them for a time I expect. Except of course Ayro, I arranged that you two be placed in the same company, he will be among the graduates you will be joining tomorrow."

"Yes, sir."

Fusna then slowly, almost tenderly, saluted. Sory saluted back, his true feelings showing in his as well. Fusna then, in a way that seemed purposefully slow, as if he wanted these last few moments never to end, lowered his hand to his side, gave a nod, and turned around. Then rather solemnly, he began to walk away. "Sir," Fusna stopped, "thank you." Fusna smiled as Sory flew out of the Iron Structure, possibly for the last time.

*

The next morning, Sory reported to the Knight's Corps barracks where Ayro had been trained. Sory was given a uniform, and fell-in with the rest of his company, Dust Company, as it stood in formation at the entrance to the camp with their families all gathered around. A company being a small unit of soldiers, each about one-hundred strong. "Sory," whispered Ayro, "I want you to meet a couple friends of mine, this is Crio and Kyvor."

They shook hands as the commanding general of First Knight Corps stepped onto a stage in front of Dust Company, the very same general who had talked to Fusna about what he thought the Raishans were planning on Platu. Though thin and moderately tall, he cut a formidable appearance. Ayro leaned into Sory's ear, "that's General Zlade."

Now at the front of the stage, the general began to speak. "Good day, today, is a good day, for yesterday you were mere griffins, but what happened yesterday does not matter. Nothing that happened in your lives before today matters, because before today, you were not Knights. Well today – you are! And from now on, you will serve a greater cause, the cause of the liberty and the freedom of your country. A cause – that is as I speak – under threat. We are under threat from the menace known – as Raishany, and it is you – you who will fight this Red Empire from here on out. You will be the ones on the front lines from here on out, you will be the ones asked to give your lives first. Not because you have to, but because you choose to, because you know, you *all* know that if you don't risk your lives, then those whom you are defending will lose theirs'. Having this knowledge is how you made it this far, that is why you will fight, and that is why I am certain that we will win this war!" The crowd of families then cheered and clapped.

"Present arms!" commanded the boot sergeants in unison. And ex-recruits, now soldiers, unsheathed their swords and held them straight up in rigid attention.

And so, that was it, those who had family to say good-bye to did. Sory tried to find Dyricio, but couldn't find him. After their own Field of Tears, the First Knight Division reformed into their ranks and headed for the eastern coast where a fleet of ships was waiting. Three days later, they arrived, only to find that there was not enough room for all them. The Arktorian Navy had become so overstretched that many of these soldiers, as well as others, had to share bunks.

While this chaos unfolded below deck, Sory decided to take one last glance at Arktorion. Standing the aft, he watched the sun set over the land. It painted the land and the sky red, nearly uniting them, but splitting them at the same time at the horizon with a radiant yellow sliver of luminescence. Ayro came up and looked on with him. "Something isn't it?" asked Sory.

"Yeah it is beautiful."

"No not that, I meant how only a quarter year ago we were running from the war. Now, we're heading back into it." Sory paused, "funny how things unfold."

Ayro smiled, "come on," he grabbed Sory's shoulder, "let's get some sleep."

Yet Sory remained there for a little longer. "Funny how things unfold." And with that, he followed Ayro below deck.

Chapter 15

It was nighttime in Arktorion City, Dyricio was slumped over in the same spot that he and his friends had always eaten at in the dining hall, now he was alone. He was reading a newspaper that listed the names of all the Knights who had just been sent to Platu. He fingered through the list until he found Sory's name, then he crumpled the paper and threw it away. "You seem lonely," said an unfamiliar voice. Dyricio looked up and it was his guard, the one with the scar.

"Go away!" barked Dyricio when a waiter came over with a pint of ale.

"Is that any way to treat a friend?" asked the guard as he sat down next to Dyricio.

"You're not my friend. I don't even know your name." Dyricio took a huge gulp of ale.

"Didn't take you for a drinker."

"What do you want?" he asked.

"Your name's Dyricio, right?"

"Yep."

"And your brother's Sory, right?"

"Oh yeah, Sory, the special one."

"What do you mean 'the special one?'"

"I can't tell you." Dyricio waived his finger, "what's your name?"

"Tell you what, if you tell me what your trouble is with your
brother," he forced another drink down Dyricio's throat, "and tell me
why he's been with Fusna so much, I'll tell you my name."

"Why does everybody want to know about Sory?! I mean – it's
that stupid Fusna! Why couldn't he train me too? Why am I not good
enough to be a Fyzar?" He turned to the guard, but he had vanished.

✳

Meanwhile, Sory was laying in his bunk in the middle of the
ocean alongside his fellow Knights. The gentle swaying of the waves
helped put him and the rest of his company to sleep, when a nightmare
began, a familiar one. The same one he had had before. Sory was
standing in front of Sairus, whose face remained shrouded in darkness,
Ramous, and the third figure who was still just a silhouette. Sory still
felt trapped but could now see nearly every detail of the dream. As his
eyes wandered about Sairus started speaking. "You are the Fyzar." Sory
flinched. Sairus was talking to him. "Raishany thanks you for joining
your fatherland." Then a vision with the aura of a burning hatred
stabbed into Sory's head. He rejected it, but caught a glimpse of a

procession of a couple dozen griffins in chains, and great flames burning behind them. Yet that flash of that profound hatred seared his mind the most. It burned his mind like a fire. A moment later though it had all disappeared. "You have been trained," Sairus' words reignited this feeling, which then poked at his mind like a swarm of wasps.

The insurmountable persistence of this vision pressed on Sory. He almost seemed to know that it would never go away. It seemed futile to resist and so he let it in for a second, but then pushed it back out in fear of what would happen should he not continue to resist. However, it came again, scratching at him. Sory started to think of how to escape but this feeling buzzing around his skull just kept him from concentrating. He couldn't think. He was trapped, "and I can sense that your powers are great," finally, Sory let it in, "you will lead Raishany to the defeat of Arktorion!" And as Sairus spoke these last few words Sory saw the vision in its entirety, his mind completely and utterly exposed to the fiery terror that burst through. Now Sory saw not just a couple dozen griffins, instead there trudged thousands stretching to the horizon in a great column of misery, all of them non-Reds, their shackles rattling as they traipsed on. Their heads hanging, lash marks covering their bare backs, many limping, all thin and emaciated, feathers filthy and falling out, and an overwhelming feeling of such hopelessness it emitted the foulest of stenches as they all

moaned along, vibrating the air. The wanting to die so as to escape –
gradually over powering the will to survive.

Cities in rubble burned all around them, entire castles laid
destroyed. And, in the distance, Sory could see the Obelisk, intact, but
burning, flames climbing up it like vines up a tree as billowing black
smoke blocked out the sun, lighting exploding from the midst of those
black clouds. *"Tysorious, look, look what the Lesser Races have made
us do for trying to save the world from them. Look upon Raishany, all
pure red griffin, and look at how far it has come while Arktorion can
barely defend itself! You can stop this, Tysorious. You know what I say
is the truth."*

Sory jumped up, his eyes wide open, his heart pounding, sweat
drenching him. After realizing he was safe he laid back down,
knowing sleep would elude him for the rest of the night. He needed to
know what that was, he needed help, and he remembered what Fusna
had said about always being able to ask him for help. *Fusna, can you
hear me?* He waited a minute but nothing happened. *This is
ridiculous.*

Sory, what is the matter? asked Fusna.

Sir. It worked!

What is troubling you?

I had that dream again, sir.

The one with Ramous and Sairus?

Yes, silence, *sir?*

Yes Sory, I am here.

Does this dream mean something, sir?

I don't know. Was it the same as the last time, your body being stuck as your mind fell under attack?

Yes sir.

And was it clearer than the last time?

Yes sir.

Another pause as Sory waited in anticipation. *Sory, what you had was a vision of the future.* A terror detonated in Sory's heart. *All that you have told me are characteristic of a vision. It becoming clearer is but a sign that this event is fast approaching.* Sory's horror grew, he was going to betray them all, betray his friends, betray his new home, Ruby. *I apologize that I did not tell you sooner. I was not sure if it truly was a vision, but I did not want to frighten you for no reason.* Sory didn't reply, *Sory?*

Sory didn't answer for a while, *Thank you, sir. Good night.*

Good night, Sory.

Sory laid there wide awake thinking about what Sairus had said, about how Raishany had purged itself of all the other races and thrived, and how Arktorion hasn't and is suffering. *Could it be true?* Sory stopped himself. *Of course not!* Yet what Sairus said was fact, Raishany was prospering and Arktorion was crumbling. He stopped himself again. *How could I think such things? Maybe I am like Sairus. No, he cannot be right. What's the difference anyway? I know my fate.*

*

Rathimus, Raishany, the Monolith a few days later. The sun had just barely poked through the smoke of the huge pyres circling the city as Ramous entered the Throne Room, the King on his throne. Ramous sensed someone to his left and turned to see a hooded griffin with his arms crossed leaning up against the wall just next to the door. Ramous didn't know who this griffin was, but he smiled a devious grin at the general anyway. "General," said King Sairus.

"Your Greatness," Ramous stepped in front of the throne, kneeled, then bowed his head.

"Do you know why I summoned you?"

"His Greatness always has his reasons."

"This is my spy in Arktorion City. He says he knows the whereabouts of both of your sons."

Ramous knew what this meant, he had failed to find his sons and now he would be punished. Silence permeated as Sairus waited for a response, "Your Greatness, even though it was my responsibility-"

"You will have the opportunity to redeem yourself, General," Ramous was filled with the utmost relief, yet through all of this he remained a rock on the outside, still and emotionless, "by going to Arktorion to retrieve your youngest."

Ramous was confused, "but Your Greatness-"

"That will be all, General." Ramous rose to his feet, clicked his heels and saluted. Then he rushed to the door where Sairus stopped him, "and General, when you find your youngest, I want you to tell him that he is the one from the prophecy."

The general was now even more befuddled. "Yes, Your Greatness." He then exited, the spy still leaning up against the wall.

Sairus turned to the spy, "find the rest of my military command, tell them to ready themselves for my arrival, and for attack." Meanwhile Ramous charged to the end of the hall where there was an open window and flew through it, rushing toward Arktorion.

Chapter 16

It was nighttime in the Obelisk as Dyricio sulkily slumped to his room. It had been twenty days since his conversation with the guard, which was also the last time he had had a real conversation with anybody. Midnight had come and gone as he opened his bedroom door, the curtain over his window blocked out the moon and shrouded the room in pitch black as the door closed behind him. He felt something move behind him and turned to see, but saw nothing in the dead of night. He reached to the dresser for a candle and lit it with a match. His father's grimacing face glared down at him. "Father!" Dyricio jumped back and dropped the candle. It went out. Then burst into a tall flame that rose to meet Ramous' cupped hand.

"Hello, son," he said, walking around the flame.

"H-I-I-I, um," stuttered Dyricio as his father approached him.

"Shut-up," Dyricio closed his beak and looked down. A second later, and a burning slap and four scars ripped his face. "If you weren't my son I'd have you bludgeoned to death for deserting!" Ramous snatched Dyricio by the collar and lifted him off his feet. "Count yourself LUCKY!" Dyricio's eyes dilated with fear. Once Ramous was sure that the young one understood he dropped him. "King Sairus wishes me to inform you of something," Dyricio remained in his ashamed posture, "you are the Fyzar from the prophecy." Dyricio's eyes then glimmered up at his father. "Come, we must get to Rathimus as soon as possible." Ramous thrust his hand forward and shattered the window without touching it. He then ripped aside the curtains and stood on the windowsill.

Dyricio remained still. "So, you came back for me, not Sory?"

Ramous stared off into the night. "If I wanted Tysorious I would have gone to Platu," he brought his eyes to Dyricio, an infuriation about them, "and don't you dare call him Sory again!" Dyricio bowed his head. "Understand?"

"Yes sir."

"Come now, we best get moving." With that, Ramous charged into the night with his son fast behind. Dyricio was not accustomed to flying so far so fast so it wasn't long before they had to stop while still in central Arktorion. Gradually though they made it passed the southern border and over the lawless tribal lands which spanned for thousands of leagues in every direction. Ramous would have practically been within sight of Rathimus by now, yet Dyricio had to stop at least twice a day and by now he was almost completely worn out. Finally Ramous had had enough. He picked his son up and carried him the rest of the way. Finally, they could see Rathimus.

Ramous dropped Dyricio and allowed him to fly the rest of the way as they flew over the city's perimeter wall. Dyricio eyed the city with awe and reverence as they headed straight for the Monolith. When they landed at the foot of the entrance, the same one Ramous had entered when Dyricio and Sory had first disappeared, the general approached the doors as Dyricio stood transfixed by the grandiose edifice. It nearly touched the stars that dared show themselves through the smoke, which revolved like a cyclone over the peak of the great castle. "DYRICIO!" the general belted. Dyricio flinched like something had been thrown at him, then followed his father to the elevator. There, Ramous gave his son a quick lesson in royal etiquette, "now remember, this is your King that you are meeting, do not speak unless spoken to, address him as Your Greatness, and most of all," he leaned into Dyricio, "do not make an fool out of yourself." Dyricio's heart was pounding, he felt nauseated. "Understand?"

Dyricio nodded his head timidly, "yes sir."

The elevator stopped. "We are here." Ramous opened the door and Dyricio cautiously stepped out. Dyricio's eyes then became fearfully fixed on the menacing Royal Guards to his right and left. He looked at each and every one of them, as if afraid they were going to attack, as he skittishly approached the cascading doors ahead. Ramous then grabbed Dyricio's arm and pulled him toward the open doors as a hooded griffin emerged out of them and passed the pair. Dyricio caught a glimpse of his face, it was his body guard with the scar. The bodyguard stepped into the elevator and as it descended, he caught a glimpse of Dyricio. He grinned, and then winked.

When he reached the doorway, Dyricio leaned in to see inside. Ramous stopped him, "you must wait until the King bid you enter."

From inside came a voice, "General Trajetton," the ancient voice made Dyricio shiver, "come in." Together the pair entered slowly, warily. Dyricio bowed his head in fear, yet simultaneously wanted to at long last see his King's face after all these years. When they reached the throne, they kneeled. "I see you brought me my Fyzar."

"Yes, Your Greatness, I have," replied Ramous.

"It took you longer than I expected. Perhaps your age is surpassing your value."

"No, Greatness, my son slowed me."

Dyricio frowned as the King continued, "ah yes, your traitorous son." The King stood and approached the frightened boy. "Dyricio," Dyricio then peered up into the terrible face of the King, a face as ancient as his voice. His grayed, fixed brow gave him a permanent expression of anger, as if he had been frowning for a century. Under his eyes were carved countless bags, beside his eyes crow's-feet sliced his scraggly skin, not to mention his scarred beak. His ears were fixed flat against his massive, stream-lined head, his beak massive enough to decapitate the young Dyricio. All of this though remained trumped in comparison to the King's enormous neck. King Sairus towered over Dyricio as they locked eyes for a moment. Finally though, the King spoke. "Rise," slowly, they both did, "not you, general!" Ramous sunk back to his knee. The King turned back to Dyricio, his head only reaching the King's waist. "Dyricio, why did you stray from your King?"

"W-w, well I-" Dyricio stuttered. Ramous grew impatient.

Sairus put his hand up, "that is enough. General, stand over there." He pointed next to his throne. Ramous did as told as Sairus sat back on his throne. "You are the Fyzar, Raishany thanks you for joining your fatherland. You have been trained," Dyricio was confounded, he hadn't been trained. Both his and his father's faces were scrunched in confusion. On Platu, Sory suddenly became sick. Sairus' voice stabbed through his ears. He collapsed as he listened, "and I can sense your powers are great. You will lead Raishany to the defeat of Arktorion."

On Platu, Sairus's voice then evaporated, and so did Sory's sickness. Sory knelt on the ground, bewildered.

Back in the Monolith, Dyricio stood motionless before he finally spoke, "y – your Greatness, I thank you – for your mercy, but I must beg your pardon," he said cautiously, "I have not been trained."

Ramous cringed as he waited for Dyricio to be dragged away to the gulags. "Yes, I know." Dyricio was about to ask a question when, "go wait outside, boy." Dyricio gawked for a moment before bowing, then hurriedly scampering out the door. Sairus raised his hand and the doors closed.

Ramous stepped in front of the King, "Your Greatness, I will go retrieve my eldest."

King Sairus scorned back at him, "no, Tysorious will come," he looked to the doors, "by himself. Now leave me, Dyricio will be sleeping in your quarters."

Ramous clicked his heels before exiting, then raised his hand to open the doors. Outside, Dyricio shuffled about nervously when Ramous grabbed him by the arm and dragged him down the hall. "What happened, where are we going?"

Ramous halted and put his face in his son's, "first, I am your military superior from now on. I do not know why His Greatness said that you were trained, but either way, I do have to train you now. And second, do not correct him. If you were not the Fyzar you would be a

head shorter by now. Now come, we will be sleeping in my quarters."
In his quarters, Ramous removed a sheet from his bed and laid it on the
cold, wooden floor. "Get some sleep, you will need it for tomorrow."

"On the floor?" Ramous did not answer. "Very well." Dyricio laid
down while Ramous gazed out the window, it had started to rain
outside. Dyricio watched him, his father appeared to be searching for
something. "Father," Dyricio waited for a response, but none came,
"thank you."

"For what?" he asked bluntly.

"For coming back for me."

"You have a duty to this empire."

"As well the other reason why you'd come all this way to get me
back."

Ramous turned around, "of what other reason do you speak?"

"I'm your son."

Ramous hesitated, "all that matters now is fulfilling your destiny,
Dyricio." He turned back to the window. Dyricio laid back down,
doubt written on his face.

The next day they commenced training in a field just outside of the city. Yet Ramous had never taught someone how to be a Fyzar before and Dyricio could barely handle the exercises he was given. Soon, Ramous showed Dyricio the Run, taking him to a field covered in ash from the coal mines not too far away. Dyricio started running, but nothing. Since he was the true Fyzar though, Ramous expected that he would be able to get it the first time. So he made Dyricio do it again, and again, and again. After a few times, Dyricio could barely stand, let alone run, his chest contracted as he gasped for breath and laid on the ground. All the while Ramous glowered down on him with frustration. "Get up." He hauled Dyricio to his feet. "You shall never defeat the enemy at this rate of progress. Now run again." He pointed out to the black field.

Dyricio was wheezing. "I – I can't do it, hih-huh-hih-huh." For the rest of the day, Ramous made his son exercise. But the new student was failing miserably.

Sunset, a relief for both of them as they retired to their quarters. Dyricio stood next to his sheet on the floor with Ramous at the doorway. "That was disappointing," said Ramous. Dyricio hung his head.

A guard opened the door, "general, sir, His Greatness wants to speak to you."

Ramous nodded and the guard exited. "Wait here," he told his son, "you still have the Ark stench on you and I would not want you to be arrested." He slammed the door behind him. Dyricio slumped down on his father's bed and replayed the whole day in his mind.

All that surfaced was his father's incessant shunning. The constant bombardment flooded back to Dyricio as he covered his face with his hands. Tears trickled between his fingers. Dyricio then leapt up and marched to the Throne Room. Once there he could hear his father and the King speaking. Dyricio heard his name. They were discussing him. He put his ear to the door. King Sairus was speaking, "has there been progress, General? How has your youngest been faring?"

"Terribly, it will be a long time before young Dyricio amounts to anything even close to the most basic of soldiers, let alone a Fyzar."

"How long, general?"

"The war may be over by the time he's ready, sir."

"That is not acceptable, seeing as though he is the one to win this war for us."

"I am afraid that Dyricio is a weakling runt and is not the one to lead Raishany to victory." Dyricio thrust his head away from the door, then stormed off down the hall back to the room.

Inside of the Throne Room, "do you think he heard us?" Ramous asked.

"Oh yes, General Trajetton, he heard us."

"Your Greatness, why do you think Dyricio is the Fyzar of the prophecy?"

"I do not," confusion grew on Ramous' face, "Tysorious is the Fyzar." He paused. "We are leaving for Platu tomorrow. Get your son ready, you will train him there, and when you do, be as harsh as possible, strike him if need be."

"Yes sir," replied a bemused Ramous.

Chapter 17

The next day, Ramous, Dyricio, and the King left for Platu on the King's yacht, the very same grandiose vessel that had once brought Ramous back to Raishany months ago. It departed amidst a fleet of hundreds of all manner of warships from galleons to caravels, the largest of which had as many as four masts. The great fleet bobbed about in the angry southern Longstin Ocean, gradually making its way to the Raishan colony on Platu. When the ships docked the massive army which they hauled took flight for the interior. Dyricio watched from the Royal Yacht in awe as tens of thousands of soldiers in V-formation blocked out the sun, and created a gale below.

*

Midday, the Royal Camp was assembled next to a cliff that overlooked the ocean. From the camp its inhabitants could hear the rumbling waves strike and brake at the cliff's base. The waves shimmered in the sun's light. This vast dark-blue ocean stretched to the south and west of the camp, the rest of the continent of Platu extended to the north and east.

Just outside of camp, on a windy and grassy field where two guards stood watch, Dyricio practiced hand to hand fighting with Ramous, yet had little improvement as his father never failed to exploit every opening that the young-one gave. Dyricio was never able to strike a single blow either and soon became frustrated. Within only a few minutes, he had had it. "ENOUGH!" he screamed at last, his voice choking, his eyes tearing, his beak bleeding.

"There is never enough." Ramous wound up but Dyricio backed away.

"I will fight you no longer!" Dyricio declared.

"You do not have the choice. Your enemy would never give in whether or not you did."

"I WILL NOT FIGHT!" Dyricio then stormed off with his father's eyes burning a hole in his back.

"You will never be remembered." Dyricio halted. "Your name will never be uttered after you die."

Dyricio turned around. He could take this abuse no more. A tear rolled down his cheek. Then, with his ears flattened, and his talons extended, he screeched and sprinted. Then he jumped above his father with his hands back as he prepared to stab them down. Ramous grabbed him and threw him to the dirt. Dyricio rolled over but Ramous stomped his throat. Dyricio grasped at his father's foot as he fought to breathe. Ramous looked down on him with condescension and cocked his head to one side. He then wrenched Dyricio up by his collar and held him to his face as another tear rolled down Dyricio's cheek. "Do not cry!" Dyricio didn't care. "You will not be the one to lead Raishany to victory if you remain like this."

Just then, Ramous felt a sharp pain in his gut. He looked down and saw Dyricio's talons stabbing him. Ramous then tossed his son to the ground when a soldier came up. "Sir, His Greatness has called a meeting." The general then marched off into the planning tent, then the soldier turned to Dyricio. "His Greatness requests your presence as well, sir."

Inside the tent stood a table with a map of the entire continent; red lines, which indicated where the Raishans planned to attack, covered it. Most of these lines stabbed right through the middle of the Ark colony, cutting it in half, with another indicating a strike in the north on a fortress. The colonies of Raishany and its allies were in red, the Arktorian in blue, those colonies belonging to neutral countries were in purple.

Around the table stood ten generals, admirals, one field marshal, and of course the King at the far end with his son, Prince Saitick, at his side. The field marshal, the overall commander of Raishan forces on the continent, was pointing to the map on the table, describing the battle plan to the King who was making sure that his son paid attention, as did Ramous who pulled Dyricio right up to the edge. He studied the battle plan and focused on the small bit of lines that indicated the attack on the fortress in the north. Dyricio saw the name written next to it in Raishan. "Fortress Mountain Foot," he whispered.

The field marshal was tall, nearly the same height as Ramous, a bit older, but he had a chiseled, commanding face. "Now, Your Greatness," he began, "the first phase of our plan is to attack an Ark fortress in the north named Mountain Foot. Attacking there will convince the Arks that that is where we are beginning our thrust. In reality though, we will wait until they have moved their forces to the north. At which point we will then drive our troops through the center. However, Your Greatness, moving the amount of forces necessary for this will take considerable time so we will need to assemble this army as the Arks are moving north. It should take a quarter-year before we are ready to drive through the center, sir."

Dyricio nearly flinched upon hearing this. He knew that bad news was a risky thing to give to a king like Sairus. Which is why Dyricio was surprised when the field marshal giving it didn't seem the least bit anxious about the King's reaction. Dyricio expected the King to be steaming, but he didn't seem to mind this delay. "Very well, field marshal." Sairus turned to Dyricio. "Dyricio, I seemed to have left my spectacles in my tent. Fetch them for me so that I may examine the map." Dyricio nodded and left.

When he left, Ramous turned to the King. "Your Greatness, I have never seen you wear spectacles."

"That is because I do not have any, general." Sairus turned back to the field marshal. "Now, field marshal, what are the true plans of attack?"

The field marshal pulled out another map from underneath of the table and laid it on top of the old one. This one was different, there were still plenty of red lines showing where they planned to advance, as well the same colors indicating which colonies belonged to which country, and the lines showing their attack on the Ark fortress in the north were still there as well. Yet there was one major difference, this new map showed that their attack wasn't cutting straight through the center. Instead, there were two main sets of lines, one set coming down onto the Ark colony from the north, the other from the south. These two fronts then met in the middle, on the coast.

"Now, our real plans are more complex," Ramous leaned in to see. He had no idea that there were two sets of plans. As he looked around he saw that none of the other commanders were surprised. An unnerving feeling crept into his heart as the field marshal continued, "with the false plans young Dyricio will give to the Arks," Ramous flared his eyes at the field marshal who paused and remained facing down at the map, refusing to make eye contact before continuing as if he had said nothing unusual, "they will be fooled into believing that we will be attacking from the north, then the center when in reality we will attack Fort Mountain Foot in the north to convince them that the plans that young Dyricio's given them are real. Then, once they've moved their army to the northern most area of the continent we will advance from the very south of their colony. The advance will begin by seizing this small port city on the border, Cayza, at which point the enemy will panic and split its forces. That will then allow us to crush them between the army already advancing in the south and the other we will then send in from the north." The field marshal then faced the King rather proud of himself. "I like to call this tactic – a super-pincer, Your Greatness."

King Sairus examined the map closely. "Very good, field marshal." Ramous did not feel the same sentiment, he did not like being played. He had never been informed of the role Dyricio had in this, he had been kept out of the loop. King Sairus then asked another question, "How soon can we launch this offensive?"

"Right away, Your Greatness," replied the field-marshal.

"Well then field marshal, attack now, and soon Platu will be ours."

"Yes sir." The commanders clicked their heels and marched out, all except the baffled and agitated Ramous.

"Your Greatness," Ramous began, "there seems to be much you have kept from me. I am confused as to why you had me retrieve Dyricio when you know that Tysorious is the Fyzar, and also that you did not inform me that you were planning on using Dyricio as a double agent, sir."

"You are speaking out of turn, General Trajetton, but I suppose I do owe you an explanation. You see, general, all that you have just described, as well so much more, is all part of an elaborate master plan to secure victory in Platu, and so then inevitably, the war. It began when I sensed that young Tysorious was slipping away, that he was becoming sympathetic toward the enemy. So I gave him a vision, the vision of when I first met his brother and told *him* that *he* was the Fyzar. In the vision though, young Tysorious could only identify me and you, and would assume that the third griffin was him from what I was saying. And I knew that he would eventually ask Fusna what he was seeing and that Fusna would tell him that it was a vision of the future. Thus, this implanted the idea into the boy's head that he would soon betray the Arks for us."

"But sir, we knew where he was, why not simply bring him back?"

"Because we need him to come voluntarily, otherwise his heart and mind would still be with the enemy. I knew that he had truly sided with the Arks when he resisted the Slithus."

"I see, but why Dyricio, Greatness?"

"We needed someone who was initially on the enemy's side so that he would be trusted when giving them our false war plans, which is why I am pushing young Dyricio away. Between what he heard us saying about him in the Throne Room and your enhanced training he may soon flee to the arms of the enemy."

Ramous was astonished. "Your Greatness, forgive me but I never figured you for such a great tactician."

"There is much about me you do not know, General Trajetton. Now, it is crucial you continue to force your son away. I want you to use any means necessary."

"Yes, Your Greatness," Ramous said just as Dyricio entered.

"Your Greatness," Dyricio bowed, "I apologize, but I was not able to find your spectacles."

Sairus looked to Ramous who knew what he had to do. "It was a simple task, Dyricio," the general started, "how do you expect to win the war if you cannot even accomplish this? You are in this war now. The enemy is but a few miles northwest of here."

The general then heard Sairus' voice in his head. *You must make him fly away. Silently implant the thought into his head.*

"I can do much more than you think," snapped back Dyricio.

"Prove to me that you are not some sniveling little hatchling who cannot carry out the simplest of tasks." Dyricio was about to reply, but then stomped away.

"Very good, general."

Later past midnight, Dyricio was resting wide-awake in his bed, staring straight up, slowly working up the nerve to fly away. Finally, he sat up and put his feet on the ground. With his body in absolute stillness, he moved his eyes about the room for something to happen, yet nothing did. He didn't know what Sairus was capable of, that King could read minds for all he knew, he may have been reading his mind right then, but nothing happened. Feeling safer, Dyricio stood. He was still in his day clothes as he warily moved to the opening of the tent. He poked his head through the opening and made sure no one could see him. Nothing, not a guard in sight, to his left stretched the forest, in front of him and to his right rested the camp. Upon arrival, Dyricio and his father had been given separate tents, Dyricio's being at the edge of camp. It would be so easy to fly away, but he couldn't. He brought his head back inside.

Yet then, Dyricio remembered all that his father had done to him, all the times he had been pushed around and yelled at, and struck. He darted out and charged into the forest. He ran and ran until he was sure he couldn't be seen when in the air. "A few miles northwest, huh?" he said grinningly as he looked up at a tree, then clawed his way to the canopy and took flight. He was determined to reach the Arks. *I'll show father. I'll show them all. I'm not just some sniveling little hatchling. I can do things, I could be a threat, and that's exactly what I will be – a threat. How could I not be? I know their plan of attack.*

The next morning, Sairus emerged from his tent to a panic outside as his soldiers scampered around. General Trajetton came up to him. "General," Sairus said.

"Good morning, Your Greatness."

"What is the matter?"

"My son has flown away and cannot be found," the general said with a neutral expression.

Sairus smiled. "Excellent."

Chapter 18

It was midday in Fortress Mountain Foot in the northern area of the Arktorian colony, the Raishan border was just within eyeshot. Thick clouds grayed the sky and chilled the air as lunchtime came and the soldiers of the fort sat down to their meals inside of the smallish mess hall. Ruby had just gotten her luncheon and had sat down across from Bahren at his crowded table. Around them the bustling of dozens of troops filled the air. Ruby couldn't take her eyes off the sludge on her tray. "You know, it wouldn't be too much to ask not to be served mud every day," she said. Bahren smiled and shook his head before bravely slurping down a spoon full as Ruby watched him. "Ugh!"

Across the border at Raishan Fortress Smokescreen, a courier flew inside while the commander rested in his quarters. He was reading in his chair, the light of the fire allowing him to see in the windowless room. One of his guards then entered. "Sir, dispatch from His Greatness." The commander took the envelope with the Royal Seal on it and read the parchment within.

General, you are to attack the Arktorian fortress Mountain Foot. Do it at supper, when the enemy soldiers will be gathered eating in the mess hall. Once the attack is over make sure that there is at least one survivor to tell the rest of the Arks what has happened there. Do not fail.

*

Supper, Fort Mountain Foot. Ruby and Bahren tried to eat the same meal again, forcing themselves to gulp down as much as they could before having to go on sentry duty, but they simply couldn't eat. "Maybe if we don't look at it while we eat it," suggested Ruby.

Bahren bravely took a spoonful and held it to his beak, then squeezed his eyes shut and opened his mouth. He dropped the sludge onto his tongue but spit it out immediately. Through his coughing he managed a few words. "No, no, that doesn't help at all," he sighed. "Well, if we're not going to have supper we might as well leave."

"Yes, please, anything to escape here," Ruby said as she stood. They left the mess hall and walked through the main hall. All around them, their fellow troops went about their lives either on duty or off. The light of day had been replaced by the glow of torches in the early evening. Then Bahren spotted an empty archer's post, one of a dozen posts that protruded from the fort's roof. These cylindrical posts had domed roofs that could be opened at will. This allowed archers to see all around them during an attack, but way out in the wilderness, far away from any city or even small town, all of the stars could be seen through this opening. Ruby and Bahren flew to the post and opened the roof, then stood in awe of the night sky.

"The war seems so distant," sighed Bahren.

"I think the last time we saw battle was when Sory's father attacked us on Zat's ship. Remember, you heard him call Sory by name and you thought he was a spy," she smiled.

"Yeah," he said quietly, his eyes on the floor.

"And then it turns out, he's the one who's supposed to save us all from a Raishan occupation of the whole world. That's fun to say, Raishan occupation, Raishan occupation." She turned to Bahren. "You say it, Raishan occupation, Raishan occupation."

"Are you alright? You're all," he held his hand up and shook it, "jittery tonight."

"I think it's just my hunger. I think it's starting to reach my head."

"Yeah, maybe," he started to reach his hand around her back. A shockwave then flung them forward.

Dust blinded them. A ringing in their ears defended them. "WHAT WAS THAT?!" Exclaimed Ruby as they stumbled to their feet.

"The Raishans are attacking!" yelled Bahren who then dove out of the post with Ruby following. Meanwhile griffins scrambled about. Officers tried to organize their companies. Soldiers ran to retrieve armor or weapons. Others manned their battle positions. Raishan boulders had leveled the eastern wall and mess hall. Rubble and blood was spread across the floor.

The Raishans then aimed and fired their ballistae, giant crossbows that fired flaming spear-sized arrows, toward the gaping hole in the eastern wall. The trebuchets then whirled great clay spheres filled with flaming tar at the roof.

Only seconds from this ordinance raining down, Ruby and Bahren heard a whizzing. Then the flaming bolts streaked by and impaled griffins as they scurried about. The pair ducked between a supporting column and the wall when the clay spheres smashed through the roof, broke apart, and unleashed their fiery liquid torrent onto the soldiers below who then wriggled and riled on the floor, screaming as their bodies were devoured by flame.

Ruby and Bahren closed their eyes, but the volley had ended. "We must reach the armory," said Bahren. She nodded. The armory contained all of their armor and weapons and was clear across the other side of the fort. They bounded over rubble and charred bodies alike, the living still writhing. The whizzing returned. They jumped inside just as more bolts and fireballs thundered down. They then scrambled to dress themselves in armor as their friends screamed and cried from outside. Ruby couldn't help but look. They all seemed helpless. Those who were unscathed darted about in a chaotic daze, jumping from one wounded soldier to another, trying to save all at once, only to be crushed under flaming pieces of the roof as it fell apart.

"FORGET THIS!" cried Ruby. She snatched her sword and charged to the door with only her chest plate on.

"RUBY WAIT!" yelled Bahren. She stepped outside just as the next volley came. She froze. The carnage overwhelmed her. Then the roof came crashing down under the force of another tar-sphere volley. She looked up. Then Bahren thrust her back inside. The planet shook as fire roared and the walls of the fort came crumbling down. Dust and smoke then filled the air.

Then the ground stopped shaking, the dust began to settle, Ruby and Bahren gradually rose to their feet coughing. "Are you alright?" Bahren asked Ruby who nodded. All but the top of the entrance had been blocked by rubble. They peaked out of it – onto a fiery moonscape. Not much later the Raishan grenadiers descended out of the dusk sky like demons out of hell, they were searching for survivors.

"AHHH!" Ruby leapt up and tried to squeeze through the opening, but Bahren grabbed her.

"NO! Ruby!" A grenadier heard the commotion as Bahren pulled her to the floor. "There's nothing you can do."

"Yes there is! I can kill them! I can kill them!"

"Ruby-"

"All of our friends are dead!"

Bahren heard a Raishan voice, "come on, there's an underground tunnel at the other end! They have them in all forts," he said as he opened the trap door, Ruby still at the door. "Ruby! There's nothing killing yourself will accomplish! Now come on! We must warn the army!" She stood still as a statue, her eyes locked in front of her. "Ruby!" Then a grenadier poked his eye into the opening, then starting yelling in Raishan when Ruby stabbed him in the eye. "Ruby!" Bahren jumped over and grabbed her, then forced her down the escape.

In the pitch black of the underground, they could see nothing as they felt their way to the end. Behind them, the sound of Raishans yelling and digging became more and more distant, soon though the two survivors reached the end of the tunnel. Bahren charged through the trap door and into the forest above. Despite the thick trees, he could still see the fortress. He stood in awe of it, as did Ruby when she emerged. Together, they watched, they watched as their fellow soldiers, their brothers, burned in a rocky funeral pyre, griffins they had known for months. "Come," said Bahren, "Ruby, we must leave." He ran off. Yet Ruby remained for another moment before turning and following. Above them, an army of Raishans flushed the air around, as if the wind itself feared this advancing force.

They ran as fast as they could toward the coast, they ran because flying would allow them to be seen. It wasn't long before they had found a trail. "These trails lead to the coast," said Bahren, "we follow this, we can reach the fleet and warn them." So they followed this trail, sprinting along its edge under the cover of the forest. In some ways though, it would have been safer to fly, far greater dangers than Raishans lurked in those wild and untamed trees.

They ran all night, adrenaline their fuel, stopping every now and again to catch their breath, always searching the skies for enemy soldiers. Every so often though, they'd hear a twig snap, or a strange noise or cry come from deep within the woods. Soon they kept their eyes on the trees – as much as the sky. They couldn't wait for morning. The night blinded them. Anything could be following them and they wouldn't even know it was there.

When morning came, more clouds blotted out the sun. Bahren and Ruby were still jogging, the adrenaline that had once drove them had drained. They could see columns of Raishan soldiers in the distance in almost every direction. They heard yelling and when they turned a corner, they saw, just about fifty feet in front of them, about a half dozen Raishan troops. They were circled around something, kicking it, and yelling at it. Bahren and Ruby crouched down and watched from the trees when a general emerged from up ahead. "Alright," he said in Raishan, "he's had enough." The soldiers stopped kicking and backed away from it, an Arktorian soldier. Ruby jumped up but Bahren pulled her back down.

The Arktorian soldier had no armor, and was covered in bruises and bumps. Both of his eyes were black and swollen as he lay in the fetal position, trembling, shaking, terrified. The general bent down over him. "Now," he said softly in Arktorian, a heavy Raishan accent in his voice, "I will only say this one final time, you are to go to the Ark fleet just off the coast and tell them what has befallen here at this fort," he said with a smile, staring into the Arktorian's blackened eyes. Then the smile was erased. "What are you waiting for?! Go! Go!" The soldier scrambled to his feet and flew off, the Raishans yelling after him.

Ruby had seen enough and leapt out of the trees. "H – no!" whispered Bahren, but it was too late, she was in plain view in the middle of the dirt road with murder in her eyes. "Damn it all!" whispered Bahren.

The Raishan general turned around to return to the fort when he spotted Ruby. "Well well well, what do we have here?" She stood still as granite, the soldiers cackling as they approached her. "Looks like we have found something to keep us entertained, boys," said the general. She unsheathed her sword. "Whoa!" exclaimed a couple of the amused soldiers.

"Now what's a lady as pretty as you doing way out here by herself?" asked the general.

"She's not by herself!" yelled Bahren from behind them.

The general's eyes skipped back and forth between them, then he waived his hand. "Kill them," he ordered in Raishan. There were six soldiers, four went for Bahren as the other two nonchalantly strolled over to Ruby and drew their sabers, smiling. The one on Ruby's left swung at her neck, she leaned backwards, then the other stabbed at her gut, she twisted her body and swung her foot into his face, knocking him to the ground. The other stabbed at her neck again and she side-stepped, then stabbed him in the neck. Then the other struck at her abdomen, but Ruby managed to hit the saber away, then rip his gut.

Ruby was about to help Bahren, but he, being outnumbered four to one, had been defeated. She found him with an enemy saber at his throat, two dead at his side. "It's over," said the general in Arktorian, "give up, drop your weapon, or we kill your lover." She tightened her grip, she saw that one of the Raishans was falling asleep, then she spotted the blood pouring out of his leg. The dying griffin's eyelids were beginning to droop as he leaned more and more onto Bahren. Ruby then started at them. "Stay back!" She ignored the general, fire in her eyes. "Kill him!" The general screamed in Raishan, watching Ruby as she reached arm's reach. "Kill HIM!" But the soldier closed his eyes and fell over. Bahren grabbed his saber and stabbed the other one holding him before pointing it at the general.

Ruby's blade was already at his throat. "Now, sir, it is over," she said.

He put his hands in the air. "Please, I am unarmed."

"So was I," replied Bahren.

The general trembled, Ruby tipped her head. "Awe, Bahren, he must not be a field officer, he's never had his life in danger before," she put her face in his, "have you?"

"N – no."

"I thought not." She smashed her sword's handle in his eye and he fell to the ground.

"Please!" He begged with terror in his eyes and his hands in the air as Ruby knelt down. "What do you want? You wouldn't do anything to me, right?"

"Well that depends if you cooperate, if you do we will do nothing, if you don't, well," she smiled at Bahren, "we'll leave that to our imaginations." She swiftly pointed her sword in the Raishan's face and he flinched. "Now tell us who you are and what you know about the attack on that fortress!"

The corners of his beak trembled, "n – nothing."

"Give me that other saber, Bahren." She held up her hand. "I will need two blades for this."

"No! No!" He waived his hands in the air. "I am the general who led the attack on Fortress Mountain Foot and I know what their plan is. This is part of a much more massive attack, this was just a diversion, the main attack is coming on the southern border, at Cayza, that's all I know."

Ruby turned to Bahren who said, "you know, normally when someone you're interrogating says 'that's all I know', it means – he knows more."

"Is there something you're not telling us?!" she screamed and pointed the sword in his eye again.

"NO!" She gradually moved the blade forward until its tip remained but half a feather's width from the water over his eye.

"Alright!" Then he sighed. "After you have been distracted in the south, they'll launch another attack from the north, through here."

Ruby gleamed into his eyes, squinting, searching for the tiniest particulate of deception. "If you're lying again-"

"NO! NO! I'm telling the truth!"

She kept at him until Bahren interrupted, "we should go, we have to warn the fleet." He started taking the armor off of the Raishans.

"What are you doing?" Ruby asked.

"We will not reach the fleet in time unless we fly," he put on a Raishan chest-plate, "and this is the only way we can fly safely."

"Should we take him with us?"

Bahren eyed the general. "No, he would only slow us down."

"But he's a general!"

"If we weren't fighting time it would be different." Ruby then also changed uniforms. Once disguised, they charged into the sky with legions of enemy troops in all directions and the red and orange morning sun penetrating the clouds. Ruby and Bahren pumped their wings to the point of total exhaustion and beyond, to the point where their wings stung and felt as if lit aflame. The Raishan armor wore them down even more, yet the fate of thousands of Arktorian troops pushed them on.

The sun was setting by the time Ruby and Bahren could see the coast. The fleet they needed to warn was stationed in a harbor town named Moozma, one built a century earlier specifically to harbor war-fleets. The vessels stationed in it were the same ones that had brought Ruby, Bahren and the other soldiers that had once shared the Field of Tears with them to Platu and that had rescued them from Hyleeda, something that seemed such a long time ago. The pair landed on Captain Zat's ship as he stood at its wheel. "Captain Z–" started Bahren.

"Shhh," he held up his pointer finger, "do you hear that, boy?"

"No."

"Exactly! You don't hear it. It's the silence before the storm." He smiled and looked up, then his eyes traversed from left to right.

Bahren looked to Ruby, then back to Zat. "Actually the saying is the calm before the storm." The captain faced them.

"Zat," urged Ruby, "we need your help."

"What's wrong, my dear?"

"The Raishans are setting a trap and we need to speak to the commander of this fleet, Commodore Pdosvine!"

"Aye, he's probably pushin' paper in his-" a sneer grew on Captain Zat's face, "office, somewhere."

"Where is his office?"

"Aye, probably the flagship."

"Yes but where is that?" asked Ruby.

"I have no idea."

"Come on Ruby, it can't be far." The pair darted off in search of the flagship not sure of what it looked like, but they knew it was probably rather grandiose in appearance.

Within a minute though, Ruby spotted what could have been it. "There!" She pointed. They landed on the ship's chaotic deck with soldiers marching all around, couriers running back and forth, and officers standing around discussing retaliation. Ruby and Bahren stepped below deck where Ruby stopped one of the couriers. "Hey! Where is the commodore's quarters?"

"Right down there," he pointed toward the end of the hall.

"Thanks." They then ran to the door where two tall guards stood at attention on either side. They crossed their spears into an X when the pair reached them. "Please, you must let us through," pleaded Ruby.

"No one but couriers and officers," one said with a voice so deep it sounded like a groan.

"What if they were with me?" asked Zat from behind, Ruby smiled as he limped over. "Let these two in."

"Yes sir." The guards then removed their spears.

Ruby and Bahren burst inside, with Zat behind, where Commodore Pdosvine sat hunched over his desk. Maps, logistics, weather plans, and all other manner of war plans covered his desk as a half dozen other commanders stood about him, pointing at things on the papers on his desk, making suggestions and what not. Ruby and Bahren stood at attention and waited in-vain for the admiral to acknowledge them. After a minute, Bahren discreetly cleared his throat, but he wasn't heard. He did it again, nothing.

Captain Zat had had enough. "Oh for goodness sake!" He brushed the two aside and slammed his cane on the commodore's desk. He and the rest of his staff flinched, snapping out of their paperwork trance.

After the initial shock passed, the commodore collected himself. "Captain Zat, what a nice-" he cleared his throat, "pleasure."

"Sir," Ruby stepped forward, "sir we must send this fleet to Cayza."

"Hah, my dear," he leaned in, "why would you think such a thing?"

A fire grew in her eyes and Bahren realized that she was about to say something she'd regret. "What she's trying to say is that we found the Raishan commander of the attack on the fort and that upon the threat of torture he told us that that was just a diversion, that the main attack was going to occur in the south, in Cayza, and then through the north."

The commodore smiled, "alright, so you found some Raishan general out in, somewhere, and you assumed he led the attack on Mountain Foot-"

"Sir-" started Bahren.

"Let me finish. You find some Raishan general, you assume he's the commander, and then you threaten to torture him and he tells you this – a little anecdote to which you have no proof?!"

"Sir I-" started Ruby.

"I said let me finish!" He took in a deep breath. "How do you know he was telling the truth? He could have simply made it all up. He may have just told you all this so that our entire northern force would go south, which would then allow the enemy to take the north with no resistance!"

"Sir," said Bahren, "we threatened to torture him again if we thought he wasn't telling the truth. Not that we necessarily would have."

"Oh really? Tell me soldier, have you ever even tortured anyone before? Do you know how to do it? Do you know when they're being honest and when they're BLOODY WELL SAYING JUST ABOUT ANYTHING TO GET YOU TO STOP?!" Bahren bowed his head. "Well do you?!"

"No sir," he mumbled.

The commodore sat back in his chair. "That will be all." With no choice, they clicked their heels, saluted and exited with Zat following.

"Stupid idiot," Ruby whispered to herself.

"What are we going to do now?" asked Bahren.

Zat pushed them aside and led them above deck. Together they flew back to his ship where he landed at the wheel. All around, his crew scurried about as they prepared for battle. "My crew!" They all halted. "My crew, you have all served me well over the years, and it is today that I ask you one last favor."

"What is it, Cap'm?" yelled up a sailor.

"The enemy thinks it can pull a fast one on us. Well they can't trick this old sod! The enemy is attacking south and so we will go there to meet him! Even though – it would be disobeying orders."

"Why is that disobeying orders, sir?" yelled up another.

"It doesn't matter, for tonight–" he unsheathed his saber, "we feast on Raishan flesh." In unison they cheered. "Let down those sails! Raise the anchor!" The deck exploded with energy as the crew prepared to set sail.

Bahren then whispered into the captain's ear, "you're going to risk the careers of this crew?"

"To save the lives of those who are in danger I'd risk anyone's *career.*"

Bahren turned to Ruby, "he's out of his mind! You agree with me, right?"

Ruby smiled, "yes, and he's just crazy enough." Once the ship was prepared, Captain Zat turned to port, then began to weave his way through the jumble of war vessels in his way. Zat himself screamed at them from his wheel. He soon attracted attention and other captains began yelling back, asking what they were doing. "The enemy's going to attack south!"

"Why weren't we told?" many would respond.

"Well you're being told now!" And with that, one by one, they would move out of his way before following. As word spread, other ships began to follow as well.

Meanwhile, the commodore and his staff were still working out their strategy when a young, baby faced member of the crew came barging in. "Sir, there's something you need to see."

"Son, I have had about enough of hatchlings coming in here and telling me what to do," he stood up and pointed his finger at the sailor, "now-" then the ship turned. The commodore and his staff nearly fell over at the sudden jolt. "The ship's moving! Why is my ship moving?!"

"That's what I was trying to tell you, sir." All of them then rushed to the deck. The entire fleet was moving out of the harbor with Captain Zat at its front.

Captain Zat spotted the commodore. "Commodore!"

"That crazy-"

"So glad you decided to join us!"

Awestruck, the commodore just gawked for a time. "Stop!" he finally ordered and pushed the griffin at the wheel away from his station. "Stop turning the ship!"

"I'm sorry, sir," he apologized with an annoyed tone.

"Why are you turning the ship?! Who told you to turn it?!"

"I thought we were supposed to. Look, the rest of the fleet's going too."

The commodore peered out over the rest of the ships. "Blast," he then stood at the gunwale. "Hey!" He waved his arms in the air. "Stop! Halt! That's an order!"

One of his staff then approached him, "sir, if I may ask, how do you know the enemy isn't attacking in the south? Perhaps those two soldiers were right. It could be a diversion."

"How could it be a diversion?"

"Why couldn't it be?"

"Well—" he thought for a moment, "fine!" He pointed his eyes to the sunset. "We head south." He turned to his second in command. "General,"

"Yes sir," he snapped into attention.

"Order the troops back onto their ships."

"Yes sir." A minute later, and an arrow lit with white flame was fired, ordering that all of the soldiers return to their ships.

Chapter 19

That very next morning, clouds and fog blanketed the air around the small harbor city of Cayza like a great lazy ghost. Cayza sat on the northern edge of a bay that led into a river, both of which drew the border between the Arktorian and Raishan colonies, to the east of Cayza stood cliffs that gradually shrunk into the river's bank. To the city's west the coast suddenly grew into another cliff that turned northward. To the north of Cayza the land rose into the Arktorian encampment, dotted within this encampment were small, steep mountains.

To the east of Cayza hid two Arktorian scouts in a forest. From their perch over a cliff, they stood guard for any sign of attack from the enemy. They were twins and had feathers covered in different shades of green paint, not to mention the branches they had tied to their heads and limbs. Then they heard something coming up from behind and turned to see an exhausted looking red griffin emerge from the branches. He saw the twins and froze. They drew their swords. "No! Please! I'm Arktorian!" begged this stranger.

"Prove it!" the twins barked simultaneously.

"I can't but you must listen to me! The Raishans will soon attack this city!"

"What's your name?" one asked.

"Dyricio," he answered meekly, "I – I don't have a last name."

"He's lying." the other said.

"You're right," then they faced Dyricio, "you're our prisoner."
They then grabbed Dyricio. They were taking him to the stockades
which was a small, fenced and empty paddock, one meant to house as
many as a dozen or so prisoners. Dyricio struggled and yelled all the
way there, through the woods to the vast clearing on the coast where
the encampment laid, trying to convince his captors of his loyalty.
Soon the scouts had nearly had enough. Once in the camp's clearing
they were walking through the midst of legions of griffins as they
milled about, as well as thousands of small sleeping tents that extended
beyond the eye's vision. Spotted in between them were larger tents,
ones used as mess halls, command posts, or baths. Then Dyricio saw
the stockades and struggled yet more, so the twins decided to teach him
a lesson. "Alright! That's it!" one said and tossed his prisoner to the
ground. Dyricio landed face down in the wet mud, then swiftly rolled
over with muck covering his entire front side. The scouts stood over
him, "you need to learn your manners, Raishan."

"I'm not Raishan!" Dyricio insisted, but they still didn't believe
him. Soon a crowd of Arktorian soldiers had gathered around them.

Their dead eyes burned a hole in Dyricio. For more time than these troops could remember, they have stood on their toes, on constant watch. Their enemy could attack at any second. This wore on them like sandpaper on bare skin. The feeling of being watched remained constant and so these soldiers knew that if they ever let their guard down, they let everyone else down. They knew that their enemy could attack at any second.

The sight of what they believed to be a Raishan was just what they needed. Their enemy was a specter, something that cannot be seen, something that slithers in the dark and whispers your name into your ear to strike fear into your soul – just for the fun of it. Now this enemy finally had a face, and all this – this tension and raw emotion was about to be poured out onto Dyricio. In their eyes, he saw this, their blank eyes, wiped clean by the constant anticipation of death, death as both a fear, and by now, a sweet release. If they attacked Dyricio, they would not be able to stop.

Ayro was walking by when he saw the gathering crowd. Curious, he kept looking until he saw Dyricio. "What the-?" he ran over, pushing the crowd aside, "Dyricio?"

"Ayro!" His face lit up even though he had never liked Ayro, but for that moment, he was a savior.

"You know this one?" asked the scouts.

"Yeah, he's a friend."

"Ayro, tell them I'm not a Raishan!"

"He's telling the truth." The crowd then dispersed as the scouts returned to their positions in the forest.

"Dyricio, how'd you get here?"

"You must take me to your commanders!"

"What, why?"

"Where are they?!"

"Alright. Alright, calm down, I'll take you there." Ayro then escorted Dyricio to the Field Head-Quarters, a long white tent with golden edgings. It was clean and quaint, resembling the kind of place a senator might stay on holiday. Inside, Ayro and Dyricio approached the top commander as he sat with his feet on his desk and leaned back in his chair. He appeared incredibly bored. Ayro stood at attention as Dyricio remained in a normal stance. The commander eyed them with a slight flicker of annoyance. *"Some more soldiers who want something."* He thought. "At ease," he glumly ordered.

"Forgive him, Commander Relkor, sir, he's a civilian." Ayro motioned to Dyricio and his undisciplined stance.

"Then what in the name of the Gods is he doing in my command tent?"

Dyricio then responded, "s – sir, I'm here because I know the enemy's secret war plans." Ayro, the commander, and everyone else in the tent all gawked at Dyricio.

The commander smiled, "alright," he removed his feet from his desk then leaned forward, feigning interest, "and just how did you come by this intel?"

"Well," Dyricio tried to find the right words, "I had been taken by the enemy and while in captivity I was able to see their plans of attack."

"Uh-huh, and just how do they plan on attacking?"

Dyricio could tell this general had no intent on listening to him. "They're going to attack a fortress in the north, Mountain Foot I think."

"What's your name?" asked the commander.

"Dyricio, sir."

"Dyricio what?"

"Dyricio," Ayro squeezed his eyes shut, "Trajetton."

"Tra – hah! Look boys, we're standing in the presence of the greatest general of the enemy's son." A low laugh emanated from the rest of the tent.

"Sir," said Ayro, "I know this griffin, and he is the son of General Trajetton."

The commander's smile vanished. "What?"

Ayro continued, "it's true, sir. I was once even taken prisoner by Trajetton himself."

The commander's eyes grew infuriated and fearful simultaneously when a courier came running in. "Commander Relkor, the Raishans have launched an attack on a fortress in the north!"

"What fortress?" Commander Relkor asked.

"Mountain Foot, sir."

Relkor turned to Dyricio for a moment before returning to the courier. "When did this happen?"

"A couple days ago, sir."

The commander then looked back to Dyricio. "What are they planning next?"

Nearby, Sory's glazed eyes reflected his day-dreaming mind as he laid at the edge of the forest. He had the cliff that led to the bay at his feet and the encampment to his right. He was about to return to his tent when a behemoth of sense barreled through him and knocked him down. It was something evil, yet familiar. He had felt it before. Sory searched his memory until he remembered the visions – until he remembered the aura of the King. With that, Sory bolted off for headquarters. A minute later he barged into the tent. "Sir!" he stopped dead, "Dyricio?"

"Sory?"

"Soldier, you know this one too?" the commander asked Sory.

"Yes sir, he's my brother."

Commander Relkor raised his brow. "You're also a son of Trajetton?"

"You told them?!" exclaimed Sory.

"I thought it would help them believe me."

"Believe you about what?" asked Sory.

The commander answered, "your brother is giving us vital intel on the enemy's plans."

"How do you know their plans?"

"It's complicated," snapped back Dyricio.

The commander cleared his throat. "We'll have time for family reunions later but for now," he turned to Dyricio, "son, continue."

"Anyway, all I know is that they attacked Fort Mountain Foot as a decoy so that they could then cut through the border right in the middle and split the continent in half."

"Do you know when they'll flank us?" asked the commander.

"I suppose as soon as we have our forces up north."

"Alright boys," the commander turned to the five senior officers, "what do you think we should do?"

"We should ready ourselves for an attack here," declared Sory. Then they all stared at him. "King Sairus and General Trajetton are on the other side of that bay."

"Right, and how do you know this?" asked Commander Relkor. "Is it that you are all part of some sort of family spy ring?"

"No sir," groaned Sory.

"Then how do you know that the *King of Raishany* is over there?!" Commander Relkor pointed in the direction of the enemy.

Sory faltered before he answered, "I could sense them, sir."

The commander furrowed his brow. "W – what do you mean you 'could sense them?'" Sory closed his eyes, when they opened a white glow had overtaken them. At once, everyone in the tent lurched backwards as Sory floated into the air for a couple seconds, then he returned to the muddy ground. He then immediately exited trance, knowing full-well that he had to conserve his energy for the imminent fight ahead. "W – w – what kind of monstrosity are you?!"

"I am the Fyzar."

"The Fyzar? From the prophecy?"

"The one and only, sir."

The commander sighed, "alright, so you are the Fyzar, but just because you have magical powers does not mean that Sairus and your father–"

"He is not my father."

"Either way, you cannot possibly know for sure that they're over there! And how could you be sure? I mean how do you know that it's them?"

"It is difficult to explain, sir."

"Right well, I don't mean to hurt your feelings, but here in reality we base our military strategy off of facts. That is all, dismissed." Sory remained, awestruck, before the commander looked back up. "Soldier, you are dismissed!"

"Permission to speak freely, sir," said Sory.

"Denied, dismissed." He pointed his finger at the opening in the tent.

"Sir, the Raishans are world renowned for their deceiving maneuvers in war. They may have sent Dyricio to trick us."

"HEY!" screeched Dyricio. "They didn't send me – I escaped!"

"Escaped?" asked Sory.

"Yeah, they had taken me prisoner."

"Then how do you know their secret plans? Do they have their meetings right in front of the stockades?"

"Well – ugh, I wasn't really a prisoner, I actually chose to go, they thought I was the Fyzar."

The commander's eyes flared. "What?!"

"But I realized I was on the wrong side so I escaped, and it was pretty easy too, there weren't any guards or anyone around to stop me."

The commander sighed, "alright, I cannot deal with this. Private Trajetton, you said they're setting a trap, correct?"

"Yes sir."

"Well you know what? You're right, and this trap is the one your brother has just described to us, the one where the Raishans attack fort Mountain Foot, which they have done, and we send our forces to the north in response, only to be flanked in the center. That's the trap."

"No, sir, I don't think it is."

"Private you have no experience in battle."

"Neither do you, we haven't fought the Raishans in centuries."

"Guards, escort this private outside of my headquarters!"

Two guards grabbed Sory by the arms. "General Relkor! Listen to me! I don't know what the Rasihans are planning but whatever it is you're about to fall right into it!" They threw him out of the tent and into the mud. Sory spat some muck out of his mouth before punching the ground.

Back in the tent, the commanders gathered around the map of Platu. "Right," started Commander Relkor, "now that we're alone, I suggest we make it appear as though we're falling for this trap. We'll send a small force in plain view of the Raishans to the fort while gathering an even larger, unseen army in the center of the continent. It will be this hidden army that will absorb the full force of the enemy as they attempt to flank our soldiers in the north. Any questions? Good, then we're in agreement, we send our forces north."

"But sir," one of the other commanders interrupted, "we do not have the numbers in certain areas to fight what I'm guessing is a substantial Raishan force, as well as keep the rest of our colony safe."

Commander Relkor sighed, "you're right, general. Send a courier to the emperor with a request for reinforcements." This other general then signaled for the courier to come over from the corner. He then wrote the request for the extra troops before stamping the Imperial Seal on it. The courier placed it in his satchel and walked out.

The courier flew out over the cliffs of the coast while waves crashed on the razor sharp rocks below. With the thick fog, the coast disappeared behind him within a minute. Then he heard a rustling from behind. He turned and saw a Raishan crossbowman pointing a crossbow at him. The courier froze. He was about to call out when the crossbowman pulled the trigger and shot him. The courier began to fall, but not before the crossbowman rushed forward and grabbed his satchel.

*

Nighttime, the insects sang their evening song as Sory sat in his old hiding place above the bay and at the forest's edge, the same place where he had first felt the presence of his father and King Sairus. From there he watched the Raishan cliffs on the opposite side. He was sure of what the enemy had planned. The commander of the First Knights Division came up from behind. "General Zlade, sir."

"Private, do you mind if I sit?" The general extended his hand.

"No, sir."

"Thank you," he sat and then gazed out in the direction Sory was.

A silence persisted for a moment before Sory spoke. "You're the commander of the First Knight Division, right?"

"Yes, I am," the general replied.

"Yeah, I remember you on graduation day, that speech you gave."

"Thank you, I enjoyed giving that speech," another silence for another moment. "That was quite a scene earlier."

"I know, sir."

"You seem to have felt quite strongly about your little theory."

"Yes sir."

"Well, what did you say your name was again?" asked the general.

"Trajetton, sir."

"Well I remember your last name, I meant your first."

"Sory."

"Sory, right, well anyways Sory, it is my personal belief that whenever someone believes something strongly enough, then there is the strong possibility – that they may be right." He paused. "So, why do you think the Raishans are leading us into this trap?"

"Well, Dyricio said it was very easy for him to escape. Maybe they wanted him to so that he could feed us those false battle plans."

"That's very good, son."

"Thank you, sir."

"But how did they make him escape? And more importantly, could he be working for them?"

"I'd know if Dyricio was lying, and besides, it's not that difficult to drive him away. I mean look how easily he ran to their side, all they had to do was tell him he's the Fyzar."

The general smiled, "you know, you remind me a lot of Fusna."

"You know him?"

"Oh yes, one night he came down to the planning room below the Obelisk, saying to us that he thought that the Raishans were planning some sort of massive offensive, that they were saving up legions of troops for something, something – big. This was just around the time the First Knight Division was sent here, and I told him, I told Fusna I hope you're wrong about what the Raishans are planning on Platu, because you just sent my division there."

"Really? You said that to him?"

"Yes, well," he tipped his head, "something like that."

"And anyway, there's so much more we may not know. For all we know there's an entire army over there, just watching and waiting until our forces pull out."

"Is that why you've been sitting here and staring over there?"

Sory sighed, "no, I don't know. I don't know what I'm doing. Not that it matters anyway, no matter what I say they'll never believe me."

"Well, you've convinced me, maybe you'd be able to convince them."

"Really, you believe me?"

"Yes, you've made a very convincing argument."

"You don't seem very afraid."

"Well I suppose that when your life has been in danger enough times–"

"You get used to it?"

"No, I'm afraid. You just get really good at hiding your fear of it."

"Oh."

"Well, I was going to head back to headquarters," he stood up, groaning with his arthritis, "it'll be your last chance to convince them."

Sory thought for a moment, "alright."

They walked to the headquarters and when they arrived, the general entered first, "Commander."

"What?" Commander Relkor groaned from his chair as Sory walked in. "What is this? I thought I removed you from my command tent!"

General Zlade began, "Commander Relkor, sir, I have been talking to this soldier and he has made a convincing case–"

"Forget it!"

"Sir, this young griffin has pointed out many holes in his brother's story."

"Holes in my story?!" Dyricio yelled from behind them. "What do you think I am, a spy?!"

"Nobody thinks you're a spy," said Sory.

"I escaped!"

"How did you escape anyway?"

"I told you, there weren't any guards around so I just ran out of my tent."

"Why though? Why did you fly away?"

"Because I realized they were evil."

"When did you realize this?"

"When father started treating me like dirt, I mean, I think he thought he could because he was convinced I'd never do anything about it, like fly away, and those were his words. 'You don't even have the guts to fly away!'"

"Really?"

"Something like that, at least that's what I thought he meant."

"And you did fly away?"

"Yep," Dyricio proudly declared.

"After you saw their battle plans?"

"Right after actually, it was that very same night."

"And when did this conversation about you not being able to fly away start?"

"Just after I saw their battle plans."

"So they showed you their battle plans, then pushed you to fly away, and when you did there were no guards around to stop you?"

"No, they never had any guards around me."

"But you are the Fyzar, at least to them you are, so why wouldn't they protect you? When Fusna first figured out who we are, not only did we have guards, we weren't even allowed to tell anybody who we were."

"So?"

"So? It's all just one big hoodwink!"

General Zlade cut in, "we believed Dyricio because he knew about the attack on Fort Mountain Foot before anyone else."

"Exactly!" said Sory. "We'd believe him so that we'd fall right into their trap!"

"What trap?" asked Commander Relkor.

"I don't know, but I think that they showed Dyricio false plans that somehow coincide with real ones."

"Alright soldier," said Commander Relkor, "I'll humor you, you said that your father was over on the other side of the bay. Fine, tomorrow morning I'll send out a scout to see for sure. Actually you know what, I'll send two scouts out. But that is it, that is the end of the matter and you are dismissed!"

"Sir—"

"I SAID – you are dismissed." Sory clenched his fists. "Don't make me throw you out again, private." Sory took a deep breath, straightened up, snapped his heels, and marched out. Dyricio watched him before jumping up and chasing after him.

Sory was stomping with a fire to his stride as Dyricio came up behind him with the same fury. "WHAT THE HELL SORY?!"

Sory halted, "what?"

"You heard me!" Dyricio boomed as he put his face into Sory's. "Is there something wrong with me?! Do you have a problem with me getting attention, is that it?!"

"Dyricio I don't know what you're talking about."

"Oh you don't, well, let's see, you always got all the attention from father, then you got all the attention from Fusna and the emperor when they chose you to be the Fyzar, and now that I know something you just have to bring it down don't you?!" Dyricio put his finger in Sory's eye with each accusation.

"I was not chosen to be the Fyzar! If you were the eldest brother you'd be the Fyzar!"

"You don't understand!" Dyricio threw his arms in the air.

"No, you know what, I don't understand! I don't understand why you act like this! Why are you so sensitive – and paranoid?! Why do you think everything is about you?!"

Dyricio shoved Sory. "I do not think everything is about me! But whenever something isn't about you you must make it about you!"

Sory shoved Dyricio back. "I am not making this about me! I am trying to save countless lives!"

"Oh yeah, Tysorious Trajetton, always has to be the hero!"

Sory calmed himself. "You know what, think what you want," he started to turn, "I can't take care of you anymore," and he started walking away.

"Hey! Hey! Don't you turn your back on me!" Yet Sory ignored him and kept walking. Dyricio was fed up, for him this was the final straw. Dyricio jumped into the air to tackle Sory, screaming as he launched himself up. Sory twisted around and slapped Dyricio down like a bug, knocking him straight into the dirt.

Sory stood over him, both heaving. "Good night, Dyricio." And he left his brother in the mud grimacing at him.

The next morning, a rumbling woke Sory in his tent and he sat up. The three others he shared the tent with were beginning to stir as well. Sory put his shirt on and stepped outside to witness thousands of Arktorian troops marching to the north end of the encampment and flying off.

Sory's stomach turned as others awoke to the sight. He wondered if all of these griffins were doomed. Though he denied it, he knew that all of these soldiers who signed up to give their lives were about to do so in a pointless battle. Sory flew to the southern end of the encampment, next to the bay, where he had a better view of this mass procession. To his left he could see Commander Relkor outside of his tent with two scouts. They saluted him, then flew off toward the Raishan border. From a great distance, about a quarter-mile, the commander met eyes with Sory, before returning to his quarters.

Far to Sory's east, the two scouts, the same twins that had captured Dyricio were gliding low over the forest canopy so as not to be seen. Then they dove into the trees just before reaching the river, which marked the border. They bounded between trees and over logs like gazelles and soon reached the river a couple miles inland. From there, through their telescopes, they could see tens of thousands of Raishans as they formed into columns. Accompanying them, a myriad of war machines, ballistae, catapults, trebuchets, siege towers, and even cannons, all lined up and at the ready.

The twins met each other's petrified gazes. Then they whipped themselves into the air. Sory had remained in the same spot, his eyes fixed on the disappearing soldiers. To him the twins being picked off by Raishan crossbowmen was nothing more than a blip in the corner of his vision. He turned his head but saw nothing. Then he looked out to sea. More fog was gathering, only allowing the enemy to hide with much greater ease. Sory sighed before returning to his tent.

Chapter 20

Midday in the Throne Room of the Obelisk. Emperor Mecila was sitting on his throne with his head resting on his hand and his elbow on the armrest when the doors opened. He then straightened himself up as they strained ajar. *Finally something is about to happen.* He thought. A courier then moved quickly, almost nervously straight toward the throne with a hood covering his bowed face. The emperor didn't care though, he was just glad to have a visitor. This courier then kneeled before the emperor once in front of him, then handed him the message bearing the Imperial Seal. This mysterious griffin's head remained bowed as Emperor Mecila read the message aloud, "'Your Highness, this is General Relkor, chief commander of all Arktorian forces on Platu. I am pleased to inform you that the Raishans are showing no signs of aggression and that we will not need any reinforcements.' Hmm." The emperor nodded. *At least I have some good news now,* he thought. "Thank you, soldier."

The courier stood up. "The pleasure is all mine, Your Highness."

"Dismissed," said the emperor. The courier clicked his heels, then left in a hurry, still mysteriously nervous. He fast stepped toward the stairs as he removed his hood and revealed the scar and the devious grin on his face. Then Dyricio's former guard disappeared into the bowels of the Obelisk.

It was midday on Platu and the fog had persisted for over a week. By now the forces that Commander Relkor had ordered north had just about reached their final destination at the center of the colonial border. "Where are those damned scouts?!" stormed the commander from within his tent. Sory could hear him yelling from outside and decided not to go in. He was about to try to convince him one final time, but decided against it. So he returned to aimlessly meandering through the rows and rows of tents searching for Dyricio. If Sory was going to die he was going to be on good terms with at least one member of his family. He soon found Ayro though. "Ayro, have you seen Dyricio?"

"No, sorry." Sory's search grew more and more frantic as time passed, but then he remembered the command tent where just about the only griffin that Dyricio still liked, the commander, spent most of his time.

Sory returned to it, then peaked inside. It took a mere moment for him to spot Dyricio sitting in his same little corner. "Dyricio," he whispered, trying not to attract the attention of Commander Relkor.

"Go away," Dyricio grumbled as he trudged outside. Sory followed.

"Dyricio! Dyricio listen to me!" Dyricio stopped. "If you have something to say just say it!" Dyricio pondered Sory's offer, he didn't want to talk though, he wanted to fight, but he knew the consequences of executing such an idea. Dyricio instead then just flew off with Sory watching

Then Ayro came up beside Sory. "Is he still mad?"

"It's complicated," silence overtook as they watched Dyricio begin an aimless flight. "Come on," he led Ayro to the edge of the cliffs where he stared out into the sea.

"What are you looking at?" asked Ayro.

Sory sighed. "Nothing, I'm just waiting."

"For what?"

A mile inland from where the river opened into the bay a bridge crossed. On its northern bank twelve Arktorian soldiers stood guard, yet on the opposing side, no enemy force stood.

Back at the cliffs. "I don't know," answered Sory, "I mean I do know, I just don't know what's going to happen to all of us when it comes."

Back at the bridge, a unit of Raishan crossbowmen sprung out of the woods and fired at the Arktorion soldiers standing guard.

Back at the cliffs, "when what comes?" asked Ayro. Sory saw something out on the sea shrouded in the fog. It was large and dark and only about one-thousand feet away. A slight shadow of it leaked through where the fog met the ocean's surface. "Sory – what is it?"

Back at the bridge, the Raishan crossbowmen made sure that no Arks had survived. Once they had, one of them pointed his weapon with a red flaming arrow straight up, then fired. The flame pierced the fog.

Back at the cliffs, Ayro had his eyes fixed on Sory as his remained on the mysterious thing out at sea. Sory squinted and leaned forward when something bright moved in the corner of his eye. He turned to see a red flame rising into the air.

Sory then darted his eyes back to the dark mass on the waves, a slight breeze then shifted the fog just enough for him to see the bottom of a battleship. "Ayro," he said still glaring at the vessel, "do we have any ships-of-the-fleet in the area?"

"No. Why?" Ayro replied.

A series of flashes then flared out from the side of this ship, as did hundreds more along the coast. "GET DOWN!!!" Sory screamed. He tackled Ayro. Then the booming of hundreds of cannons from dozens of ships cracked the air and shook the planet. Cannonballs roared overhead at the speed of sound. Searing hot iron sliced the air towards nothing but soft flesh and weak canvas tents. They struck and the entire encampment went up as dirt, blood, shrapnel, and tents, with soldiers still in them, were flung around as infernos. Those outside were shredded by shrapnel, splintering wood, rocks ripped out of the ground, and all sorts of metal objects, everything from armor to tea pots. The force of the exploding shells blew some to bits, while others backwards. Ayro and Sory leapt up. "Are you alright?!" asked Sory.

"Yeah," Sory ran off, "where are going?!"

"To find my brother!" Sory had arrived at the camp within a minute, then the Raishans fired their second salvo. The ordinance blasted through soldiers and sprayed blood and entrails all around. Some bounced off of the ground and shredded yet more. The wounded started to scream, while those in shock just lay there, moaning, amongst the dead. Those who had not gone into shock rolled around on the ground, writhing and crying, feeling at their wounds. Those who could still stand darted about like ants with their hands or shields over their heads while some collected themselves and attempted to help the wounded and cried out for a medic.

Sory landed in the midst of this red soaking chaos. The wails of the wounded defended him as he slowed, taking it all in. He wanted to help, but he had to find his brother. Then the most awful of ideas entered his head, what if his brother was one amongst these half-dead bodies. "Dyricio!" he swiveled his body around, "DYRICIO!" The ground and air then rumbled again as exploding black powder split the atmosphere. Sory grabbed a dead soldier's shield and hid himself under it against the red mud. The Raishan ordinance then detonated all around, making the air in Sory's ears burst. As he covered them the water in the dirt jumped up as little droplets tapped his face. Meanwhile he could hear shrapnel dinging against the shield as yet more troops screamed, both in fear and pain.

More screaming as a cloud of dirt hung over Sory. The cannon balls were explosive, hollowed out and filled with black powder and small twisted pieces of iron, allowing them to kill three or four times as many. The fate worse than immediate death was being covered in the scars from this shrapnel, and being awake as they became infected, slowly killing you.

Sory tossed the shield and flew off, "Dyricio!"

From below Ayro yelled at him, "Sory! Get out of the air!"

Sory ignored him and surveyed the fires that devoured the encampment, his eyes whipped about. He didn't know how long he had been flying, how long he had until the next volley. Then he saw his brother, standing and unwounded, mesmerized be the dead.

"Dyricio!" The booming returned, then the growing roar. Sory landed just as a shell struck just in front of Dyricio and flung him away. Sory hit the mud, not able to take his eyes away from where he had last seen his brother as he waited, waited for any sign of life when Dyricio coughed and rubbed his head. Sory then felt as if the weight of the world had been lifted off of him. He stood next to Dyricio and put his hand on his head. "I'm sorry," said Dyricio when a medic came over.

"How is he?! Will he live?!" asked Sory.

"Doesn't look that bad,"

"My chest hurts," said Dyricio.

"It may be internal bleeding from the blast, but it's probably minor."

"And if it's not?" asked Sory. The medic just ignored him as he continued. Sory knew that he had to reach headquarters. He turned to his brother, "I have to leave. I'll be back when I can." Dyricio nodded.

A minute later, Sory barged into the command tent only to bear witness to a demoralizing scene. Caught off guard, the commanders panicked for a plan. No one's voice could be heard as they all melded together, yet Sory focused on the top commander's as he ordered their artillery to be positioned at the edge of the cliffs so as to fire on the enemy's fleet. Once at his desk, Sory asked, "sir, what can I do?"

"You?! You can get out!"

"Sir, I can help–"

"No you can't – NOW LEAVE!" Commander Relkor pointed to the exit.

Outside, Sory pondered what to do next when he noticed movement in the corner of his eye. From the south, a great red cloud lanced toward them. Sory darted back inside, "sir!"

"That's it! Take him to the stockades!" another salvo shook the tent.

"Sir there's a huge Raishan attack group headed our way!" they then all rushed outside where they stood in awe of this tremendous army. After overcoming the initial shock, Commander Relkor turned to First Knight Division's commander, the one that had believed Sory, "you're my second in command now. Gather a few brigades and COUNTER THAT ARMY!"

"Yes sir!" saluted General Zlade. Commander Relkor then raced back inside as the Knight commander came to Sory, "my boy."

"Y – yes sir."

"I am making you my second in command, understand?"

"Sir, I-"

"I have always been religious – and I believe in the Fyzar."

Sory nodded, "yes, sir."

"Now I need to be here, but I want you to organize and lead a force against those Raishans! Can you do that?"

Panic struck Sory and it showed in his eyes, "but sir-"

"CAN YOU DO THAT SOLDIER?!"

"I – I will do what I can, sir."

The general was disappointed, "good," he said half-heartedly, "you'll need this," he gave Sory his helmet, "so that you'll be recognized. NOW MOVE!" Sory saluted then flew off. The next salvo erupted just as he did.

Sory first went to his miraculously undamaged tent, grabbed his sword and shield and then sped off to hopefully find an area untouched by the enemy's artillery. The eastern most area of the camp, as well those areas hidden behind the small and steep mountains seemed perfect. Griffins scrambled about in these areas, some prepared for battle, while yet more ran into the areas that had been hit so as to aid the wounded. Meanwhile Sory stood in the middle of it all. "Attention!" he called. His soldiers acknowledged him as he fumbled to find his words, "the enemy is approaching! If we do not organize they will overrun us! Battalion commanders, form up your troops, spread the message and meet back here! We seem to be safe from the enemy's cannons here," and several high-ranking officers saluted and flew off. "I think that I may soon be good at this." Sory said to himself as another volley was fired.

"But sir, what about the wounded?" one soldier asked.

Sory pointed to a group of soldiers, one being the particular trooper who had asked the question, "find all the medics you can and tell them to bring the wounded either behind these mountains or to the far eastern part of this encampment!"

"Yes sir!"

Meanwhile, the Raishan army, slowed by its own numbers, had nearly crossed the bay. Sory knew that it wouldn't be long before the enemy was standing right where he was. Within a minute though, after the next salvo had struck, the first few officers arrived with their soldiers one battalion at a time. By then the enemy was losing altitude over the city of Cayza. A colonel approached Sory, "sir, the Raishans will be here before we have enough soldiers to fight them!"

Sory then realized something, "no, the Raishans want the harbor." In due time, more battalions formed up just as the front of the Raishan formation landed on the harbor's docks. "That will buy us some time," Sory said to himself. Yet his patients had worn thin. He turned to the colonel, "don't even have the soldiers form up! Just see to it that they are here now!" As the enemy dispersed itself in and around the harbor Sory addressed his growing army, "the Raishans are trying to seize the docks, if they are successful they'll be able to land their siege weapons and artillery. If that happens we lose the battle, if we lose the battle, we lose Platu and all of our forces on it, and if that happens, we may lose the war." He made sure this sunk in.

Then a captain flew up, "sir, we only have about twenty thousand all together, a – a – and it seem as though the enemy has at least thirty or so thousand, perhaps forty. But we cannot bring in any more or we won't have enough to guard the artillery or the coastline!" Sory's mind blanked out, another salvo from the ships off of the coast, "Sir!"

"They have numbers on their side. They assume that they will win so we play that to our advantage. We will fly low so as to be unseen by their fleet and once over the city their army will attack. When they do, we will seek shelter within the buildings and pick them off through the windows."

"Sir?"

"Do we have any wingless griffins?"

"Yes sir."

"Find them. They'll be perfect for this kind of fighting."

The captain flew off for the wingless battalion as Sory watched the last of the Raishans file into the city. "We can wait no longer," he said to himself, then turned to his army, "soldiers – WE MOVE NOW!" Sory then drew his sword and charged forth, flying as low as possible. So low that Sory felt as if he could reach down and touch the tops of those tents that remained standing.

"Sory!" Sory looked down to see Gyric running behind him. He nodded back, then accelerated while making a hook around the eastern edge of the encampment and avoiding the enemy cannon fire. In just over a minute though, they reached the depression that Cayza rested within, by then his archers had formed up at the front of his army all around him. Sory then watched as the Raishans reformed their battalions to defend their position. The city was larger than he had anticipated. He turned to his commanders just behind him, "I want one company per building. Aim to take the taller ones!" A second later and they were over the outskirts of Cayza. His aerial archers then commenced firing, as did the wingless ones in the streets below. Their opposites immediately returned fire. Sory could see the arrows screaming through the air. "Shields up!" he ordered. He raised his own just as an arrow bounced off of it. The enemy now within a couple hundred feet, Sory dove into a building with a few dozen soldiers following. "Lancers against the windows! Put your shields against the windows! Form a barricade!"

The Raishans slammed their barricade, knocking many of Sory's troops off their feet. They then responded with a hail of arrows and spears. The Raishans stabbed back but could only fit a few soldiers through each window, allowing for them to be picked off rather easily. They came at the Arktorians incoherently. For a good six or seven minutes they were cut to pieces while the Arktorians lost almost no one. Soon though, the Raishans fell back, disappearing into the sky.

The silence broke when Sory and his soldiers all started to cheer, hugging each other, and shaking Sory's hands. Then the enemy burst through the only door on the floor, cutting down those closest to it as the rest tried to unsuccessfully form-up. In the free-for-all, Sory slashed and cut incoherently in a panicked rush, his loose strikes soon allowed those he fought to exploit his openings and cut him up, then he heard Fusna's voice, *Calm down, Sory. Breathe.* Sory paused, only to be whacked in the face with a shield, knocking him to the floor. He leapt up, recalled his training, and with a sort of cool and collected manner, managed not to let himself be struck again.

Cries sounded out as Arktorian soldiers were stabbed from behind by the Raishans who started to spill through the windows. Too many griffins were in the room, everyone, on both sides, could barely move.

Blood, half of it his own, soaked Sory, yet he refused to fall. He screamed with each blow he gave, stabbing and slashing with ever greater madness. Then a horde of huge wingless griffins barged in through the door, clobbering the enemy as they fanned out, and soon scampered out the windows. Gyric came over to Sory who said, "impeccable timing."

"Thank you," said Gyric.

"Where's the rest of the wingless?"

"My platoon's in this building-"

"Find your commander and tell him to follow me." Sory then turned to the rest of his soldiers, "the rest of you, I need ten volunteers to tell the rest of the companies to start running toward the harbor. Tell them to jump from building to building until I take flight." His soldiers all exchanged addled expressions, "well go on! You ten!" he pointed to a random cluster, "MOVE!" and they dispersed.

"What are you thinking?" asked Gyric.

"I have an idea, Gyric. Now go find your commander." Sory then bounded to the next building over, a building that was south of their present one. With his soldiers on his heels, as well the rest of his army, Sory ran faster and faster. Soon they had come within a quarter-mile of the harbor itself while Raishan companies flew overhead. Sory broke into one last building then halted, "CHARGE!" he screamed and broke through a window. He then reared up and chose a single enemy company out of the many around him. More and more of his army began quickly emulating.

The Raishans gawked down at them in disbelief, having never been trained to fight in this style. They waited for their commander, but he too could not believe his eyes. Sory and his soldiers formed a phalanx by creating a wall with their shields and sticking their spears out in front. Then they rammed the enemy formation, which then shattered like glass. Then the Arktorians picked off their enemy individually, though some escaped.

Sory then led his troops back into the building that they had just flown out of. Concurrently, the wingless stood out on the rooftops and streets and fired their arrows in support.

Watching from a lighthouse at the bay's edge, it didn't take long for the Raishan commander to catch onto this tactic as his army came scrambling back. Once he realized the scale of the Arktorian forces in those buildings he ordered his retreating soldiers reform and for more troops so as to annihilate the resilient enemy.

Sory had just finished off another company and was diving back down, when he saw the extra Raishans coming in from across the bay. He knew that they had figured it out. Once inside he looked for volunteers for another mission, "I need another ten soldiers to send another message." Many raised their hands. Sory pointed to another random group, "tell the other commanders to hold up in the buildings they're in. The enemy's about to attempt to dislodge us," the troops nodded and dispersed. Sory then walked over to a window and leaned out, "Gyric!"

"Sory?" Gyric yelled from a platoon of wingless on the street.

"Bring your company inside and distribute them throughout the floors of this building, and tell your commander to do the same! One company per building!"

"Yes sir!" Gyric saluted.

Sory brought his head back inside and watched as his enemy reorganized. From where he stood he could also see his soldiers readying themselves as the wingless left the streets and rooftops and dispersed themselves all around. Sory looked south again, the reinforcements from across the bay were now leading the charge, with those that had just been defeated close behind.

Thousands more Raishans were barreling toward them. Now a mere thousand or so yards away, a torrent of arrows then thrashed down onto the Arktorians, stabbing into several griffins at a time in the crowded room. Troops then yelped and fell to the floor. "Put your shields to the windows!" ordered Sory. His troops did. A second later and the next volley rained down. Arrows dinged against their shields for but a few seconds. Then silence.

Sory desperately wanted to see outside but feared being shot or stabbed in the eye. Yet he had to take the chance. So he worked up the nerve, moved his shield, and saw a hundred Raishans dive-bombing them in lines, "Raishans!" he yelled. The enemy whammed through. Those against the windows were walloped backwards including Sory.

Sory then stood back up and fought, but the enemy had squished them against each other. No one could maneuver. His soldiers started to surrender. Sory soon found himself surrounded with eight Raishans pointing their sabers at him. Their breathing was deep and intense as they grimaced at him. They enclosed around the rest of his soldiers who then raised their hands in the air and dropped their weapons.

Then, from the stairwell, came a distant battle cry, one that rapidly grew ever louder. Everyone turned and looked at the door. It then blasted open as wingless griffins burst through shooting their arrows and swinging their axes down onto Raishans who held their shields up only to have them nearly cut in half and their arms broken. Sory then started fighting his way out as the rest of his soldiers picked up their weapons and did the same.

Then the enemy soldiers who remained retreated outside with Gyric and Sory both chasing them all the way out. After the Raishans had fled, Sory turned to Gyric, "again, impeccable timing."

Gyric smiled as the remainder of the Raishans retreated to the harbor, getting chewed up by the Arktorian crossfire from the wingless and archers as they all yelled and cheer. They were holding out.

Back at the lighthouse, the Raishan commanders began to formulate a new plan.

Sory's soldiers could not help but hug him and each other as they yelled and swung their swords and spears in the air. For them all, this was a victory in more than one way. Not only had they stood talon-to-talon with the enemy and won, but they had all also finally looked him in the eye. They had finally seen him after all those endless and tortuous months of waiting.

A minute later though, a soldier ran up to Sory, "sir!" he yelled over the celebrating, "the Raishans, they are going to trap us!"

"What do you mean?" The soldier took Sory to a window and pointed to the west where a red cloud was rising from the city just adjacent to the harbor. The cloud grew as Raishan companies fell-in four and five at a time. This army started to circle around the eastern edge of Cayza in a hook. The soldier then pointed to the south where two more forces, each larger than the first, were rampaging towards them in hooks as well. The enemy was about to attack them from three directions, the hook allowing them a greater distance to dive and so allowing for more momentum.

"They will crush us," Sory said silently. The cheering from his and the other buildings slowly stopped as the sun became blocked out.

Gyric came up to the window and peered out, "those are so many Raishans."

"Sir," said the soldier, "what are we to do?"

Sory faced his soldiers, thinking, "archers, ready your bows, don't fire until ordered. Pike-men form a perimeter. Everyone be at the ready." From another window, Sory eyed the three vast Raishan forces slowly lumbering towards them like three great titans from ancient mythology. Soon these vast forces made the wind rush into an eerie breeze.

The Raishans closed in, closer and closer. A grim gloom overtook the city. Soon the clanking from the enemy armor could be heard. "Archers!" yelled Sory, "ready, aim," now he could see the whites of his enemy's eyes. Arrows then raked through the windows. The Arktorians raised their shields as a few fell. Then the Raishans reared up to land, "Fire!" screamed Sory. The foe was then whisked out of the air, groaning as they fell, yet some still managed to land in the windows. There the Ark lancers slashed desperately, yet still the Raishans came, forced in by the ones behind them. Under the sheer weight of numbers, they muscled their way in from what seemed like all sides.

"Hold the lines!" Sory ordered as their nemeses tumbled in and squashed the Arktorians together, just as before. "Retreat!" Sory finally ordered. He then cut his way to the door which he kicked open and let his soldiers flood through; when an archer dropped dead right in front of him. He then put this archer's quiver full of bows on his back and took the arrow in his hands.

Sory let loose an arrow every couple of seconds as the Raishans chased him down those stairs. When he reached the bottom he jumped into the next building with his soldiers mere feet in front and the enemy mere feet behind – screaming like savages.

In the next building though, there were already Raishans. The front of Sory's column barreled right through but was also slowed just enough so that those Raishans behind could catch up. Sory shot a Raishan pointblank. Then he dropped the bow and unsheathed his sword but was knocked to the ground by his own side in the bedlam.

Sory looked up to see a Raishan grenadier about to impale him with a broadsword. Then Gyric jumped out from the crowd. He then swung his axe down with all his tremendous might and decapitated the Raishan. Sory picked the bow back up, then ran after his troops as they entered the next building.

There, Raishans chased them through the halls. Sory reached the window as a Raishan closed in on him with a spear at his hip. Sory then turned and took a shot at him, then leapt into the next building.

Back at the bridge a couple miles inland, the ground shook, the trees trembled, the river rippled as a Raishan trebuchets rolled out of the trees and onto the stone bridge. Behind them followed yet more siege weapons and artillery, the ground quivering in their wake. Once on the Arktorian side they began to follow a road that led directly into Cayza.

Sory and his army had, for the most part, managed their way out of the pincer. As the Raishans reorganized for one final push the Arktorians paused to catch their breath. Almost as soon as they had though, their foes had taken flight. In one building, Sory had his back against somebody's nightstand inside somebody's bedroom, somebody who lived in that building but was nowhere to be found when the soldier next to him looked out a window. "S – sir," he quaked, "the Raishans are returning."

"If we retreat any further we might as well surrender Cayza."

"What do we do then, sir?"

Sory pondered this, he raised his hand to his head but was stopped by his helmet, the very same one given to him by General Zlade. That gave him an idea, "you hold out. I'll distract them."

"How?"

A candle was burning on the nightstand behind Sory. He grabbed it then hopped to the nearby bed and ripped off the sheet. Then he charged outside where a column of tens of thousands of Raishans were hulking towards them, almost over them by then. Sory then lit the sheet with the candle and started waving it around while yelling so loud his throat nearly bled. Those soldiers of his that could see him gawked at this odd sight. "What is he doing?" wondered Gyric.

All of the Raishan soldiers noticed this peculiar sight as well, yet it was a general at the front of their column that noticed the helmet on Sory's head.

The sheet had almost been burned all the way through and Sory was beginning to lose hope that his desperate plan might work, when suddenly the entire army of Raishans shifted towards him. Sory then dropped the sheet and headed eastward, pumping his wings so fast one could barely see them. Soon the entire Raishan army had made a great U in the air as Sory turned south, but they were gaining on him.

An arrow zipped passed Sory's head, then another, and another, then spears. Sory looked behind him to see countless Raishans screaming with their beaks wide open and savagery in their eyes. They flung all that they could to kill him. Sory could see unbridled rage in their eyes. He entered trance and used his qi's sight to dodge the deadly metal rain around him. He then dove vertically. The enemy army followed and resembled a great serpent in the sky. The arrows and spears and axes and swords and anything else the Raishans could throw torrented down. Sory crashed through the window of a building. A second later so did one-hundred Raishans. Sory took two flights of stairs in two leaps. All sorts of projectiles continued to be flung at him. The roar of thousands of troops deafened him. Then Sory made it to the ground floor.

From there he jumped through the entrance door and straight into the door of a building across the street. Dozens of enemy soldiers landed within mere feet in every direction. Before they even knew who Sory was he had made it to the next street over. More soldiers landed all around who also reacted too late. Sory leapt to next street, then the next, with fewer and fewer enemy soldiers around him each time.

Finally, Sory ducked into a rather shabby looking place and ran to the top floor. From there, he watched the Raishans scatter about the streets. He had lost them. Relieved, Sory slumped down in the corner of this room, releasing a sigh as he exited trance. When he did exit trance a wall of illness leveled him and he vomited. He remembered Fusna's words about being in trance outside the presence of another Fyzar. After the nausea and migraine had subsided, though not disappeared, he started toward the doorway, broken glass cracking under his armored feet.

Once at the doorway, he only let his head stick out as he peered left, then right, before stepping out. Instantly a Raishan appeared from a stairwell just in front of him. The Raishan smiled, "you're mine, general."

Sory could think of nothing else, he reentered trance and roared, his eyes and drawn sword glowing.

"Ah!" the soldier ran off. Sory stood there, fearing what might happen should he exit trance again. He worked up the courage and let the glow wither. Then a hammer of pain cracked his skull and he slumped to the floor unconscious.

Chapter 21

That night, with a full moon overhead, Ayro, Gyric, and a company's worth of soldiers guarded the front line in an alleyway. Half of the city remained to their north while the rest was occupied by the Raishans. In the alley, Gyric stood watch at its end. He peaked around the corner every now and again, the air filled with the moans of the wounded when the sound of running footsteps made Gyric jump to his feet. Another soldier stood, "I hear it too." The rest stood as well. Finally, Gyric could see someone running down the street. He raised his axe, then swung when the figure had reached him.

"Ah!" yelled Sory.

"Sory?!" Gyric exclaimed in a whisper. "What happened to you?"

Ayro jumped down from the rooftop overlooking the alley. "Sory!"

"We need to fallback," protested Sory.

"Why?" asked Gyric.

"The Raishans are sending their siege weapons onto our side of the river."

"How?" Gyric asked.

"There's a bridge a little ways inland. I saw their weapons while I was looking for the front lines."

"So why retreat?" asked Gyric.

"Those weapons will be in range of Cayza by morning!"

"If we retreat then the Raishans will be able to take the rest of Cayza without a fight. If they do that then they will be able to fire on the encampment!"

"I – I need to think!" Sory slumped down.

Then a courier came up, "are you General Trajetton?"

"Yes I suppose."

"Thanks the Gods! Sir I have been looking for you all night. Commander Relkor wishes to see you." Sory gave his brothers one last look of solidarity before flying off with the courier. The courier led him a few blocks north, flying in between the buildings so as not to be seen, to an indiscrete brick building. They landed just outside. "The commander's in there," informed the courier.

Sory stepped into the darkened structure, it was nice to enter one without having to smash through a window. He followed the hall into a room where Commander Relkor, General Zlade, and a few others who Sory still didn't know the names of stood gathered around a table with a map of the city. This map had red and blue circles scribbled all over it. Sory guessed that the blue were Arktorian positions while red were Raishan. "General Trajetton," started Relkor as he approached Sory, "I believe I owe you an apology." They glared at each other. Sory could see that Relkor hated having to apologize to him, his eyes protruding scorn. An eternity passed before Relkor extended his hand to shake.

Sory shook his hand, "why wasn't there any artillery covering us?"

"It had not been positioned in time. And as I am still your superior you will refrain from speaking to me in such a tone."

"Sorry sir." Silence. "Is it in position now?"

"Yes."

"Where?"

"Some has been positioned on the mountains within the camp, that are closest to the city. The rest on the ridge just outside of it."

"What is the range of our artillery, sir?"

"The farthest out it can reach is about halfway to the harbor."

"That's not very far."

"This is Cayza, all the best weapons are given to those who are guarding much bigger and more important cities, and besides, halfway is far enough to cover our army." Then they heard the distant sound of something rushing through the air, then it turned into many something's. Everyone in the room looked up in bewilderment.

"Incoming!" yelled Sory as he jumped under the table. A boulder ripped through the ceiling. Dust filled the air. Blinded by the thick dust, Sory couldn't even see his own hand in front of his face. He crawled out as the air began to clear, allowing him to see the boulder which had cracked the stone floor like glass, and the debris all around. Sory walked to a dazed guard on the floor. "Are you alright?" The guard nodded back as he stood.

Sory searched for other survivors as they coughed and rose to their feet, but he couldn't find Relkor. As he looked about he noticed how one of the corners of the command table was underneath the boulder. As the dust continued to settle, Sory could soon see General Zlade slumped down in a corner of the room, his body covered in soot, a piece of metal through his chest. "General!" Sory bolted over. "Sir–!"

General Zlade coughed, "I've had worse wounds."

"Come, let's get you out of here." Sory began to lift him.

"No. No. Leave me. You have a responsibility to your soldiers."

"Sir I must get you out of here. Where's General Relkor?"

General Zlade looked to the boulder and Sory followed his eyes. Only then did he notice the blood for the first time as it oozed out from underneath. General Zlade coughed again, "do you know what that means, my boy?"

"What do you mean, sir?"

More coughing, "It means you're the top commander now. Relkor's dead, and I am about to be."

"Sir, I – I-"

"You can do it." General Zlade pointed at Sory. Then slowly – he closed his eyes.

"Sir! Sir!" Sory cried as he shook the general, but to no avail. Sory stood, his eyes fixed on the general for one last second. Then he stumbled outside.

Sory, with his head hung, and his stomach in knots, sat down on the muddy street as his soldiers ran about him. All of their lives, as well the lives of countless others now rested heavily on his shoulders. The fear manifested itself as pain and Sory curled up with his arms around his navel. He couldn't do it.

Sory limped out into the street, weak and horrified, only to slump down against another building and put his head in his hands. Then Ayro scrambled up, "Sory! What happened?!"

"You want to know what happened?" Sory gave Ayro a burning glare, tears rolling down his cheek. "Do you really want to know what happened?! We all just lost the battle that's what happened!" He put his head back in his hands.

"What do you mean?"

"The commanders were all just killed – and left me in charge! And now we're all doomed!"

"Why are we doomed?"

"Because I can't command an entire battlefield!"

"Why not? You saw this attack coming didn't you?"

"Ayro–"

"And you've managed to keep the Raishans from taking the city."

"Those were smaller fights, not an entire battle field."

"Still though, and there are some other generals left right? They can help you."

Sory removed his head from his hands. "Yes, perhaps you're right." He then marched back inside through the griffins still within as they recovered from the shock. Sory snatched the map off the table. "Come with me," the others exchanged looks as their new commander rushed back outside into an undamaged building across the street. A café with a few roundtables spread around with barstools upside-down on top of them. Sory knocked the barstools off the closest table with one swipe of his arm then laid the map down.

"Hey!" yelled the bartender, "what's happening out there?"

"Leave!" Sory ordered, and two guards hauled the bartender outside as Sory's half-dozen commanders gathered around. "What we must do first is organize. Bring all the dead and wounded back to the encampment, anyone who can fly and or run does not count as wounded. We also need to set up a system of communication. We'll use the side streets and back allies as safe passageways for the couriers."

"The streets?" a colonel interrupted, "why the streets? Why not have them fly?"

"They can still fly but in between the buildings so as not to be seen. Now I want half the medics treating the already wounded, the other half in the front lines ready to receive casualties."

"But sir," a rather tall general cut in, "what about the coast? The Raishan fleet continues to pound us."

"We'll divide the medics into thirds then. Now how many battle ready soldiers do I have?"

"About sixty thousand, sir," answered a somewhat older general.

"That's more than I thought," said Sory.

"It used to be seventy five."

"We took fifteen-thousand casualties in one day?!" The general's face grew sorrowful. "Damn. How many does the enemy have?" The officers hesitated as Sory waited. "Well?!"

The older general finally spoke, "sir, we estimate they now have about fifty thousand in the city alone." Sory hung his head. "They may have as many as another fifteen to twenty thousand on that fleet ready to take the coast. Of course we have no idea how many more they yet have across the bay." Sory's head ached again, he grabbed it and cringed. "Sir?"

Sory looked at his hand. "They could exterminate us now if they wanted." Sory turned his hand into a fist and slammed the table. He let out a weary sigh, his head still hanging. He then looked to the map, at all the little red circles and counted fifteen. "What do these red circles mean?"

"Raishan strongpoints, sir," answered the colonel.

"Strongpoints?"

"Large buildings where they have a good number of soldiers, fortifications, and high up hidden sentry points so as to see as far as possible," said the colonel.

Sory studied these strongpoints. At first glance they appeared random, but he soon realized the design was deliberate. "Clever Reds."

"Sir?"

"The arrangement of their strongpoints, they're checkered so that if one's attacked there's always two diagonal to it that can act as support." The generals didn't know what he was getting at. "We must take Cayza back to win the battle. The only way we can do that is to get the enemy out of their strongpoints."

The colonel cut in again, "but sir, you just said that if–"

"I know what I said. We are going to get the Raishans out of their strongpoints, but not by attacking, but by retreating."

"Sir?" asked the confused colonel.

"It's a full moon. They'll be able to see every move we make. We can use that to our advantage by sending small amounts of soldiers a little ways up north. The Raishans will think we're retreating when in reality those soldiers will hide in the forest where the enemy cannot see them. Then those soldiers will sneak up to the Raishan siege weapons on the road to the east. Meanwhile, with our forces depleted and the enemy already outnumbering us, they'll advance." Sory paused. "Does this city have a sewer system?"

"Yes I believe so," answered the colonel.

"Perfect, while some of our forces are flying into the forest we'll sneak the rest into the sewers. Meanwhile the enemy will advance onto our half of the city where they'll find no one. Then our forces will come out of the sewers on their side and take out their undefended strongpoints."

"Sir, when do you plan on doing all of this?" asked the older general.

"We'll start tonight so that we may take the southern half of Cayza by tomorrow afternoon at the latest."

"Sir we cannot accomplish all of this in one night and day!" exclaimed the older general.

"We can't but we must."

"What happens when they notice they've been tricked and turn around?" asked another general.

"They'll be on our side of the city, and our side is in range of our artillery. After that we'll-" Sory thought, "we'll disguise ourselves as Raishan soldiers."

"Disguise -? Sir-?" said the older general.

"We'll take the uniforms of the prisoners we capture in the strongpoints."

"And that's another thing, how do you know this surprise behind the lines is going to work?" asked the colonel.

Sory smiled, "because the Raishans, like you, underestimate the power of surprise. Also, as we're attacking their rear in the city, we'll give some sort of signal to tell the soldiers in the forests to attack the siege weapons."

"What about our artillery on the ridge?" A general pointed to the ridge that defined the depression that Cayza rested in, where the artillery was placed. "How many soldiers will we need to protect those guns?"

Sory tipped his head and thought for a minute. "We need none."

"Sir?"

"The Raishans will be advancing at the same time as our attack behind their lines, they will not have enough time to reach our artillery before having to turn around. Plus they'll have to divert even more soldiers to defend their siege weapons."

"And that's something else, sir. What if they call in reinforcements? For all we know they could have another army in reserve across the bay." the older general commented.

"We must take that risk." Sory turned to the others. "We have about sixty-thousand troops altogether, how many are in the city?"

"A little over fifteen thousand, sir," answered the colonel.

"How many are guarding and manning the artillery?"

"About ten thousand."

"How many are guarding the coast?"

"About twenty-five thousand, sir."

"Fifty thousand, leaving ten thousand in reserve." Sory tapped his fingers to his beak as he thought. "We leave five thousand in the encampment and ten thousand on the coast, the rest go to Cayza. Any questions? No? Then let us begin." Within minutes, Arktorian soldiers were being snuck into the city within supply carriages. Meanwhile, other soldiers were dispersed to find maps of the sewers. All the while the Raishan siege weapons fired at Cayza every once in a while.

By a couple hours after midnight, with the extra soldiers in and distributed around Cayza, Sory began to send other soldiers northward a few companies at a time. They flew high and their armor glistened in the full moon. Sory wanted them to be seen, he wanted his enemy to think that they were retreating.

Ayro was among the first of those Arktorians to retreat north. They had been told to fly to the bank of a river about ten miles north. From there they were to rush back to the battlefield and silently position themselves as close to the Raishan siege weapons as possible. They were to attack upon seeing a flaming arrow in the sky.

Ayro and the four hundred other griffins around him flew as calmly and orderly as possible so as not to arose enemy suspicion. When they reached the riverbank, with another group of soldiers a minute behind them, they dashed south through the cover of the thick woods. Sunrise was but a couple hours away.

A low but constant rustling followed this small army as it hurried through the trees, an army able to run quite quickly despite their battle armor. Forest animals looked on then scurried away. The moon's light split through the tree branches in slender shards of silver and shimmered against their armor.

In Cayza, the Raishan commander requested they move their siege weapons closer to the city, but was denied. Ramous feared that the Arktorians would attack those weapons if given the chance, unaware of those that moved through the forest. Meanwhile the Raishans in the city itself were calling in their own reinforcements. By morning, that garrison would be restored to its original size.

Morning was nearing and most of Sory's army had entered the incomplete and shoddy sewers. With not enough room, many were forced to wait on the ground floors and basements of buildings. Sory made sure though that the Raishan scouts could not see them. It was then that the Raishan high command decided to advance, as well to bring their siege weapons closer to the city, away from the forest. By then the sun could almost be seen.

*

The very top of the sun could be seen as blue-gray light filtered through the buildings. An Arktorian sentry was hidden underneath of a wheat bag on the roof of a building when he saw the storm of Raishans rise into the sky. He pushed off his wheat bag and darted down to the basement where a trap door was. He opened it and poked his head inside, the fowl stench of the sewers filled his nostrils. "Sir, the Raishans are here!"

"Good," said Sory, he drew in a deep breath, "let's go," and so he led his army south, moving silently and not all that quickly so as to give their foes as much time as possible to move north.

Back in the forest, Ayro and the rest of the retreating forces had made it to the edge of the forest only to find the Raishan siege weapons lumbering toward Cayza. Ayro looked on and leaned into their commander, a colonel, and whispered, "why are they moving away, sir?"

"I don't know, son. Maybe they have caught wind of us." Dread filled the colonel's eyes.

Back in the sewers, Sory's army had reached enemy territory, the minute of reckoning upon them. Sory stood below one of the street covers. "Archer," one with a lit arrow walked over next to him, two soldiers then lifted him up. The archer lifted the street cover, then scanned the street. Finding it empty, he threw off the cover and fired his arrow. All at once, the rest of the troopers stormed up.

Each and every soldier knew their targets, the strongpoints scattered about the city. Most of the Raishans were still asleep and only had a hand full of active sentries. They had been told that the

Arktorians were retreating and that the battle was won, thus diminishing their readiness. As the Arks took back the city one block at a time, the Raishan high command awoke to the situation around them. They called in the siege weapons and navy.

Back in the forest, Ayro and the rest of the griffins he was with watched as the siege weapons, the ballistae and trebuchets, halted to be prepared for firing. By now the distance between those giant weapons and the forest was such that they resembled toys. Ayro then spotted the arrow rising into the sky. "There's the signal!" He waited for his colonel to order attack, only for him not to, he simply stood there and watched. "Sir! That was the signal to attack!"

The colonel faltered, "soldier, if we attack now with those weapons so far away they'll have enough time to see us and maybe even form up and defend themselves!" Then those weapons commenced firing.

Sory surveyed the battle while flying over the city. His soldiers had stormed almost all of the strongpoints when he heard a whizzing. He looked east, hundreds of rocks and even more bolts had been fired. The bolts, those giant arrows, impaled several griffins at a time, Arktorian and Raishan. The rocks walloped buildings and knocked them down, killing dozens at a time. Screaming and dust filled the air.

Sory could see nothing. He had lost control of the battlefield and could no longer see his or the enemy's soldiers. He glowered toward where he knew Ayro and the others to be, "TAKE THOSE SIEGE WEAPONS!"

Back in the forest, "sir!" yelled Ayro, "we must move!"

"You will be mindful of your place, soldier!"

A soldier behind them pointed north, "look!"

"Oh no," said Ayro.

Back over the city, Sory forced himself to think of a new plan when another red cloud caught his eye. The army of Raishans that had seized the northern half of Cayza were returning. "No," he peered to the siege weapons, "COME ON! ATTACK!"

Back in the forest, "SIR!" screamed Ayro.

The colonel finally raised his sword into the air. "Attack!"

"Finally," groaned Ayro. They then all took flight without even bothering to form up. They cried out until they could taste blood. Those Raishans guarding the siege weapons panicked and flew off, leaving a few behind who were then captured.

Relieved, Sory flew down to a pre-agreed meeting point in the city. There he met some of his officers, "are we ready?"

"We're ready, sir," a lieutenant replied.

"Excellent," and Sory removed his helmet. He and the rest of his fellow red griffins changed uniforms as the remainder hid.

As the Raishans flew over the presumably Arktorian occupied section of the city, they were surprised when resistance did not meet them. Their commander spotted a high ranking officer flagging him down and landed before him. "Where are the Arks?" he asked.

This soldier, a captain, answered, "they attempted to launch a surprise attack but we repelled them, sir."

"Are there prisoners?"

"Yes sir, this way." This captain led the commander to a nearby building where about fifty bound and gagged prisoners rested within.

"They're all red griffins," commented the commander. "Shouldn't there be Lessers with them?" The captain then looked at the commander, showing him his face for the first time.

One of the prisoners was wriggling about and managed to spit out his gag. "Sir!" he screamed in Raishan, "they're the Arks!" A soldier slammed him in the head with the butt of a spear.

Sory removed his helmet and pointed his sword at the commander's neck. "Reach for the sky, sir." In unison, the Arktorians pointed their weapons at the commander and his entourage, then a dozen non-red Arktorians charged in. "Order your forces to stand down," commanded Sory.

Just outside the forest, the Raishan prisoners were being escorted back to the camp along with their siege weapons as Ayro and the rest of them celebrated. One particularly happy soldier climbed atop one of the catapults, flapping his wings and yelled uncontrollably. More joined in. Everyone else cheered on from below.

Arrows then split the air, knocking the ecstatic Arktorians from the siege weapons and sending the rest scattering under the cover of the forest as legions of Raishans swept toward them from their encampment. "Damn that's a lot of Raishans," said Ayro.

Back in the city, more celebrating as soldiers jeered their prisoners. Cayza's inhabitants, natives and colonists alike, emerged from their basements and attics. Then they all began to pelt the prisoners with rocks, bricks and whatever else they could throw. Some even flew overhead and dropped rocks and bits of debris while others tossed stuff from the windows of their apartments. Soldiers padded Sory on the back, hugged him, and shook his hands in an ocean of euphoria. Sory smiled back at the jubilated faces of the colonists in

their windows above as he strolled along. Then Sory caught a glimpse
of something in the sky. He stopped, then sprung to the roof of a
building. Petrified, he absorbed the sight of the flying doom rumbling
toward them.

Sory then faced his army, only terror did not fill his heart, guilt
did. "Soldiers," he mumbled, "Soldiers!" he yelled. "SOLDIERS!" he
cried, and gradually their euphoria terminated as they too saw what he
had.

"Sir!" a soldier yelled and pointed to the bay. From the thinning
fog emerged a few Raishan warships, followed by more, and more, and
more.

Sory flew to the docks with more officers gathering around him,
their eyes immovable from the monster vessels leading this fleet.
"Super-monitors, sir, warships with mortars at their bows, mortars
powerful enough to level entire castles with one shell."

A colonel beside Sory then cried out, "SIRS!" He pointed to the
Raishan ships that had originally bombarded the coast, as thousands of
troops departed from them, toward the Arktorian artillery positioned
along the ridge of the depression that Cayza laid in. "We had them, sir.
What happened?"

"If I knew – it would not have happened."

Chapter 22

The super-monitors faced their broadsides toward Cayza, whilst loading their mortars. Sory watched as one-dozen sailors per ship loaded each mortar with a shell large enough to comfortably fit three griffins. Once loaded, the mortars were pointed up and Sory looked on helplessly as the artillery commander on the ship closest to him, a ship so close he could see the whites of their eyes, raised his hand into the air. Then he thrust that hand down. The explosion walloped everybody off their feet, burst their ears, and battered their skulls. The entire bay rippled and the air crackled. "RETREAT!" Sory screamed.

The asteroid of a shell struck a nearby warehouse, which was then annihilated in a fiery detonation. Then the rest of the super-monitors opened fire with their mortars and cannons. So disturbing the air that the sound could almost be seen. The cannonballs shredded the city. The ground quaked as if a god had stepped onto it. Bricks, splinters, and body parts sprayed about. Airborne shrapnel impaled soldiers and colonists alike as they fled. Entire buildings imploded and walls crumbled, crushing yet more. The meteor shower of mortar shells atomized entire edifices in a flash. Soldiers and colonists grabbed those of their loved ones who could not run or fly and dragged them away, all sobbing and screaming, only to be crushed under tons of bricks or wood. Some made it into the air when the Raishans began firing their flack. The flack exploded and shredded all those nearby with thousands of bits twisted red-hot iron.

Sory flew amongst these griffins. Once more he flapped his wings to a degree of near invisibility. Yet an excruciating guilt weighed him down. He would have stayed behind and let himself die, but the will to live superseded his heavy stomach.

It took an eternity before these tens of thousands of soldiers and colonials had made it out of range of the Raishan fire. Ahead, their artillery was firing like mad at their attackers, attackers who began to retreat. A soldier flew up next to Sory, "they're retreating! Why are they retreating?!"

Sory did not care why, he was too relieved. He looked around at those who had survived, soldiers and colonists alike, there were many more than he thought. That was when he realized something, "they think we're all soldiers. They think that they're outnumbered!"

Within minutes, the Raishans had returned to their ships off the coast. These ships that had begun the battle had fallen back out of firing range of the coast, floating eerily silently. Sory went directly to headquarters. Inside of headquarters, the commanders sulked with their heads in their hands. Some sobbed silently. All were utterly demoralized. Sory had felt guilty before. Now though disappointment flooded his heart. "WHAT IS THIS?! WHY ARE YOU ALL MOPING ABOUT LIKE SLUGS?!"

A general shot to his feet, "BECAUSE WE HAVE LOST SIR!"

"No we have not! Not yet! How many troops do we have?"

This general collapsed back to the muddy ground. Another answered with his head in his hands, "not enough."

"How many?!" Sory insisted. He went over to, then leaned into this general's face, "I want an exact number."

The general removed his head from his hands, "approximately fifty thousand remaining, sir."

"We suffered that many casualties? Fifteen thousand?" The general's head fell back into his palms. Sory stared forward into space for long while. "We must form a perimeter."

"Oh, what?" another standing general grumbled with his finger pointed. "You will keep fighting? What about the soldiers?"

"What about the soldiers?! What about the soldiers that will be lost if we do not hold?!" The general's brow lowered. "What about the soldiers that have already died?! They died fighting for this city, and if we stop fighting for it their deaths would have been in-vain!"

"How many more will die if we do not retreat?" Sory opened his beak, but didn't answer. "You do not know! You are not a general! You're a foot soldier! You cannot lead an army into battle – you're too young! You don't know how!" The general looked to the others. "What we must do is organize a tactical retreat! We could then choose our battleground and could reinforce ourselves. What say you, Trajetton?"

Sory thought, "we do not have time to reinforce?"

"No, sir."

"If we retreat the Raishans will be able to land their siege weapons."

"This is a risk we must take, sir."

Sory sighed, "very well, we retreat." They commenced organizing all of their materiel. They folded their tents. They stored their munitions. They mobilized their cannons. They gathered their food, and everything else in possession. The Raishan soldiers on the coastal fleet departed for Cayza, as were thousands more from across the bay. They consolidated just east of the city.

The Arktorians had organized their materiel and began to load it onto carriages, some of their heavier things could not be loaded. Sory decided to leave that which was heaviest. In that time though the enemy had situated their siege weapons. They were readying them for advancement. The Arktorians separated the wounded from the dead. They separated the wounded between those who were and were not savable. The Raishans had landed the last of their troops outside of Cayza.

Sory realized the enemy was nearly ready to strike. He ordered his troops to fall into their battalions. Yet they had been scattered about to such a degree that they could not find their battalions. The situation devolved into chaos as tens of thousands of griffins scrambled about like so many ants. Sory peered over to Cayza, the Raishans mere minutes from taking flight. He had an idea and gathered his generals in headquarters, "our soldiers cannot organize," he drew squares on the map of the battleground, "we designate certain areas for each battalion, then their commanders will fly out there and yell out what he is commander of." They drew up the designated zones. The Raishans had reloaded the cannons on all of their ships.

Sory watched both his and his enemy's armies consolidate. The Raishans finished before his did, yet did not take to the wing. There was something that Sory did not know.

When Sory's troops finally formed up relief filled his heart. A junior officer approached him, "we are ready, sir."

"To the wing then," proclaimed Sory.

"Yes sir," the officer saluted, then motioned for an archer to give the signal for Sory's order. The archer fired an arrow with a green flame into the air. The army then took flight starting with the battalions in the front who gradually, almost at an excruciating speed, climbed into the air. The enemy followed suite.

Sory saw this, "they are flying much faster than we are! Order our forces to accelerate!" The archer gave the signal. The Arktorians did as ordered. Their pursuers continued to gain on them. There were still thousands of Arktorians on the ground. The enemy came within crossbow range of the Arktorian army's rear.

The Raishan crossbowmen fired in unison. A wall of arrows slaughtered entire companies. The Raishan fleet along the coast opened fire. Shells whined over Sory's head next to headquarters. The flack shredded his army's western flank. Sory collapsed to his knees. The junior officer ran up to him, "SIR! SIR! WE MUST DO SOMETHING!"

"O – order them to bank east!" The archer gave the signal, but to no avail. Sory's army began to break apart all the way down to the platoons, units of only one-dozen soldiers. The crossbowmen picked the Arktorians off individually. The Raishan hoplites and lancers swooped down in formation. They shattered the Arktorian army.

Sory stood there helplessly. His eyes wide and tearing. His beak half open and quaking. His mind imploding in on itself with the comprehension of his unspeakable failure. He dropped to his hands. He dug his talons into the mud. His body trembled. The Raishans shells refused to cease annihilating his troops – who never ceased screaming.

Sory heard even more cannon fire, twice as much. He felt that he could kill himself. "sir look!" the junior officer pointed north.

Three-dozen warships were lined up. They broadsided the Raishans. More followed behind them. An Arktorian fleet had emerged from the fog. They fired onto the northern flank of the Raishan fleet. The rest ceased firing onto the Arktorian army and retreated.

As the first few Raishan ships slipped below the waves an Arktorian army swooped in from the fog. They swung in a semi-circle straight into the scattered Raishan army over the encampment. The Arktorian archers fired like mad. The lancers and hoplites sliced through like a red hot knife through warmed butter. The Raishans stumbled for the bay, abandoning their siege weapons. Their King watched, "we cannot allow the enemy to possess those siege weapons. Destroy them," he ordered a senior general.

"But sir, their crews are still manning them," argued the senior general.

"DESTROY THEM!" screamed the King. Down in the bay, the Raishan fleet then opened up on its own siege weapons. Those manning them died with faces not of fear, but of confusion. Further north, the Raishan coastal fleet had begun a fighting retreat back to the bay, a third of them already sunk. The Arktorians landed in Cayza screaming at the tops of their lungs in celebration, for once. Sory heard a voice from behind, "anything else that you needed cleaned up?"

Sory whisked himself around. "Ruby!" she hugged him.

"How did you – how are you-?"

Ruby smiled, "it's a pleasure seeing you too." Sory smiled, and they hugged again.

Over on the Raishan side of the bay, General Trajetton watched his soldiers fly overhead. Another general stood beside him, "the enemy has received substantial reinforcements, sir. Shall I order retreat?"

Trajetton opened his beak when the King interrupted, "no," he growled from behind, "we will annihilate them yet."

Chapter 23

Ayro sprinted to headquarters from Cayza, smiling from ear to ear. "We've done it, Sory! We've done it!" Sory smiled, but then he looked back to the encampment. The smile vanished as he looked over the countless wounded and dead. Ayro did not understand why the happiness had fled Sory's face. "What's wrong?"

Flies swarmed around the bodies. The air was so thick with blood one could stick out their tongue and taste it. "Look," said Sory. His friends looked where he was. The wounded were segregated from the dead and carried off. Many of the survivors could not handle the scene and collapsed, sobbing like hatchlings. The sorrowful wailed more than the wounded. That noise stabbed into the four friends next to headquarters. "There are so many dead."

From behind came Zat's voice, "count them lucky," Sory turned to the old sailor, "only the dead have seen the end of war, my boy."

A general called to Sory, "General Trajetton, an officer's meeting has been called in the command tent."

Sory nodded. Bahren turned to him and asked, "General?"

"It's a rather long story." Sory said before going inside. Headquarters, which now also had the generals and admirals from the newly arrived army, contained a mixed atmosphere of hope for victory, and sorrow for the dead. More than anything else though, there was the question of retreat – or fight. "What are our casualties?" Sory asked.

One old general sighed heavily. "Not including the newly arrived soldiers, I'd estimate," he thought, "at least ten thousand, sir."

Commodore Pdosvine, from the newly arrived army interrupted, "how many have you suffered so far?"

The old general replied, "plenty."

Sory turned to Commodore Pdosvine. "How many soldiers do you have?"

"Forty thousand, sir," the commodore replied.

Sory sighed. "I don't know if I can ask our soldiers to go through any more." He glared forward with an unsteadiness in his eyes. "Prepare our forces for battle."

The old general grew enraged. "You cannot be serious! Why would you continue this hell?!"

Commodore Pdosvine answered in Sory's stead, "well of course we should!"

"You have not been here! You do not know what hell these soldiers have endured!"

Commodore Pdosvine turned to Sory, "if we are to fight we need a plan, sir."

The old general pointed his finger, "I will not have this entire army lost because of you!"

Commodore Pdosvine jumped to his feet, "I am trying to save this army!" Then they all stood and started yelling and pointing at each other as Sory watched. His eyes darted back and forth while being all too aware that the Raishans were to attack soon. He knew that even though so many soldiers had been lost, many more would be should his army retreat.

Sory's chest convulsed as his heart pounded. Fear-laced adrenalin fired through his veins. He had to escape. He ran outside to the cliffs overlooking the edge of the ocean. *Sory,* came Fusna's voice. *You are lost.*

I don't know what to do, sir. I know that we must stand, but I also know that if we do we may lose anyway. He paused, *and I don't think my soldiers are willing to fight anymore either. I have been with them the entire time – and I know that I have had enough.*

Have they *had enough? They know what is at risk as much as you.* Sory thought about this, *and Sory, you are a remarkable tactician. You* can *figure a way to victory.*

My idea to take Cayza failed, sir.

Did it? You captured Cayza and then only lost it due to an unforeseen factor.

"Yes, yes that's true."

And Sory, if you remember anything from your training, remember that all that stands in your way – is yourself.

Fusna's voice disappeared. Sory turned to see thousands of his soldiers watching him, their lives waiting on his words. He could not lose this battle, not because of what would be lost, but who. He stared into the faces of those who would perish. Yet so many had already gone. How many more would be before, and if, he achieved victory? There was no real hope of victory. Hope was gone. But hope does not heal wounds, nor does it comfort those driven insane by battle, or do anything else. It simply teases you. It gives you a fantasy that distracts from reality. So then perhaps it was good that they had no hope. Perhaps it was good that they had nothing to lose. "Soldiers…do you still wish to fight? I ask you honestly. Through all that I have put you through, will you still fight for me?"

No one spoke for a while. Then Ruby answered, "Sory, we would go through all for you."

"Why? Why have you followed me through all that has happened?"

Ayro answered, "there would have been many more dead if it wasn't for you, Sory."

Gyric yelled up next, "and we know what's at stake."

Sory nodded. "You are all willing to continue then? Good, because we have an enemy to fight, and he may be strong, and he may have greater numbers," he paused, "but despite this we have stood against him! And we have stopped him! WE have all fought valiantly! Many have died valiantly, and it is they that we fight for as well, just as much as our nation! We will FIGHT for them, and we will DIE for them! For that is what they have done for us! And we are all united in the fight for our fallen brothers just as much as our still living ones, and just as much as our country's FREEDOM! Because we ARE brothers! We ARE soldiers," he paused, "and we are KNIGHTS!" Sory unsheathed his sword and thrust it into the air. All of his fellow soldiers cheered and swung their weapons in the air in a unified battle cry. Sory stepped down and toward his generals. He stared them in the eyes, "let us then end this battle."

Chapter 24

Whilst Sory and his generals contemplated their final stand, King
Sairus stood at the mouth of the bay. Watching. Waiting. Waves
crashed against the rocks far below, and the winds gusted without
remorse. Ramous came up beside him, "what do you think, Your
Greatness?"

"I think that your son is planning something."

"Perhaps, sir."

"It is very odd that he has become their commander. Though, I
must admit, he has proven himself a worthy adversary. He is young
and inexperienced, yet those only make him–" he searched for the
word, "braver."

"Or foolish perhaps."

"Perhaps, but he certainly has his father's blood within his veins.
He has held out longer than I ever would have expected. Our next
offensive, however, should be his undoing. Young Tysorious will lose,
and Platu will belong to Raishany, as will Tysorious. Yet if by some
miracle he does not lose," his voice suddenly became harsher, his pupils
glowed red, and Ramous could see the grass under the King's feet
burning, "then I will be forced to take measures into my own hands."
Then the Arktorian army began to rise into the air, only it was moving

in a great vortex. King Sairus could not believe it. "They are forming a wall. Your son is very tenacious, Trajetton." Ramous just looked on. "Very well then, we shall do the same."

In his tent, Sory had dressed himself in battle armor. He reached for his general's helmet until, from the corner of his eye, he saw his old one laying in the mud. He picked it up and rubbed the mud off. He clutched it within his hands before putting it on. Out on the rocky cliffs, he watched his army as if formed up while his new fleet assembled for battle as well. Then he saw the Raishans assembling as well. He watched them for a moment, then was about to go to the front of his army's formation when Dyricio flew up, "Sory wait! I wanted to say good-bye, and-" he slumped his head to the side, "sorry." he mumbled.

"Nothing to apologize for."

Dyricio nodded. "Well, good-bye, Sory." They shook hands and hugged.

With that, Sory flew to his position at his army's front as it slowly advanced. Below, the Arktorian fleet began its advance as well, rocking with the rough sea. The Raishans watched from their side. One of Ramous' subordinate officers spoke, "what are they doing?"

The Ark fleet reached the bay's mouth and spread across it. Ramous knew what was happening. "They are attempting to trap our fleet." The Raishan vessels then headed for the Arktorians'.

Zat looked on with a telescope. "They're taking the bate!" he yelled to his crew who all cheered. "Battle positions!" He then turned back and peered through his telescope again. "Damn."

Far above, Sory noticed what Zat just had, "no!"

"What's wrong?" asked Bahren.

"Only half of the Raishan fleet is moving out of the harbor." Silence overtook. Sory could see a squall coming in from the ocean. They could not fight in a squall. He didn't know what to do. His soldiers all looked to him.

Finally Ruby had to ask, "Sory! What do we do?"

Back on the Raishan side, Ramous turned to a subordinate general, "move the wall forward." Their entire army then lumbered its way forward. The last few companies fell in at the rear. The army's front gradually fixed itself into a flat plane, resembling a great flying wall.

Their opposites had done the same. The two rumbled to collision. Sory made his decision, "we press our advance."

"Sory!" exclaimed Bahren, "this will not work! When two armies face off in wall formation it is always the side with the greater numbers that wins, and we have far fewer!"

"Which is why we will not hit them straight on!" Sory then gave the order. "ASCEND!" He reared up. His army followed. His father watched intently. They rose at a shallow angle, pumping their wings as their armor dragged them down. Cayza was just to their south. The Raishans still advanced horizontally. Sory estimated the distance. He estimated when the perfect time would be to spring his trap.

From the Raishan cliffs, Ramous finally realized what was about to happen, "ORDER OUR ARMY TO ASCEND!"

"CHAAARGE!" Sory screamed. He pointed his sword downward. His lancers held their shields and spears out in front as they all shredded down. Seconds passed. The Raishan army seemed to be coming up to them. Sory looked up, the top of his army slammed the Raishan's above him. He closed his eyes. BAM! He smashed through the Raishan lancers. He swept his sword and shield about without even aiming. He slashed armor and flesh alike. The deafening roar of one-hundred thousand soldiers ripped his ears and the inside of his skull.

At the mouth of the bay, Commodore Pdosvine stood at the wheel of his flagship. "OPEN FIRE!" he ordered. Their cannons released their fiery hell unto their adversaries. Hot iron blazed through ships. It sent nails, glass, splinters the size of swords, and all sorts of tiny bits of twisted metal through the air. This shrapnel sliced all in its path as the atmosphere crackled like thunder. Masts collapsed. Sailors were flung into the sea. Blood and debris already filling it. Cries in between the cannon salvos filled the air.

Ramous watched in an enraged horror. "ORDER OUR ARMY TO REFORM!" he screamed at his generals. Meanwhile, the Arktorian army had blasted its way to the heart of what was once the Raishan formation, a formation which now crumbled. The Raishans scattered like a swarm of locusts and scuttled back across the bay.

The rest of the Raishan fleet then went to the aid of it sister ships. Meanwhile, wingless griffins helped run the Arktorian land cannons into Cayza, terrifying those few Raishans left in the city. The fled alongside those already fleeing. Within a few minutes the Arktorian cannons were positioned and prepared on the docks, pointing at the Raishan fleet. "FIRE!" yelled the artillery commander. They let loose at the exact same time as the Arktorian ships. The black-powder magazine of one of the super-monitors was hit, exploding the vessel in two.

From the Raishan cliffs, Ramous and King Sairus watched, a deathly infuriation in Ramous' eyes when his King spoke, "so it *is* true then."

"Your Greatness?"

"Tysorious Trajetton is the Fyzar from the prophecy…but not for too much a greater time." A red glow then filled the King's eyes, then spread to his face, beak, and then the rest of his body. He glowed as an inferno, burning all but his armor away, which disappeared within the flame as the grass below his feet turned to ash. Sairus then leaned forward, flapped his wings, and blasted like a comet through the air and into the stormy gray clouds above.

Chapter 25

From the corner of his eye, Sory saw a red flash blast into the sky. Ayro saw it too. "What was that?"

"I'm not sure," said Sory. The air rumbled. Sory could see a faint red glow bleeding through the clouds above. He squinted as it grew brighter. "BREAK FORMATION!" A fireball tore through the army, throwing screaming griffins, some with their bodies burned.

"Whoa!" exclaimed Ruby, "what was that – an asteroid?!"

Sory watched the fireball as it turned back toward them. "No, it was the King." The formation scattered as the King then levitated in midair over the Arktorian half of the bay. As Arktorian soldiers flew towards camp he swung his arm up and a flurry of rocks and boulders from the cliffs were thrown into the air. The smaller rocks smacked soldiers as they flew, the larger ones knocked some out of the air.

An outrageous hatred swelled within Sory's gut. His veins became warm, his heart beat faster, he tightened his grip on his sword and glowered. He dove for the King. Ruby tried to stop him, but it was too late. "Sory – NO!"

"SAIRUS!"

The King turned as Sory's eyes and blade then glowed white. He smiled, "finally." Sory belted out a battle cry. He pulled back his bolt sword to swing. The King swatted him with his great hand. Sory tumbled down and dropped his shield. He righted himself a second before crashing onto a rocky peninsula on the Arktorian coast. Out of trance, he struggled to stand when a fireball exploded underneath him. He dropped his sword as he hurtled head-over-heels through the air before falling back onto the hard rock.

Sory opened his eyes with the ground against his face and rubble all around. Sheer pain struck the inside of his brain as he struggled to his hands and feet. Then the pain suddenly pounded and he winced. His ears rung so loudly he couldn't even hear the crashing waves below. On his knees, Sory squeezed his head, he could feel a stinging in his skin and counted four long ribbons of this pain, four burning scars from Sairus' talons, he could smell the burning flesh.

A deep and powerful, yet low and base groan rumbled from overhead. Sory removed his helmet and clambered to his feet. Sairus thundered down onto the peninsula and shook it, making Sory fall over. He sat back up and grimaced at the King who returned his glare with one of utter condescension. "Tysorious Trajetton, I would have expected more." His glowing redness slowly began to disappear.

"My name is Sory." Sory whispered as the last of Sairus' red glow disappeared, moving toward his eyes like water toward a drain. His glowing red feathers glowed the same way Sory's eyes glowed white, but it reminded Sory of the red glow of the Slithus' open wounds when the rain hit them.

As if correcting the bad behavior of a child, the King snapped, "What did you just say?" Sory didn't reply. Sairus smiled. "Fusna seems to have taught you all but to stand up for yourself – too bad." Sory rubbed his head, his migraine persisted. "Your head hurts, and I suppose that you have been vomiting as well, Fusna must not have impressed upon you the impact of trance sickness. Did he not warn you about entering trance outside of the presence of another Fyzar?" Sory didn't answer. "I remember when I had to fear such things. That was a long time ago though. Someday you too will no longer have to endure the limitations of this half-mortal state – that is if you are taught by me."

"You assume much."

"Hah! I assume nothing," Sairus paused, "you have much to learn, Tysorious. Someday though, someday you will know your highest potential. It may take as much as a century, but you will."

"And how do you know that?"

"Because, boy, I have had the time to hone my skills. I suspect you have heard the three century old story of the Raishan Queen who wed an Ark Fyzar, giving birth to a Prince?" Sory kept staring. "Well Tysorious, I was that Prince. And do you remember how the prince killed all of those Ark Fyzars except for one little hatchling?" He paused. "Do you know who that hatchling was?"

Through his gasping Sory managed the name. "Ramous."

Sairus smiled. "Clearly, Tysorious, you know not with which you mess. For I do not know if Fusna taught you this or not, but when one Fyzar kills another – he absorbs their power!" His voice then calmed into an eerie way as he continued. "So centuries ago, when I terminated those Ark Fyzars – one can imagine my omnipotence." He paused. "I can feel your hope ssshhhriveling, boy. I also know about the dreams." Horrified awe filled Sory's bewildered eyes. "Visions of the future. You know your destiny. It has already been written. You know this, Tysorious, deny it to yourself you may, that will change nothing. For Raishany will take this retched planet and turn it into something spectacular!" Sairus shook his fist, then brought back that eerie tone. "To achieve this dream – this war must be led with unprecedented brutality, for it is the only way to subdue the Lessers – those creatures that are destroying this world and have the nerve to defend themselves!" The King shook his raised fist again, then calmed himself. "Tysorious, you know that what I speak is true, and now you know – what must be done."

Sory thought to himself, *Demented old fool, the Lessers are not responsible. Destroying them will achieve nothing. What is responsible for the rise of Raishany is something entirely different.*

"The rise of Raishany and the subjugation of its Lessers is no coincidence. Listen to only my words and ignore your doubt about them." And that reminded Sory of something, of what Fusna had taught him a long time ago – to believe in what he himself thought and to ignore his doubt. Only here, Sairus was doubt.

Sory peered into the King's hellish eyes, eyes that began burning once more. "No," King Sairus tipped his head, "no I will not listen to your words."

"Do not talk to me like that, boy."

"I can talk to you however I want to, I am not Ramous...I – am not – your puppet!" Sory stood. "And another thing, Arktorion is not dying!"

"It is a nation falling apart."

Coolly, Sory continued on, "what do you care anyway? The worse Arktorion is, the better for you. So what? What are you going to do?

Try to make it better? If you did take it over I doubt you would. I have seen the future! I have seen how you intend to run the world and it's hell! And if making the world worse makes one a Lesser – then what does that make you?!"

King Sairus snarled and Sory felt the rocks under his feet vibrate, but then the King collected himself, trying to hide his anger. "Look at you, the Lessers have gotten to you."

Sory's anger then fired up from the pit of his stomach. "You knew that tricking me would be the only way to get me on your side, and I'm guessing it's the same for the rest of your disciples."

"The dreams, Tysorious, you remember the dreams. You remember how you felt in them. How you felt when you had your epiphany of the Lessers."

"How do you know about the dreams anyway?"

Sairus hesitated, "I can read minds, remember, boy?"

"No, no because I was not thinking about the dreams when you brought them up." Sory paused, then he squinted. "You gave me those dreams."

"Tysorious, you know nothing about telepathy."

"Exactly, and you were counting on that so that I wouldn't be able to figure it out!"

"Your dreams were a sign that you belong on the Raishan side, the side – of the Red Empire!"

"Liar!"

"You cannot argue about something you know nothing about! Why is it that you think you know how these advanced powers work?!"

"Because, Sairus, I have figured out how to follow my instinct. And by the way, I am not afraid of you anymore am I?!"

"Tysorious, we – are destined – to fight in the same war – on the same side!"

"WE ARE destined to fight in the same war – but not on the same side!"

"Tysorious, you will listen to me!"

"My name – is SORY!" Sairus' body lit up in red fire. He clutched his right hand around a non-existent handle, red flame then appeared within his grasp, flame which formed into a saber in a flash. Sory was enthralled yet appalled, "I did not know we could do that."

"*You* cannot, Tysorious." Sory reached for his sword. Sairus raised his saber over his head. Sory's sword flew toward his hand. Sairus swung down. His saber thundered against the white blade of Sory's sword. The blades shrieked as they cut into each other. Sairus bore down, forcing Sory toward the ground. Sory then angled his blade so that Sairus' slid off.

Sory dodged a jab that clipped his wing and let out the scent of singed feathers. He took flight. A red-hot rock pelted his ribs. "AH!" He curled up. Then he was hit by another in the head. He hit the rocks near Sairus. Sairus down swung. Sory jumped away and was sprayed by the molten rocks being flung by the impact of the King's bolt sword. Sairus swiped at Sory again who bent backwards, then ran for the edge of the peninsula. Something odd then occurred, the face of the cliff turned horizontal rather than vertical. Everything was turned on its side.

"You have discovered a secret of being in trance," said Sairus as he approached his quarry, "just one of many." Rocks tumbled out from under his feet and along the ground, toward the thrashing sea. Sairus stabbed and swung at Sory who dodged every blow by a feather's width. The King's saber instead hit rocks and created a rain of lava. Bits of Sory's singed skin began peeling off. He had to escape, now realizing that he had been backed to the edge of the violent tide. "Come on, FIGHT!" The King pointed his saber, which shot out like a flash of lightning. It detonated the ground underneath Sory who ducked under a boulder. BAM! The boulder shattered into a million liquid pieces. Sory ran away, hopping about as searing beams of energy cracked around him. Sory couldn't handle this anymore. He crouched down behind another boulder gasping for air. His hands trembled as he waited for the inevitable.

"SORY!" Ruby screamed from the top of the cliff. The King pointed his saber at her.

"RUBY!" screamed Sory. The King shot a beam. She disappeared in a cloud of dust and fire. Sory sprung at Sairus. He cut the King's wing who cried out and wheeled around to face him.

"You have finally decided to fight," said the King.

"I don't take too kindly to my friends being threatened."

"Or perhaps – even more than a friend?" he smiled, then down-swung. Sory deflected the blow. Then he jumped up and swung at Sairus' face. The King leaned back at the last moment. He then swung his blade at the still airborne Sory who bent his body. The King's blade cut a few inches into his ribs, exposing the bone.

"AH!" Sory slammed into the rock. The King charged at him. Sory stood and fought back. He avoided the humongous swings and inflicted wounds whenever possible. However, his own injuries mounted.

Sory, remember, running does not have to be retreating, whispered Fusna's voice. Sairus pointed his saber at Sory. It shot out another beam. Sory smacked it with his sword, walloping him backwards. He then took a long leap and darted off through the air, the world readjusted itself as he swiveled his head to avoid more flying rocks and beams. Sairus then took flight himself, roaring, swinging his saber and exploding the cliff's face just as Sory hugged the end of the peninsula.

Sairus opened his great beak and a stream of fire rampaged out in a billowing inferno. Sory dove, but was singed. Sairus closed his beak having lost sight of the Fyzar. He landed on the cliff's face, but found nothing as gravity shifted again, so he scanned about in the stabbing silence. Then, the camouflaged Sory shrieked and pounced on the King, biting and stabbing him. Sairus flung him off. "HA!" the King shot a beam at Sory who jumped aside. Then Sory ran over the top of the cliff. The King sprang up, put his hands at the top of the precipice and peered over. Sory stabbed one hand while scratching the other. "AH!" The King went full flame again. He shot a beam at Sory who darted up into the stormy clouds as thunder rang out.

Hidden within those stormy clouds, Sory smelled the rain not too far off. He looked down at the red glow of the King as it pierced through the clouds. The clouds were shifted about by the wind. Then the glow vanished. Sory looked in all directions but saw nothing. Then he closed his eyes and pressed on that little blue speck. He saw further and further out. *Qi's sight, you have far to go,* whispered Sairus in Sory's mind. Sory whisked around, nothing. He looked up, not because he sensed something, he just had the instinct that Sairus would be there. The King roared out of the clouds, his fire saber cutting through them. Sory folded his wings and dove. Lightning struck and Sairus redirected it at Sory. Sory's body jolted, then fell limp.

From the encampment, a wounded Ruby watched with heart-shredding horror as Sory fell out of the storm. "SORY!" she cried as a wall of anguish swept through her and brought her to her knees.

The cliffs were streaming up at Sory as his eyes opened a peak. He looked up and saw Sairus levitating above. Sory then dove toward a small space between two peninsulas and flattened his limbs and wings against his body. Sairus growled, then went full fire and charged down, an asteroid roaring through the atmosphere.

Sory entered trance and accelerated. His body felt as if it were extending, as if slowly morphing as he streaked toward the ocean. He could sense Sairus behind him. He passed the tops of the cliffs, two peninsulas on either side, his chest facing the encampment. Sory began to lean up as the fabric of space seemed to stretch with him. The sharp boulders below extended into great knives the size of castles that reached up to impale him. He strained as the G-forces crushed him and grew stronger and stronger the more he leaned up. He groaned from the pain, but fought it. He was soon facing forward. A second later, he darted in between two sharp, gargantuan boulders stabbing into the sky, a whoosh sounding out as he did.

Sory lost altitude as he emerged from in between the peninsulas just out to sea over swelling waves. The sea's surface bent into a U-shape as Sory neared it. A wake formed around and behind him as water sprayed into the air, hitting Sairus. Sory turned around just as Sairus winced from the pain of the water. The King saw Sory noticing this. Sory rolled over when he was struck in the head by a rock from the cliffs. He then tumbled into the ocean.

From the edge of the Arktorian cliffs, a soupy thick depression leaned down onto the Arktorian soldiers. Sairus abruptly stopped. The flame retreated to his eyes, he faced upward, held his fists up and roared as a torrential flame erupted from his great beak, rain then drenched him. Dyricio fell to his knees. Ayro put his hand on his shoulder. Ruby spread her wings and was about to fly off to Sairus when Gyric pulled her back down. She screamed and flailed around, yet soon gave in, crying into Gyric's chest.

Sory was sinking, bubbles floating up from his beak, his eyes closed, his body limp, around him the sound of churning water from the storm. Soon, as the water became dark, it began to crush him. Form within the Iron Structure, Fusna levitated and smoked a pipe as he communicated to his student. *Sory, wake up.*

Back on the Raishan cliffs, the Raishan army was already readying to fall back. Ramous eyed the King as he landed then started walking to his tent. Then the rain began to subside.

Back under water, Fusna continued to try to wake his student. *I know you can hear me…they need you Sory…they all do…now – WAKE UP!* Sory's body flinched as a jolt of energy struck him. Back at the Iron Structure, Fusna inhaled a deep breath from his pipe, then exhaled a puffy cloud of smoke. Near the encampment, the storm rumbled as a single cloud shifted out to sea.

Sairus was still walking when he felt this presence. He halted, then gazed up to the storm cloud. "Fusna."

Sory could feel his body. It was weightless. With his empty mind, he didn't know where he was.

Sairus rushed back to the cliffs.

Fusna sucked in his energy. Concentrated it. Compacted it into a volatile sphere at the core of his mind. He put his fists up to his heart. He held his breath. Then, he exhaled, and a burst of energy flushed out in a wave that rippled through the smoke like a ripple through water.

Sairus had reached the edge of the cliffs when he felt a burst of disembodied energy. He halted when a wave went through the storm cloud.

The Arktorians felt it too. They peered up to see the wave go right over them. Ruby smiled, "Fusna."

Ramous searched the water, then did Sairus. "NOOO!" screamed the King. A lightning bolt struck down from the clouds. It split the air apart as it snaked its way to the ocean's surface. When it hit the surface, the bolt split into hundreds, then thousands, then millions of branches like the roots of a tree.

Sory was still sinking. Then – BOOM. A searing strike of energy ripped through Sory and awoke him.

Thunder cracked the air and echoed through the mountains and hills as Sairus watched the ocean's surface with a profound intensity, his eyes wide open, his beak clinched as he rapidly breathed through it. One-hundred thousand griffins watched the surface.

Then an explosion ripped the surface. Sory boomed into the air, his eyes closed. "SORY!" screamed Ruby over the deafening screams of the rest of the army. Sory levitated with his wings all the way extended out at his sides, his body still.

From the cliffs, Sairus growled. He pointed at Sory. He formed his bolt sword. "TYSORIOUS!!!"

King Sairus' voice was thunder as it echoed through the mountains and hills. Sory heard it, and with his qi he saw it. Then, a second later, he opened his glowing white eyes, so bright were they – they lit up the gloomy air like two micro stars. Everyone, from the Arktorian encampment to the Raishan cliffs fell silent.

Sairus crouched down, then launched himself like before, fire once more overtaking his body.

Sory's body remained stagnant, when all of the microscopic droplets of water in his feathers began to stir. They shifted sideways, orbiting his body, and soon droplets farther and farther out commenced orbiting as well. Far below him the ocean's surface swelled. A funnel reached up out of it and toward Sory. Above him, the clouds did the same. The King could see what was happening. He accelerated, roaring. His bolt sword over his head until within striking distance of his foe a moment later. Sairus ripped his weapon downward. Sory closed his eyes. Sairus screamed. And a wall of water crashed into him.

"AHHH!" screamed Sairus as he backed away from the waterspout. The King then raked the tornado with his bolt sword only for it to be dragged by the current. "TYSORIOUS!" The vortex rammed the King. He snarled. He shot fireballs and beams at it. Then he circled the tornado. "Come out of there Tysorious!" But the water kept spinning. Sairus snarled.

"Kill him Sory!" yelled Ruby from the cliffs. Sairus looked at them, thousands of enemy soldiers concentrated in such a tight space. He grinned.

From within the towering vortex, all that could be heard was the deafeningly rumbling roar of millions of gallons of rushing white water. Yet above this, Sory swore he heard a scream, which he tipped his head in the direction of. Something flew into him. A griffin with a profoundly unequivocal horror in his eyes so great it terrified Sory, clung to him, half of his feathers having been burnt off. "Put down – the tornado." This griffin mumbled. He then let go only to be thrashed about by the water. Then another came, then another.

The waterspout dissipated. Sory could finally see the cause of the fear in the first griffin's eyes. "SAIRUS!" The King froze for but a moment before rotating around and eyeing he who had dared utter his name. He then folded back his wings and lunged forth. Sory lit up his bolt sword.

The King cupped his hands. A beam of fire shot out at Sory's face. Sory stabbed the beam with his bolt sword and it deflected around him. Sory could barely hold his weapon. He gritted his beak and strained as he was forced backward. The scream of burning metal thrashed in his skull. "You wanted to combat a Fyzar, Tysorious, and so I am obliged to grant you that wish!" Sairus announced as he circled around Sory who turned with him until the King hovered above him. As Sory strained yet harder, a crazed look grew on Sairus' face as his eyes grew and a demented smile went from ear to ear. He then gave a push and Sory's bolt sword was pushed into his own face, burning it.

"AHHH!" cried Sory as his own weapon seared into him. Then the fire beam vanished. Sory lunged forth with his bolt sword pointed forward. The King rematerialized his bolt sword then raked it at Sory. Sory reared back, dodging it by so little his eyes instantly dried from the heat of his enemy's weapon. Then he swung only to be blocked. Sairus then unleashed another white-hot fiery torrent from his beak. Sory darted underneath of him and sprang for the coast. Sairus pursued and swung again. Sory blocked, but the force flung him toward the sea. Sory could nearly feel his energy draining one blow at a time.

Sory made it to the cliffs, his back right up against the rock. Sairus stabbed at his face. Sory bent backwards and hit his head on the rock. Hot embers rained down on him as the King's sword burnt its way to his face. Sory exited trance and let himself fall. The King gave chase, his piece slashing a red scar in the cliff as he dragged it down. Sory pointed himself downward as the rumbling crashing waves flew up at him. He then reared up and landed on a rock just above the highest reach of the crashing tide.

Sairus thudded down, then ripped his weapon out of the cliff. "You are out of trance," Sory said nothing as Sairus noticed Sory's hand had no weapon. He smiled, "and you have lost your sword."

Sory entered trance, and a confused Sairus tipped his head as Sory lifted his open palm. An unlit sword then fell and stabbed right into the King's shoulder just beside the neck, slashing deep into his lung and almost all the way to his heart. Sory twisted it around. "AH!" screamed the King as his eyes burned toward the impaling metal. He then pulled it out. Sory dove away. "I WILL VAPORIZE YOU!" shrieked the King before charging down after him.

A huge wave crashed into the rocks and sprayed upward. It engulfed both of them. It burnt into Sairus' entire enflamed body and flooded into his open wound. "AHHH!" screamed the King. An explosion from his body vaporized the wave. A blast-front knocked the Arktorians off their feet. A mushroom-cloud rose up.

King Sairus laid motionless on the rocks below, waves crashing over him, his armor in smoldering shambles. The Arktorians stared intently. The King opened his eyes, then clambered to his feet. He squinted up them, glowering. The rain started pouring again. The King then rushed off to the Raishan cliffs holding his open wound, guarding it from the water, flapping erratically, gasping in pain. "Sairus has surrendered!" yelled Ayro, and they all cheered. Sairus heard the commotion and turned around only to witness the personification of his humiliation.

"SILENCE! You damn Arks!" Yet they only screamed louder and more deliberately.

Sory grabbed his sword and landed at the edge of the cliffs, his brothers in arms swarming around him, screaming. The gratefulness of an entire army cascading out in yelps and tears as they never seemed to be able to stop giving thanks. As Sory's brothers gathered around him he greeted and hugged them back, but in the back of his mind he knew that the King had only been wounded. He looked over there, over the bay, over to the Raishan cliffs.

Back on those cliffs, Sairus had landed, his own blood streaming out and dripping down his arm. Around him, his army watched their scarred King as he stood defeated. Next to him stood Ramous as he peered out at the Arktorian cliffs, "Tysorious is still alive, Your Greatness."

The heat of the sun then churned in Sairus' eyes as they then pointed out toward those cliffs. "So be it then. Tysorious and I – we shall meet – on another battlefield." He could hear the cheering of his enemy as it persisted.

*

The throng around Sory conveyed their gratitude unto him all at once. A soldier then pointed to the sky as the inhabitants of Cayza began to fly back to their city. "Look!" Sory watched for a moment before following those griffins.

Sory landed in Cayza's debris filled main-street as thousands of others scampered about. He could have walked all the way up and down that street and never touched the cobblestone. "Sory!" cried Ruby. She ran up and hugged him. "I'm so glad you're alive!" He hugged her back as Ayro, Bahren, and Dyricio came up. Then Ruby turned to Cayza and tears rolled out of her eyes. "Look at this! How could this happen?"

Anger and empathy overwhelmed Sory when a bright-eyed little hatchling shyly stepped in front of him. They locked eyes for a moment, then the hatchling handed Sory her stuffed toy. Sory held it, then squeezed it in his hands. Then he looked back into the bright and innocent eyes of this hatchling. Eyes that had been drowned by sadness, yet were also confused, innocent eyes that could not comprehend the carnage that had befallen. Sory rubbed this little hatchling's head. "We will rebuild this city," he declared. "We will."

Bahren came up next to Sory, "how? Where will they live?"

"They may live in our ships for now."

Ruby then stood next to Sory, "how will we feed them?"

"We will find a way."

Ayro came up next, "they will need much more."

"Then we will give it to them."

Dyricio walked up last, "there is no way we can do this."

Sory then faced them, "yes there is! We owe them that much."

Around them, some soldiers carried the elderly, hatchlings, and the wounded and brought them back to the encampment, while others began collecting the tons upon tons of debris into piles all around

Cayza. Others brought in food, fresh water, and medical supplies as the medics began to treat the injured.

Sory then kneeled down so that he was face to face with the hatchling. "What is your name?" he asked. She said nothing, she simply just kept staring at him. "Are you hurt?" She shook her head. "Are you hungry?" She nodded and Sory smiled. "Come, let's find you something to eat."

Dyricio stopped him, "Sory…you were right. We should have left Hyleeda long ago. Thank you."

Sory smiled and said, "you're welcome." Dyricio took a step when Sory continued, "and I'm sorry too. I'm sorry that we are in this war fighting against our own father. I'm sorry that we're in this war."

"Because of you, less griffins will have to be in it. You can shorten this war, Sory. You have to."

Sory smiled, and then started walking with the hatchling's hand in his, then Ruby took the hatchling's other hand and together they walked in search of food. All around them, his soldiers no longer seemed like an army. Armies were meant to fight, to kill. Yet his was doing the opposite. For a moment, Sory thought this to be perhaps the most unnatural sight he had ever seen. Then he remembered all that he had seen, all of the monsters and beasts, all of what Fusna had

shown him, what the King had been able to do, what Sory himself had
been able to do. He then looked at the stuffed animal in his hand one
last time, as if it would return him to reality – to what he had known all
his life up until a mere few months ago. The memory of this oblivious
past came as strangely comforting. It was a time when he was just a
boy living out in the middle of nowhere with his brother and father. To
a time that he almost wished he could return to. Then he heard a
familiar voice in his head, *You have done well, Sory,* said Fusna. *You
have learned beyond what I have taught you. You are not a Fyzar yet,
but you will become a great one someday.*

www.ingramcontent.com/pod-product-compliance
Lightning Source LLC
Chambersburg PA
CBHW060144260626
47160CB00001B/107